What the critics are saying...

"… a wonderful collection of exceptional storytelling… will stay in my 'keeper' stack." ~ *Romance Junkies*

"Truly impressive and a lot of fun to read." ~ *The Romance Studio*

"…a talented author with a knack for writing wonderful, sexy stories of love and BDSM." ~ *Coffeetime Romance*

"Three delicious stories from three extremely talented authors, this anthology will stimulate and tantalise the senses." ~ *Love Romances*

"The love scenes are hotter than a jar of jalapeno peppers..." ~ *Coffeetime Romance*

"Dominique Adair always creates memorable and interesting characters and Gia and Drake are no exception" ~ *The Romance Studio*

D1519843

Silver Star Award. Must Love Music by Jennifer Dunne. "This short story hit each key within my "great book" meter. The emotions are so varied that I felt every single change, including trauma, fear, distrust, satisfaction, reawakening, and intense passion…" ~ *Just Erotic Romance Reviews*

4 Hearts "Jennifer Dunne has crafted a very sexy and touching story about a man hiding behind his past and the woman who finally makes him want to live again. … as a fan of BDSM themed stories, I found the scene to be particularly engrossing and very important to the growth of their relationship. Single White Submissive is an interesting anthology featuring three eclectic stories that experience the many levels of BDSM. Endearing and lots of fun…" ~ *The Romance Studio*

Must Love Music - Jennifer Dunne "A gripping tale that is more than just kinky sex, Jennifer Dunne tells the story of a tortured soul finding the road to healing. The characters are well written and will reach into the hearts of the reader. The sex scenes between these two lovers are dripping with sensuality and emotion and will grip the reader, not only making her panties wet, but her eyes too." ~ *Love Romances*

"A poignant story that was not only sensual but also emotionally intense. The slight essence of danger was just the right touch to put this story over the edge." ~ *Enchanted In Romance*

Single White Submissive

Madeleine Oh
Jennifer Dunne
Dominique Adair

ELLORA'S CAVE
ROMANTICA PUBLISHING

An Ellora's Cave Romantica Publication

www.ellorascave.com

Single White Submissive

ISBN # 1419953761
ALL RIGHTS RESERVED.

Sunday AfternoonWith Mac Copyright© 2005 Madeleine Oh
Must Love Music Copyright© 2005 Jennifer Dunne
Gia in Wonderland Copyright© 2005 Dominique Adair

Electronic book Publication August 2005
Trade paperback Publication March 2006

Edited by Sue-Ellen Gower and Mary Moran
Cover art by Syneca

With the exception of quotes used in reviews, this book may not be reproduced or used in whole or in part by any means existing without written permission from the publisher, Ellora's Cave Publishing, Inc.® 1056 Home Avenue, Akron OH 44310-3502.

This book is a work of fiction and any resemblance to persons, living or dead, or places, events or locales is purely coincidental. The characters are productions of the authors' imagination and used fictitiously.

Warning:

The following material contains graphic sexual content meant for mature readers. *Single White Submissive* has been rated E–rotic by a minimum of three independent reviewers.

Ellora's Cave Publishing offers three levels of Romantica™ reading entertainment: S (S-ensuous), E (E-rotic), and X (X-treme).

S-*ensuous* love scenes are explicit and leave nothing to the imagination.

E-*rotic* love scenes are explicit, leave nothing to the imagination, and are high in volume per the overall word count. In addition, some E-rated titles might contain fantasy material that some readers find objectionable, such as bondage, submission, same sex encounters, forced seductions, and so forth. E-rated titles are the most graphic titles we carry; it is common, for instance, for an author to use words such as "fucking", "cock", "pussy", and such within their work of literature.

X-*treme* titles differ from E-rated titles only in plot premise and storyline execution. Unlike E-rated titles, stories designated with the letter X tend to contain controversial subject matter not for the faint of heart.

Contents

ॐ

Sunday Afternoon With Mac

by Madeleine Oh

Must Love Music

by Jennifer Dunne

Gia in Wonderland

by Dominique Adair

Sunday Afternoon With Mac

Madeleine Oh

ℰↄ

Trademarks Acknowledgement

~

The author acknowledges the trademarked status and trademark owners of the following wordmarks mentioned in this work of fiction:

Isadora Duncan: Isadora Duncan International Institute, Inc.

Meissen: Staatliche Porzellan-Manufactur Meissen GmbH Corporation

Norfolk Lavender: Norfolk Lavender Limited Company

Terylene: Imperial Chemical Industries, Limited Corporation

Velcro: Velcro Industries B.V. Ltd Liab. Co.

Chapter One

∞

You're stark, raving nutters! Ginny made a point of ignoring the naggy little voice in her skull. *You're crackers to be doing this!* her sensible self insisted.

She wasn't crackers, not really, just fed up, disappointed and, most of all, frustrated. "I have nothing to lose," she told the nag in her skull, "I'm just...er...doing market research. Seeing what's out there."

Yeah! Right. Her cautious self would not be silenced. *You're advertising for sex.*

Not exactly.

All right, yes! She was. And why not? She wanted a man. A nice man. An intelligent man. A man who washed between his toes. A clever man. A man who didn't think she was utterly twisted, perverted and in need of extensive therapy.

Not Simon—nice, presentable, a steady career in insurance, great taste in restaurants and shirts, and more than happy to indulge her with a weekend in a country hotel in Sussex. A man with a lovely bod and a stalwart erection that shriveled before her eyes when she blithely suggested he tie her to the bedposts.

Or Pete—a rather adventurous sort who'd climbed Everest, took her to rather outré art-house cinema and lived on a houseboat on the Regent's Canal. He'd responded to her sharing of her fantasy by suggesting she go into psychotherapy to resolve her deep-seated personality problems.

No, they had not understood.

Then there was Rex. She really should have been leery of a man who shared a name with her grandmother's corgi. When Ginny casually mentioned she had a fantasy of being tied to the bedposts, Rex's eyes all but popped out of his skull, he grinned wide enough to display the fillings in his molars and suggested she spend the weekend as his naked sex slave in his truck tent.

Her libido nosedived even faster than Simon's had.

She bombed out every time. She was obviously going about it the wrong way.

A personal ad was a safe, low investment—both in money and emotions—and gave her a chance to pick and choose at a safe distance.

Her one foray to a kinky club had been a less than total success. She'd researched carefully. From the outside, the building in Wimbledon looked nice enough. Inside was incredible—as if all her wildest fantasies were being acted out before her eyes. She'd have been content to watch all evening, but was hit on an average of every five minutes. After an hour of increasingly irritated, "No, thank you, I prefer to watch right now," she did what she hadn't done since she was sixteen—fled to the sanctuary of the ladies' room and, in desperation, nipped out a back door, setting off a fire alarm. Horrified, she'd fled into the night, only to realize, standing on the platform waiting for a train back to Hammersmith, she'd left her cashmere jacket behind.

Too bad! She had her handbag, front door key and her fare home—it had been cheap cashmere anyway.

That disastrous evening had stifled her kinky dreams for a good few months, but now, after indulging in the glossy pages of a copy of *Erotic Leather Quarterly*, Ginny was back daydreaming.

This time there'd be no hit and miss, no horrifying of nice actuaries and definitely no invitations to fuck on a truck bed.

She would be in control.

Sort of.

It wasn't the most brilliant prose of the twenty-first century but clear, concise and to the point counted for more than style—at least going by the sample ads she'd pored over for inspiration.

So she'd acquired a free email address, wrote a check to *Erotic Leather Quarterly* and attached her carefully typed copy.

Single white submissive ISO intelligent, inventive and creative Dominant. Perfection not necessary but common sense, wit and sense of humor are. I'm 27, employed and looking for someone to fulfill my fantasies of velvet manacles and silk scarves.

Even with her phony email address, it came in under five lines.

Double-checking the directions that asked for hard copy and disk, she copied the ad to a new disk, tucked the lot in an envelope and took it right down to the nearest postbox before she lost her courage. That done, she treated herself to a wildly extravagant designer iced coffee on her way home. The cool drink would surely steady her nerves and, she told herself as she sipped the iced double java amaretto latte, she needed to settle down. The ad wouldn't even appear for at least four weeks. The darn magazine was a quarterly after all.

Ginny took a slow, deep breath then another. She was not expecting a miracle, not really expecting anything. Maybe all she'd get would be a bunch of spam. Perhaps she'd get nothing but a resounding silence. Maybe she'd find a pot of gold or perhaps a cock of gold, attached to the man of her dreams.

Maybe.

Meanwhile, in between holding down her job as a reporter for the sports page of a national newspaper, Ginny was writing her own brand of kinky science-fiction romance in her spare time.

One paid her mortgage and the other kept her off the streets of an evening and diverted her dissatisfaction with her love life. Her characters enjoyed great sex lives even if she was left wanting.

Mac Brodie scowled at the mound of envelopes on his desk. The downside of editing a magazine in his spare time was not having much spare time. But he was doing his bit for the kinky community and—he truly believed—raising its image by producing a glossy, quality magazine. Maybe, just maybe, one day it would pay for itself. Meanwhile he had the next issue to send to the printer by Friday.

He sorted out the personal ad sales from the rest of the mail—at least they'd all have checks—and there were always a few good for a sly chuckle. One learned a lot about human and kinky nature reading personal ads. More than once, he'd been tempted to contact the senders and ask if they wrote fiction.

Still fourteen ads meant fourteen checks. It all helped pay the printer. He put the checks aside, stacked up the hard copies and the disks. As usual, there were a couple who didn't include disks. He should charge double if he had to key the wretched stuff in himself.

The first six were pretty much predictable. Mac wished them luck. Hell, he wished everyone luck. All they were looking for was a kinky partner—other than number three, "Sir Peter" who signed his check "Peter Smith" and was looking for twins for preference. The seventh caught his eye. Even if the application hadn't requested it be listed under "women looking for men", he'd have guessed it was a woman. It was clear and to the point, and no mention of body size, hair color or height. Women always seemed to skip those details and this one was no different, getting right to the point about what she wanted—a man worth the trouble, intelligent, witty, creative and…dominant.

And bless her sweet, little submissive heart, the check was for the correct amount and the disk clearly labeled with her name—Ginny Wallace. Sounded almost too nice and wholesome to be looking for a man in leather—a man wielding velvet manacles and silk scarves. Mac hoped she'd found what she was looking for.

He took the disk and popped it into his disk drive, absently noting the postcode in the return address. Couldn't be that far from where he lived but he was far too professional to contact an advertiser himself, no matter how interesting she sounded. Pity he had to live up to that standard. Ginny sounded fun.

Disk scanned for viruses, he clicked it open and stared. She'd sent him more than a personal ad. Yes, it was there, he found it neatly labeled ELQ personal ad between *Each to his Own* and *Fishing for Compliments*. He scanned the list on his screen—*Blood in the Sky, Cyber Sex Kittens, In the Vastness of Space, Wishing on the Moon.*

Mentally uttering a halfhearted apology for deliberately reading what was not intended for his eyes, Mac clicked open *Cyber Sex Kittens* and was smiling before he read ten lines.

Damn! This was good.

After five years of editing *Erotic Leather Quarterly*, and half a lifetime of reading kinky fiction, he'd become a connoisseur of pervy writing. This was smashing! He was half-inclined to slash one of the okay-but-not-brilliant stories he'd planned to use in the next issue and substitute *Cyber Sex Kittens* or…he went on reading the other stories, and after the better part of an hour, decided he'd just had an editor's dream come true—finding a gem in the slush pile. Not even the slush pile—among the personals!

He could not let this chance go. Okay, these were obviously rough drafts, but her voice was playful and her inventiveness brilliant. Small wonder she was looking for a witty, intelligent man, but right now all Mac Brodie was interested in was a damn good writer.

Glancing over the cover sheet with her contact info, he picked up his phone and punched in her number.

Ginny was indulging in a Saturday morning soak in lavender bubble bath when the phone rang. She was tempted to let the answering machine pick up, but good old guilt that it might be her mother made her grab a towel and drip all the way into her bedroom.

"Hello?" If it was a double-glazing salesman, she'd swear.

"Ginny Wallace?"

The warm, male voice had her wet toes curling, but she still didn't need double-glazing. "Yes?"

"This is Mac Brodie from *Erotic Leather Quarterly*."

"Oh?" Had she forgotten the check? Were they rejecting her ad? Did they really reject personal ads?

"Do you have time to talk?"

Not here! She was soaking the new Berber carpet she'd treated herself to for Christmas. "Hang on a minute!"

It didn't take much longer to get back into her blissfully warm bath. "Something wrong with the ad I sent?" Who'd have thought they picked over them?

"Not at all. That's not why I'm calling. It's about your disk."

"I sent one." She'd double-checked.

"You certainly did, but there's more on the disk than just your personal ad." Hell! What was on it? "You sent me some short stories."

Her face burned. How had she grabbed that disk? Too late to worry now. "That was my mistake, sorry."

"I'm not!" She could almost hear the smile in his voice. He and every sub-editor must have had a good giggle over them. "What I want to know is have you sold them?"

He was serious. Sounded like it anyway. "Er...no." Never tried to, come to that.

"I'd like to buy them."

"All of them?"

"Definitely *Cyber Sex Kittens* and *Wishing on the Moon* but wouldn't mind first refusal on the others. We only pay on publication, and since I only use two pieces of fiction in each issue, it might be a while before you see any money. I don't want to impede you from selling elsewhere."

"I see..." She should be professional and sharp, instead she was naked, stammering and soaking in Norfolk Lavender. "Er...what do you pay?"

"Not much, I'm afraid." He mentioned a sum and she agreed it wasn't much, but fair enough for a small distribution quarterly. "We give you a byline and space for a bio, and if you want to include a website URL, that's fine."

Great if she had one but... "Good." What next?

"Do you want to use a pen name?"

Yes! She could just see Sam, her executive editor having apoplexy at seeing her byline on a kinky mag. "I need to come up with one, don't I?"

"Might be a good idea. Lots of our authors do." She imagined a wide smile that matched the rich, deep voice with just a hit of Scots accent suggesting heather and windswept hillsides and… "Look, how about you think of a pen name and we meet for coffee?"

"Oh!" Heck why not? "All right. Make it lateish. I've got some things to do this morning." Get out of the bath for a start.

"Let's make it lunch then. How about one-thirty at Tarantella on the Brompton Road?"

Nice and handy, he must have worked that out from her address on the cover letter but funny that he'd picked her brother-in-law's establishment out of all the restaurants in South London. "All right." She almost hung up but stopped just in time to ask. "How will I recognize you?"

His laugh was sexy. Lovely in fact. Must come from reading all the naughty stuff in his job. "I'm tall and will be wearing a long, black leather coat." She should have worked out that last detail for herself. "What about you, Ginny? What are you wearing?"

Nothing right now, but she'd keep that to herself. "Blue jeans." A no-brainer on a Saturday. "And a sweater. I've got bright red hair, cut short. Not easy to miss."

Wasn't easy to miss his gut-tickling laugh either. "Very good, Ginny. See you then."

He hung up and she eased deeper into the now-cooling water.

What had she agreed to? Writing her wild imaginings was one thing. Selling them and seeing them in print another. Why not? It would get her a little bit extra dosh. She could treat herself to that super-duper vibrator she'd been lusting after.

Dressed, she set off, still unsure of the vital but elusive pen name. That had her worried. Meeting an editor she brushed off. On that point they'd be equals — well, sort of. Pseudonyms were another matter entirely.

She arrived early at Tarantella. Not out of nervousness or anxiety, but to give time for caffeine to get her synapses firing and to think of a suitable nom de plume.

She was going to be ready and set when Mac Brodie arrived.

Chapter Two

ဆ

He picked her out the minute he opened the door. Couldn't miss. The only redheaded woman in the crowded coffee shop. She'd also snagged one of the best tables — a large round one, with the perfect vantage spot. Although right now she was not surveying the room, but frowning over a notepad on the table in front of her. But that hair! "Red" was wholly inadequate. His godmother had red hair — or had until she went white — Ginny's was the color of burnished copper or the brilliant orange glow of an autumn sunset. Pity she wore it cropped so short. He rather fancied it as a gleaming mane over her shoulders and covering her breasts. Most unprofessional of him to nurture such thoughts but, dammit, he wouldn't mind being unprofessional with Ginny Wallace. He wanted to see her breasts, to run his fingers over the sweet, pale fullness and tease her rosy nipples to hardness with his tongue, to feast his eyes on her lovely body, preferably with her arms held immobile with the velvet manacles she favored, and to find out once and for all if she had that glorious hair all the way down.

Right! He was here on business, wasn't he? So he closed the door — much to the relief of a couple at a nearby table who'd been frowning at the breeze — and walked to the back of the cafe, telling himself he was there to discuss word counts and lead-in times, but totally failing to work up any sort of conviction. He wanted a whole lot more from Ginny Wallace than a few thousand words.

She looked up as he approached, a question lighting her face. "Mac Brodie?" she asked.

He nodded. "Ginny Wallace, I presume?"

Her blue eyes crinkled at the corners. "Yup, that's me."

"May I join you?" A line hackneyed from a fifties film but…

"Isn't that why you came here?"

That and more. Much, much more. Later. "I wanted to meet my newest fiction writer." He sat down. It beat him how she'd snagged a table this big just for the two of them. "Do you have pull here, Ginny?" He glanced at the crowded cafe. There were groups of three, even four sitting around smaller tables. "Bagging the best table?"

Her smile lit up her entire face. Nice face, too. "I used to work here when I was at Uni. Plus, my sister's married to the owner."

"Will dropping your name help here?"

"Always!" She turned and nodded to a dark-haired waiter lounging near the cash register. He was at their table, pad in hand in seconds. Minutes later, they had a basket of breadsticks, a plate of olives and crudités, and a promise their orders would be out as soon as possible.

And this was a woman who dubbed herself submissive. Lovely. Couldn't be better. Just looking at her had him hard, thinking about her naked and helpless sent his cock a-waving. Damn good thing he was sitting down. Yes, well…to business. "About your stories…"

She looked at him. "You really want to buy them?"

"You bet. You thought I was fooling on the phone?"

She shook her head. "No, you sounded perfectly serious. It was just…" She hesitated, shrugged and smiled. "I sent them by mistake. Must have grabbed the wrong disk. I never planned on selling them."

"Fortunate mistake from my angle." A flash of uncertainly clouded her eyes. "Something the matter?"

"Just curious."

"About what?"

"Why you want to buy my stories."

"I need all the good fiction I can get. Yours is good. You will let me have them? Pay's lousy, I admit, but heck, the magazine isn't a moneymaker."

"I realize that… Oh!" She shook her head, again the darn sexy smile, with a hint of embarrassment in her eyes this time. "Didn't mean that quite the way it came out but, yes. I mean, no, it's not the money. It's just I never expected to sell them."

"Now you have, Ginny, and will sell many more I imagine. Did you decide on a pen name?"

"Amy Wise."

Interesting. "You just picked it?"

"While I was waiting. Amy is my middle name and heck, I was sitting here wondering if I'd been wise or foolish and since 'foolish' sounded a bit odd as a last name, I went for 'wise'."

"Very wise of you."

Even her groans were sexy.

By the time they'd agreed on the sale, he'd promised to put the first one in the next issue and she'd bargained for extra contributor copies, a carafe of wine arrived with two glasses. Not what they'd ordered. ELQ's budget didn't run to wine with lunch. Heck, lunch was stretching it a bit.

"Roger thought you might like this," the waiter said. "He wanted you to try it before he inflicted it on the customers."

"What is it, Pete, Algerian with antifreeze?"

The dark-haired waiter shook his glossy curls. "Watch yourself, Ginny! Slandering us." He tut-tutted and rolled his eyes. "It's a very nice South African Roger snapped up. Not bad at all, actually." He picked up the carafe and poured.

Ginny's eyes met Mac's as she reached for her glass. "We'd better risk our taste buds and give it a go. Are you game?"

You bet! Game for anything that involved Ginny Wallace. He took a sip. Pete had been right. Not bad at all.

She took her time. Sniffing then eying it with a little crease between her eyebrows before sipping the dark red wine. She let it sit on her tongue before swallowing and taking a second taste.

Mac sensed the waiter's anxiety. He really did want to know what she thought. Who was she? Some wine connoisseur?

He should not be jealous of a smile at a waiter. Hell, he had no right to be, but damn, he was. He wanted those blue eyes turned on him and her smile aimed in his direction. Who was he kidding? He wanted her naked. Just as well she wasn't looking his way. He half suspected his intentions were plastered all over is face. What was wrong with him? He was the Dominant, the one in control, the one who stayed in command of himself, the one who was falling fast for a pair of blue eyes and a sexy smile that right now was bestowed on a shiny-haired waiter.

"Not bad at all, Pete. Tell Roger he can send me a case for my birthday."

Pete grinned. "I'll tell him." He nodded to Mac. "Wine seems okay?"

"Would I question Ginny?"

Pete rolled his eyes. "Not if you've any desire to survive with your family jewels intact."

"Pete, scram and rustle up our lunches. I'm hungry." She was also blushing all over her face.

"She always is," Pete said with an exaggerated movement of his head and shoulders. But he did what he was told.

Mac took another sip of wine and set his glass down. This meeting was not going as he'd anticipated. He reached for a breadstick and brushed fingers with Ginny. She looked up, flushed but didn't draw back. Instead, she smiled, picked up a breadstick and bit into it. Her teeth were strong and white and her neck muscles undulated as she swallowed.

This was rather getting out of hand. "Tell me, Ginny, do you come here all the time?"

She shrugged. "Once in a while. It's not a good idea to sponge off one's family too much."

"You could have suggested somewhere else."

She tilted her head to one side. "I could have, couldn't I? I was so stunned at your call, I said 'yes' to everything. Besides, I'm all for sending business my family's way. Plus it was close and the food's good."

To say nothing of the company.

Ginny wasn't too sure about this. Yes, he was pleasant enough and, unexpected as it was, it would be fun to see her stories in print and lunch here was never a hardship. But she'd get the inevitable family inquisition re Mac.

Yes, Mac Brodie! Somehow, she'd expected him to be fifty, thinning on top and sporting a gray moustache like her managing editor. Certainly not rather attractive, sexy even, with a voice that gave her goose bumps. His would be a good voice to hear in bed and something told her Mac would be very, very good in bed. Good and kinky. He had to be, right? No doubt an expert who could have his pick of women in London.

But there was no charge for a quiet little daydream about his brown eyes looking into hers while his wide, sexy mouth smiled and touched her lips. Instinct told her he'd be a darn good kisser. She bet his dark hair looked rather tempting when tousled in the morning. She rather fancied his hands, too. Those long fingers curled around his wineglass seemed as if they'd be particularly expert brushing her bare skin, stroking her breast, teasing her nipples to hardness and reaching lower...

Pity that this was business. Just business.

After today she'd probably never see anything of him again, apart from his signature on a few modest checks. And she'd remember him by a couple of glossy magazines she'd have to hide when her family came over.

Shame really. Mac was worth seeing again. Perhaps she'd call him for editorial advice. Already Mac knew things about her that no one else she knew suspected—at least she hoped they never did.

"Worried about something, Ginny?"

Was she? "Just thinking you're not the least like my managing editor."

"I though you'd never sent your stories out before?"

"Not fiction, no," she paused. What the heck, he knew her name and address after all. "I'm a sports reporter."

"Where?"

She told him and earned the usual amazed look. Funny how even in the twenty-first century, a woman reporting on manly pursuits like rugger, cricket and snooker got raised eyebrows. "Not what you expected, eh?"

"You know, Ginny. I wasn't sure what to expect. Your stories were brilliantly written, that's the reporter in you obviously. Sexy, heck, they turned me on. But I've learned erotica writers come in all ages, shapes and sexes."

"Maybe, but Ginny Wallace had nothing to do with that. It's Amy who writes that naughty stuff."

He raised his glass, his dark eyes gleaming like jet. "Here's to Amy, long may she make me horny."

The thought of Mac Brodie, all broad shoulders and wicked smile, being horny sent an odd thrill right through her. And she'd done it to him with a few fantasies put on paper. There were certainly worse ways of wiling away long Sunday afternoons. She raised her glass. "To Amy!"

He reached across the table and they clinked glasses. Just that brief contact left her very much aware of his hands and his long arms. Good hands, she bet, and those arms would feel wonderful wound around her—

And right now, she'd better get her mind on due dates and lead times.

Lunches arriving were a definite distraction—for a good ten seconds. Hell! Even the way he picked up the saltcellar was sexy. Or was that a clear sign she needed to get out more and spend a little less time with Amy?

"Ginny," Mac said. "About pay. It's lousy, I know, but I could comp that personal ad you sent in."

She almost choked on a mouthful of ratatouille. Reaching for her wine and taking a gulp wasn't the best idea either. "You mean not pay for it?" Duh! Wasn't that what "comping" meant?

"Yes."

Would be so much easier if he didn't smile. Or would it?

"Thanks." Second mouthful of wine a big mistake— perhaps.

"My pleasure."

Yeah, she bet he knew all about pleasure. His voice was sending warm thrills down below the waist. She really did need to eat up and go home.

"Thanks." Sheesh, her vocabulary wasn't usually this sparse but heck...

"Do we have the business settled? Anymore questions re the stories?"

She shook her head. Better than saying "thanks" a third time.

"Good, let's enjoy lunch then."

Brilliant idea. Assuming she could still swallow and chew. He was having no such problem, but thinking about Mac and swallowing in the same thought was not a good idea. She was being ridiculous. Just because the man was sexy as blazes was no reason to go bonkers. Bad choice of words there. Bonking him was a lovely prospect. Oh, hell, better stop thinking. She took another mouthful of ratatouille.

"Where did you first learn of ELQ?"

This time she swallowed without recourse to wine. She even managed a little breath. "I found it in...er..." Might as well admit it. He knew where it sold after all. "In a little shop in Soho. Great Compton Street, I think."

His mouth twitched at the corner and made a little dimple in his chin. "Go there often?"

Her breath caught. Good thing she was between bites. "From time to time."

He nodded. "I guessed as much from your writing. It definitely had the ring of authenticity."

Why did her face have to burn at that? Cripes, she bet even her neck was blushing. "I've read widely in the genre."

"Just read?"

"Why wouldn't reading be enough? I bet nobody ever asked Agatha Christie how many murders she'd committed." Testy, but he was making her nervous and she was irritated to find she enjoyed it.

"True." He reached for the wine, tilted the neck of the carafe over her glass and met her eyes. She nodded. He refilled her glass then his own, and put the now three-quarters empty carafe on the table. "But I wonder how realistic most of her nice, tidy, middle-class murders really were. No drive-by shootings, mob killings, no blood or gore."

"There's blood in *Lord Edgware Dies*."

He grinned. "You're right! Read a lot of them have you?"

"Almost all of them. One summer I was visiting an aunt and broke my leg. I was semi-immobile for weeks and read my way through her bookshelves. Lots of medical romances and murders."

"And you preferred slaughter to sex?"

"I was nine!"

He threw back his head and laughed. His Adam's apple bobbed as the laugh came from deep in his belly. A wildly sexy laugh, a laugh to keep you warm at night and…

"I see." She doubted he did but never mind. "Too young to appreciate the finer points of the opposite sex."

"Back then there were no finer points. My brother and his friends teased me mercilessly."

"But now you read my outrageously kinky periodical and write the most deliciously pervy tales."

"Yes!" She tried hard for unflustered and composed, and failed miserably.

Mac held back the smile. She was lovely. He'd gone a long way beyond professional but why not? His thoughts toward Ginny Wallace were decidedly unprofessional. If he could only convince her… "So, when did you start reading kinky magazines?"

She was silent a good thirty seconds while she broke off a corner of bread, put it in her mouth, chewed and swallowed. A nice mouth, rather tempting lips and a definitely fine neck. He waited. She was going to be worth waiting for. He knew it in his gut — or maybe his cock.

"At Uni."

Interesting. "Not part of coursework I presume?" If so, he wished he'd gone wherever she had.

"No." The giggle had to be nervous. "I found one. Nicked it actually. Someone dropped it, instead of being a good girl and giving it back, I held onto it. I read it so much, I just about memorized it, then I got up my courage and went looking for more."

"And...?"

She took a sip of wine. Only a sip. Obviously unwilling to drink too much but needing to moisten her dry lips and mouth. "I found them. Used to have to hide them when I went home, but I loved reading them."

"Gave you a wicked, illicit thrill?"

She nodded. And blushed again. He hoped the blush went lower than he could see with the damn high-neck sweater she was wearing. "Why the personal ad? Hasn't life sent a nice pervy man your way?"

She shook her head. "Not any 'nice' ones. There's a lot more frogs and toads than princes out there." She reached for her glass but didn't drink. "Maybe fiction suits me better."

Chapter Three

&

He didn't think so. "Maybe not, Ginny. I own a pair of velvet manacles and I'd be more than happy to add a few silk scarves."

She jumped and knocked over her glass. Damn! He'd jumped her too soon. Or had he? She leant toward him. "Are you serious?"

"Every bit as serious as you were when you sent in that ad."

Pause while she pondered that one. She nodded slowly and took a deep breath. "You really mean it, don't you?"

"You will learn, Ginny, that I mean everything I say."

Her mouth tightened. She was scared but willing. Lovely. But one wrong move on his part and he'd lose her. He waited. Smiled. And waited. Seemed the noise around them had receded and they were enclosed in a force field composed of their mutual needs. Needs he understood only too well, and needs she longed to have met.

"I want to say 'yes' but I'm scared witless!" Her eyes widened and held his. "Mac?"

There were a hundred questions in the single word. He understood them. Every last one. He reached over and took her hand, drawing it to him while keeping his eyes latched on hers. Slowly he brushed her fingertips, one by one over his lips. "I'll never harm you, Ginny. I can offer you velvet manacles, all the silk scarves you can imagine and more, much more, than your wildest dreams."

"My dreams are pretty damn wild!" Her voice was tight with anxiety and excitement.

"I know, Ginny. I read them, remember?"

She nodded. "When?" There was a trace of fear in her words. He bet her heart was racing, too.

"Tomorrow." The flush drained from her face. She waited, watching him. Not for a second did she try to pull her hand away. He reached into his jacket with his free hand and pulled out a business card. "This—" he pushed the card toward her "—is my home address. Before you come, let a friend know where you will be. You should make that a rule for yourself anytime meeting a contact. Come over tomorrow for Sunday lunch. How about one?"

He let go of her hand as she reached for the card and read it. It was a respectable enough address after all. She read the card slowly, as if memorizing the address. He righted the overturned glass and split the last of the wine between them. "Shall we drink to tomorrow?" he asked.

She nodded and after a couple of seconds hesitation reached for the glass. "Tomorrow!"

He called her an hour after they parted in front of Tarantella. He called and promised wicked things with velvet and silk scarves and a flogger with tresses of fur. That conversation had her resorting to her handy-dandy vibrator after he rung off and she spent the entire evening giving herself a face pack, plucking her eyebrows, shaving her legs and generally agonizing over what to wear, or not to wear, in the morning.

He called again Sunday morning, ten minutes or so before she left, and asked if she could please bring some silk scarves. He was all out of them.

He hung up before she could ask where exactly he thought she'd find silk scarves on a Sunday morning.

She rummaged though drawers, discarding her nylon, Terylene and cotton scarves, and ended up with three—two head scarves and one long, Isadora Duncan sort, she'd seldom worn, but would be perfect for tying her hands to the bed. She almost shoved it back in the drawer, but wasn't that what she'd fantasized about for years?

Why chicken out now?

She put the lot in her bag, grabbed her coat and set off for the tube. He didn't live far—just as well. If she'd had to stand about and change trains, she might well have flaked out—or at least reconsidered the option, but it was a short ride and she knew exactly where he lived—on a side street not far from Sloane Square. She'd found it yesterday evening, taking a taxi and having the driver pass very slowly. He probably thought she was a stalker or looking for somewhere to burgle, but Ginny wanted to be sure he didn't live in a lock-up storage under a railway bridge.

Mac didn't.

He lived on a street of very well-kept terrace houses. His address was the ground floor flat of the third from the corner. She'd actually had the taxi drive past twice. No doubt reinforcing his notion she was casing the joint for some doubtful purpose. What did Mac do for a living? He couldn't live there on the proceeds from *Erotic Leather Quarterly*.

She'd done what he suggested—left his address on her refrigerator, her bathroom mirror and by her telephone. "Always tell someone where you're going," he'd cautioned her on the phone. "I'm honest and trustworthy, I promise, but you never know..."

"I've only your word for your honesty and trustworthiness," she'd replied.

He'd chuckled. "Wise lass, Ginny. Always be careful."

She'd also called her stepsister Alicia. She and Ginny had covered for each other since they'd been in school together. Mind, she'd given Alicia a very doctored account of her expectations for the afternoon.

Perhaps she was foolish, but she trusted Mac. He'd always looked her in the eyes, the mark—her father always insisted—of an honest, straightforward man.

She now stood on the pavement across the road from this putatively honest and straightforward man's house, her heart racing, her hands sweaty and, if truth to be told, panties damp. She needed to compose herself. This was exactly what she'd asked for and Mac was going to deliver. Taking a deep breath, she crossed the road, mounted the five stone steps and pressed the white china button beside his name.

The bell echoed inside. Ginny imagined long corridors, high ceilings and big cavernous rooms.

"Ginny!" He had the door wide open and was smiling as if he'd just been given a raise, won the lottery or at they very least discovered a willing young woman right on his front doorstep. He reached out, took her hand in his and pulled her into the house, shutting the door behind her.

She'd done it! And now…another deep breath.

"Don't look so worried, Ginny. You're not late, if you had been, I'd have to punish you but you're not, so look on this as coming to play for the afternoon with a friend." Her cunt had clenched at the mention of punishment, and she wasn't entirely sure if she was relieved or disappointed at being spared. "Come on in, Ginny," he went on. "Let me show you around."

"Around" was a large bedroom, a small but luxurious bathroom, a narrow kitchen with packages from a well-known caterer on the countertops and a sitting room-cum-dining room that gave onto a terrace.

"It's lovely!" No two ways about it—but left her wondering again what he did for a living. Thoughts of drug dealing or illicit slave trading sprung to mind, but dissipated at the smile in his eyes.

"Don't look so worried, Ginny. Come on out back and have a seat while I get lunch together."

"Out back" was a lovely terrace overlooking a pocket-handkerchief of a garden and the backs of the houses in the square.

Sitting on a wrought iron chair in the sunshine, surrounded by stone pots of begonias and lavender and even a small lemon tree, seemed far, far, removed from their intimate conversation in the dimness of Tarantella. Everything here was in the light, and that raised her anxiety level a few more notches.

"Here!" He placed a flute of sparkling water in front of her. "Not being cheese paring, honest," he said, "but I'll keep the wine for later. We both need command of all our faculties for this. Me to know what I'm doing, and you to not miss a single sensation, and, Ginny—" he reached over and took her hand "—sensation is what I'm promising you. Agreed?"

"Yes."

"Good, remember what I said on the phone about safe words?"

"If I use it, you'll stop."

"Right, and, Ginny, never, never play with a partner who won't agree to one. You need that and so does any decent or caring Dominant. Things might not work out as either of us expect. It's a first, for both of us. I don't know— apart from a few hints you gave me on the phone yesterday—what really turns you on or how much you can tolerate. We're both learning. Remember that." She nodded. "Answer me, Ginny."

His voice was soft, but demanded a reply. "Oh, yes, right. I agree. What safe word?"

"What's your full name?"

"Virginia Amy Elizabeth Wallace."

"Let's use that then, agreed?"

"All right."

He smiled. "All right then, you brought the scarves?"

"Here." She reached into her bag and pulled them out. They sat in a heap of colored silk on the white painted tabletop.

"Good girl, now before we eat, ask me what you're dying to know."

Could she? It was downright personal, but heck, he'd offered. "How can you afford to live in Belgravia?"

"Brilliant, Ginny! Congratulations on a) doing what I told you and b) getting it out without blushing or stammering."

Now she was blushing, but so far no stammers. "Well then?"

"Let me put your mind at rest re drug deals or illegal activities. It's mine. Or at least the lease is. Left to me by my godmother ten years ago. It was horrid and run-down. Probably the only property around that hadn't changed hands during the eighties boom. I had to take out a mortgage just to pay the death duties and it takes almost every spare penny I have to keep it up. You wouldn't believe the council tax I have to pay but I rent out the top two floors and the basement. I see it as my pension plan."

"Either you are very honest, or I'm thoroughly naïve."

"Naïve you're not, Ginny. Anxious, curious and horny, no doubt, and you're sensible to be cautious, but I'll play straight with you, Ginny. I've been in the kinky scene since my university days. I'm now thirty-five. I've had more play partners than I can remember to count, but I seldom invite one of them here. We meet in clubs or a private dungeon I belong to. I'm breaking my own rule bringing you here but, somehow, I felt you weren't quite ready for either of those. They can be pretty intense. I don't want to scare you. I want to excite you, thrill you and delight you, and give you the climax—or better still, climaxes—of your life."

"And lunch, too?" Flippancy might help her ignore the damp now soaking her panties.

"Definitely." He stood. "Pop into the loo, get rid off your panties and I'll get the lunch out."

Her throat went dry, her gullet all but clamped shut, a great weight churned in the pit of her stomach and what was going on deep in her cunt was nobody's business and all this just to take off her damn knickers!

Mac was already clanging dishes and clinking china, quite unconcerned with her turmoil. Wasn't this what she dreamed of? Sitting in the sun, with a warm breeze all the way up and thinking about what she'd take off next.

Ginny stood. It took less that three minutes to nip into the loo in the hall, yank off her admittedly flimsy panties, shove them into her pocketbook and get back on the terrace as Mac brought out a platter of pate, Melba toast and black olives.

"Got them off?" he asked as he put a bone china plate in front of her.

"Yes."

"Good." He laid the table with cutlery and nipped back in for another bottle of sparkling water. "Give them to me." He held out his hand.

It took a moment or two to realize he was not talking about Melba toast or forks. "My knickers?"

"Yes, Ginny. They're mine now. Just as you are. For this afternoon you belong to me. Your pleasure belongs to me. Your climaxes belong to me." He stretched out his hand and stiffened his wrist to emphasize his demand.

She dug them out of her bag and placed them in his outstretched hand. They looked even skimpier between his long fingers.

"Nice," he said, eying them appreciatively before tucking them in his pocket. "I'll keep them for now. Be a good girl and you'll get them back before you go home."

"And if I'm not?"

"You ride home on the District line without them. The draught as you go down the escalator would be quite an—" he gave a teasing smile "—interesting sensation."

"And if I get run over and carried off to hospital?" Damn, she was sounding like her mother!

"They'll think you're a wild, naughty woman." He was obviously enjoying this. "Have some pate." He handed her the plate. "And some Melba toast. And, Ginny, I'm counting on you being wild and naughty. You are, aren't you?"

"Whenever I get the chance. Hasn't happened as often as I'd like."

He looked as if she'd offered him a new car—complete with insurance for life. "Oh, Ginny, be wild and naughty with me as often as you like."

Chapter Four

ೋ

Mac couldn't tamp down the wild elation bursting inside. She was incredible! Sharp, eager, willing and by the evidence on the panties deep in his pocket, aroused already. Some naggy part of his brain—no doubt the caution learned of hard experience—told him she couldn't be this marvelous, that she was too good to be true and would fail him utterly or run out of there crying rape. But, seeing the hope in her eyes, his heart warmed.

Perhaps he was too jaded and cynical to really believe there was a woman who would be "the one" or that love at first sight was possible. Or was he? Five lines of copy had drawn him to her, seeing her in the cafe had thrilled him and he wasn't sure there was an adequate enough word for what he now felt deep in his gut—and he wasn't thinking about his erection, but something deeper, even more persistent—hope.

"Have an olive," he said.

She took one, bit into the wrinkled black flesh, licked her lips, chewed briefly and swallowed, her eyes widening. "They're wonderful!" She popped the rest into her mouth, chewed and turned away for a second as she spat the pit into her closed hand. When the pit hit her plate, it made a quiet ping.

"Like them?"

She nodded. "Best I've tasted in years. They're like the wonderful, ripe ones you get in Greece."

"Sicily." Better put her straight. "I brought them back a couple of months ago when I visited my sister. She lives near

Syracuse." Catching the curiosity in her eyes, he went on. "She's a potter, married to a local lawyer. Went out there for a cheap holiday fifteen years ago and stayed. They're from her father-in-law's olive grove. They always send me home with great jars of olives and tins of olive oil..." he paused, time perhaps to notch up her anticipation a bit. She was getting far too distracted by the food. "I don't cook that much, but find olive oil wonderfully useful as a massage oil and a lubricant."

Oh, dear! She almost choked—not what he'd hoped for—but she coped well, reached for her water and downed most of it. Then glared. "Thanks, just what I needed while swallowing."

"Would have been worse if you'd been drinking."

Had he pushed too far? No, she smiled and rolled her eyes. "Not really. I'd just have ruined your nice linen tablecloth."

"But you didn't. Neither did you pass out. Instead you are curious about alternative uses for Nonno's first pressing."

Bingo! She smiled.

He pushed the plate of pate toward her. "Finish it up. I'll get the rest of the meal."

He gave her five minutes to stew while he decanted the contents of the little packets onto two dinner plates. Wasn't quite as elegant-looking as on the catalog illustration but appetizing. Almost as appetizing as Ginny. He glanced out of the window. She hadn't eaten the last of the pate but was sitting back, sipping her water and looking worried. Time to get back outside. He grabbed a plate in each hand.

She smiled as he came though the French door. "Looks wonderful!"

He bit back the cliché about her looking wonderful, too, but heck, her smile was getting contagious. He grinned at her. "Enjoy! Can't claim the credit, but I do know how to pick a good caterer. Hope you like salmon."

"I love it!"

She tucked in with gusto. He might as well do the same, keeping one eye on Ginny, of course. Not an arduous task. He loved the way her copper hair shone when the sun caught it, and the little crinkles at the corners of her eyes as she smiled. And she smiled a lot, not the nervous smiles he'd noticed yesterday or even earlier today, but joyous grins at her enjoyment of the lunch, and—he hoped—his company and the afternoon ahead.

"That was wonderful!" she said, pushing her plate away. "Fantastic but I don't think I can eat any more."

"I do have pudding, a rather decadent concoction of raspberries, apricots, whipped cream and hazelnut meringue, but I thought we'd keep that for later."

"Yes," Ginny replied, an odd nervousness setting in her chest, threatening to churn up the lunch she'd enjoyed so much. Mac's hand on hers and the gentleness in his eyes stirred another emotion entirely.

"Worried?" he asked. "You can leave anytime, I promise. Walk out now if you want to. No hard feelings."

"And miss that pudding? And what about all the promises you made yesterday?"

"You want that, Ginny, are you certain? If you stay, I'll demand obedience. Do whatever I want with you. Strip you naked. Tie you down with those scarves you brought. Forbid you to climax until I choose. Make you wait, make you suck my cock on your knees. I might even spank you, if you take too long to obey or resist me. Are you really ready and willing?"

It took a second or two to get her voice box operating again. A racing heart and a tight throat rather constricted her larynx. "I won't really know unless we try, will I?"

His wide mouth curled at the corners as he put his hand over hers. His touch was gentle but she felt his strength and suspected if she tried to pull away, it wouldn't be easy. "Neither of us will, Ginny. I hope I don't disappoint you."

Oh, dear, had she gone on too much about earlier letdowns? No, he didn't seem too worried. "You haven't so far, Mac."

"I'll endeavor to give you want you need, Ginny. Remember your safe word? What is it?"

"Virginia Amy Elizabeth Wallace."

"Good, use it and I'll stop, otherwise, you may cry, wail, yell 'no' or shout, moan and complain to your heart's content, and I'll ignore you completely." He stood up, raising her to her feet as he kept hold of her hand. "Ready to obey, dear?"

"Yes." Nervousness and anticipation made the hoarse whisper echo in her skull.

He stood, drew her close and dropped a kiss on her forehead. Steamed heat poured from his lips. His kiss imprinted on her skin as he pulled back and looked down at her. Her heart echoed against her ribs. There was no mistaking the heat and desire in his eyes. A need that mirrored her own.

"You never kissed me before."

"No," he replied, "I wasn't sure of you." He yanked her close, one arm around her shoulders, his free hand cupping the back of her head, holding her steady as his mouth met hers. His first kiss had heated her. This one inflamed. Her lips opened under his and his tongue touched hers. He held her against him, pressing her breasts into his chest and his erection into her belly as his tongue caressed hers. His lips

41

sent her mind whirling and her body responded like dry tinder to a match.

Somewhere in the void beyond sensation, a woman sighed and a man groaned, independent of her awareness, apart from the incredible sensations that coursed though her. She felt her own moisture between her legs, sensed her own need and his desire, and ached for more and more and more.

She kissed back, reaching up to his strong shoulders and melded her need into his. She was vaguely aware of his hand trailing down her back, lifting her skirt and cupping her naked bottom, of his fingers stroking and caressing but not quite reaching where she wanted them.

She rocked her hips and he took his hand away, breaking the kiss gently. "I need more," she whispered, her voice hoarse.

"I know, and, Ginny, you're going to get more. More than you can imagine. Soon. Right now, help me with the washing up."

Damn! She bit back the instinctive gripe, suspecting it was part of his game, and the washing up was pretty straightforward—a few plates and knives and forks in the dishwasher, leftovers in the fridge and scraps in the bin. But none of it easy with a raging libido.

She'd never been this easily aroused. Heck, her nipples hurt, and just meeting his eyes a couple of times had her close to panting for it.

It was ridiculous, but wonderful, and she couldn't wait for what came next. But she'd have to. And one glance his way convinced her he was thoroughly enjoying her all too obvious need.

Her libido simmered down enough to let her remember his comment. "Did you really mean it about not climaxing without permission?"

"Oh, yes." He put a finger under her chin and tilted it up. "You haven't, have you?"

"Not yet but—"

"But you really want to, eh?"

"Let's say your kiss got me really worked up."

His chuckle came from deep in his belly. "It was intended to, Ginny. I'm going to get you very, very worked up. Now be a love, grab the scarves off the table and meet me in the bedroom."

Taking a deep breath, she followed him out of the minuscule kitchen, turning to the left into the sitting room while he went on down the hallway and opened his bedroom door.

"I'll be here, waiting," he called glancing over his shoulder.

Right. She darted across the sitting room, grabbed the scarves off the table on the terrace, resisted the temptation to toss them in the air and watch them flutter over the gardens on either side and stepped back into the flat.

Seemed a long, long way down the corridor. The bedroom door was ajar and as she pushed it open, Mac was standing by the bed. He'd pulled down the covers and was arranging a pair of black manacles on the pale sheets. He looked up, waving a manacle at her. "See, Ginny, just as you wanted—or almost. Not exactly velvet, I'm afraid, but some sort of plush. It'll feel very nice tightened around your wrists." Just as her cunt was tightening looking at them. "And you've got the scarves? Good! Bring them over here."

The last came out like an order. Shocked, she was across the room before she considered his tone. "Here they are."

"Put them on the bed," he said. "On the edge, so I can reach them easily when I need them. How much restraint will you need, Ginny? Will arms be enough or will I have to spread-eagle your legs and leave you completely open and available for my use, hmm?"

"I want to be completely helpless!" It came out without thinking. She couldn't believe the words that echoed in her mind, but she meant them. And was terrified.

Mac looked at her, as if trying to peer into her soul and measure her fears. "You will be, Ginny, my dear. You will be."

He'd moved close. Near enough to touch if either of them reached out. Neither of them did. She was too stunned at her admission and he... Who knew what Mac was thinking?

"I'll tie you so you're helpless, Ginny, if that's what you want. I'll enjoy knowing I had you at my mercy. I'll be able to touch you anywhere, with whatever I want and you'll be unable to do anything but take what I hand out. To submit."

Her throat tightened again and her heart raced, but an odd peace settled over her. She wanted to give over power to Mac, to be helpless and powerless. A wild rush of emotion, desire and heat raced through her mind, and without thinking, she fell to her knees at his feet and lowered her head. She was close to shaking, wanted, needed, yearned for his touch but didn't dare ask.

Mac held in the gasp but nothing contained the rush of emotion, power and tenderness as he looked at Ginny, neck bowed, body quivering. He understood her need. It was a reflection of his own. She was scared. So was he. What if he disappointed her? She was excited, aroused. He could smell her and he and was hard as a poker with an erection that all but hurt. As long as he made her wait, he'd have to as well, but, oh, they'd both enjoy the release when it came.

He stroked her head, ruffling the lovely copper hair. Ran his hand over her slender neck. She was so vulnerable, so gloriously submissive, but he knew what strength it took to kneel at his feet.

Scared and anxious as she was, she begged for what she needed with every muscle and sinew in her quivering body.

Time to play.

He grasped her upper arms with both hands and helped her to her feet. "Look at me, Ginny."

She raised her eyes. They seemed bluer and brighter than before. Her face was calm but her shoulders shook. He kissed her, slowly and thoroughly, pressing his lips to hers, teasing her tongue with his, pushing the kiss deeper and harder until she gave that lovely, sexy moan again. Time to stop before he lost it, he had an afternoon of play planned. The last thing he wanted was to disappoint her.

"You are wonderful," he whispered to her lips. "Sexy and lovely and wondrously submissive. You will obey me, won't you?"

"Yes," she said, between little gasps.

He kissed her hair, took her hand, meshing her fingers with his and led her to the middle of the room. "I'm going to undress you," he told her. "Then we are going to shower together and afterwards, when you've soaped and washed every inch of your body, we're coming back in here and playing 'doctor'."

"Doctor?" A little crease appeared between her raised eyebrows. He smoothed it with his lips.

"Yes, doctor. Never played it as a child? I did, lots of times, and it's even more fun as a grown-up. I'll examine your body most assiduously. You will lie completely still, like a good little submissive and cooperate fully with whatever I ask." He paused. "Won't you, Ginny?"

She nodded, pausing to take a deep breath. "Yes. I think so."

"I know so! That's why you're here." Before she had time to worry that one, he unfastened the first button on her dress. She couldn't have picked a better style, it had a row of large pearl buttons from the open neck to the hem. Most obliging of her to make it so convenient. He undid three more so her dress was open to the waist and pulled the two halves apart. Nice bra. He always liked lace, and this warm pink looked particularly lovely against her pale skin but... "Next time, Ginny, be sure to wear a bra with a front fastening."

"Oh!" She gave a little shake as he traced the sweet swell of flesh above the lacy cups. "I will. But... Mac, I don't have any."

"Better go shopping. Your job is to make it easy for me to strip you. Impede me like this again and you may end up over my knee."

Her hand came up, grasping his forearm as if to steady herself. "I'll buy one. I never thought..." Her breath caught. She was aroused and exited. By being undressed, or the threat of a spanking? He'd find out in time.

"I know. I won't punish you, but next time, you know what I'll expect."

"Yes, next time." Another tight little gasp. Was she anticipating a "next time" as much as he was?

He ran his fingers over her soft flesh, reaching into the cup to find her nipple. It was already hard. He gave it a gentle squeeze, watching her face as she breathed hard and her lips parted. "Ever worn nipple clamps, Ginny?"

"No!"

"You will, one of these days. Tight ones that pinch your nipples. But first, let's get off this damn bra." He spun her around, pulling her dress off her shoulders and flicking open the hooks, pushed the straps off her shoulders. It was a pretty bra, but the floor was the best place for it. He spun her back to face him and gave himself the luxury of ogling her breasts.

They were large, firm and tipped with upstanding, rosy-brown nipples. He cupped a breast in each hand rubbing his thumbs over the firm points of flesh. "Do they always stay this hard?"

"N-no."

The stammer might have been because he squeezed them between finger and thumb. As she caught her breath, he eased the pressure then bent his head and licked her right nipple. She shivered as he closed his mouth on her flesh and suckled. He undid three more buttons and her dress fell to the floor. Not quite naked. She wore a thin, waist slip, but he could smell her arousal, sweet, and feminine and sexy.

He wanted the damn slip off her. Time to show her what dominant meant. Lifting his mouth off her breast, he stood upright, put both hands on her waist and lifted her. He took two steps toward the bed and dropped her onto the mattress. While she gasped and tried to sit upright, he grabbed her slip, yanked it off and fell on top of her, grasping her wrists and pinning her to the bed, arms spread.

"This, Ginny, is how it will feel when I tie you down. Do you like it? You won't be able to move. Unable to resist. All you'll be able to do is submit meekly."

"Maybe not meekly," she whispered, her voice clear, her mouth just inches from his ear.

"No?" he replied. "We'll see about that!" He was darn well tempted to skip the shower, just tie her down here and now and start playing this second. He had her naked didn't he? But he wanted the pleasure of soaping and examining every inch of her, and besides, he really fancied playing "doctor" with her.

He stood, and before she could move, grabbed her, tossing her over his shoulder and crossed the carpet to the open bathroom door. One hand held her ankles together and with her lovely arse at eye level, he couldn't resist planting a big, smacky kiss on one bum cheek and just for luck, he gave her a friendly smack before letting her naked body slide down his front. She stood, inches away from him, head tousled, face flushed and eyes bright.

Time to play in earnest. "Ginny, go stand in the corner."

Chapter Five

ဢ

Ginny stared at Mac. "What?"

"You heard me, dear. Time to start obeying. Stand in the corner, with your face to the wall while I get things ready." She opened her mouth as if to protest or argue, thought better of it, and turned and faced the corner. Very promising. "Peep or turn around before I give you permission, Ginny, and you'll learn the difference between a love pat on your delectable posterior and a thorough hand spanking."

She got the message. Good. Now he'd take his time. Let her anxiety peak a little. He whistled as he stripped off, banged cupboard doors and found towels.

Ginny stood, breathing slowly in a vain attempt to still her racing pulse. She should be scared, worried, anxious — heck, she was naked, alone and with a man she only met yesterday. Instead, despite the excitement and fast beating heart, her overwhelming emotion was peace. At last her dreams and fantasies were coming true. She'd knelt to a lover and now stood stripped, awaiting his pleasure. Her knees wobbled as a rush of emotion poured though her. Another slow, calming breath and the peacefulness returned.

Until she sensed Mac near, felt his warm breath on her shoulder and fought the urge to turn and face him. She clenched her fists and tensed her shoulders, wanting to wrap her arms around his neck, but knowing this was a test. She'd been told to stand and face the wall — and face the wall she would. She jumped as his hand touched her back and traced a slow path down her spine. When he reached her bottom, she was shaking. He stroked the curve of her hip and whispered, "You are magnificent, Ginny. Not much longer. I'm almost ready."

He kissed her shoulder and was gone.

She wanted to whimper, but held that back, too. This was so hard and so utterly right. She shut her eyes, blocking out any distraction from the sensations in her body. He'd barely started playing and she was this hot, this aroused. How much more could she take without climaxing. A lot! She'd have to. He had a long way to go.

Ginny almost jumped as the shower started running. Not much longer, surely? Slow, deep breath. And another.

"Ginny." A shudder rippled though her at his voice.

"Yes, Mac?"

His hand was gentle on her shoulder. "Turn around."

She obeyed and gaped. He was as naked as she was. Shouldn't be surprised at that. He'd hardly be getting in the shower in a knit shirt and chinos, but the sight of him took her breath away. He was beautiful from his broad shoulders to his slim waist and solid thighs, to the twinkle in his eyes and the magnificent cock rising hard and proud from the nest of dark curls at his groin.

Her mouth went dry then flowed with saliva at the prospect of sucking that lovely cock, of running her lips up its length and easing her tongue over the smooth head and lapping the hard flesh.

Her knees relaxed in preparation to kneel and worship his cock, but Mac's hand on her shoulder stayed her. "Not yet, Ginny. Soon. Very soon, you will have the privilege of sucking my cock and feeling it touch the back of your throat, but first, I want to enjoy myself a little with your sumptuous body. Come on." He opened the shower door and stood aside to let her enter.

His shower alone was worth the trip! The door was a standard shower door width, but inside, it was five times as deep as most showers and… She couldn't help staring. He must have bought up the entire stock of shower fitments from the nearest builders' supply. At the farthest end, a super-wide spray head sent a deluge of warm water pouring past the dark blue tiled wall. That was just the beginning. On each wall were three more showerheads, at various heights and angles, and to her right an array of shiny brass knobs presumably controlled the panoply of options, including, she just noticed, two handheld showers on a rail and an assortment of rails and hooks along one wall.

"You could spend a week here and still not try out everything," she said, looking around and catching his amused glance.

"Like it?"

"Yes." She was a bit dubious about a couple of odd-looking hoses at one end, but the warm cascade appealed.

"There's soap on the ledge," Mac said, "grab it and start on my back."

Where had she dreamed up the idea of being massaged with scented bubbles by his strong hands? Would have been nice but he was waiting, watching, and no doubt imagining her bottom over his knee if she hesitated too long. She reached for the tablet of soap. She'd wanted to be dominated. Better start obeying.

She lathered up the soap and started on his shoulders. Really, she couldn't complain. Getting to run her hands over his shoulders and back was no hardship, and stroking his firm arse was, quite honestly, a pleasure. She soaped up and down the backs of his arms. Kneeling, she worked her way down his thighs to his ankles. "If you lift your foot, I can soap that, too."

"Wait."

All right, she'd wait. "Want me to rinse you off before I start on your front?" Was she supposed to be asking? Hell if she knew, but he'd have to turn around in a minute and—

He did, smiling down at her crouched by his ankles. "I'm going to rinse off then you may wash my front." He walked down to the end, stood under the spray a few minutes as the lather ran off him and toward the center drain. "Stand up, Ginny," he said, turning and coming back to her. "You can't wash my chest kneeling."

No, but she would have his cock at eye level and that could never be bad. She settled for chest and nipples at eye level, nothing to be sneezed at after all, and ended up humming as she soaped his chest and belly. She got in a little tickle under his arms and earned a slap on her rump. Not hard, but she got the message. Apparently tickling was unacceptable. She'd have to be careful as she worked south. Kneeling she lathered down his thighs and legs, and was back at his ankles. Obligingly he lifted one foot then the other while she soaped his toes and insteps.

She was getting turned on. Really turned on. Every bit of skin under her fingers was utterly male and emphasized the difference between them, and the magnificent cock jutting out at eye level was the cream in the coffee. She might as well go for it. Lathering up her hands extra well, she eyed his erect and uncircumcised cock. Rather lovely in all respects, and as her hand closed around the hard flesh and eased his foreskin back, she felt his shudder. She lowered her head to hide her smile. After all, he might take exception to a big, wide grin aimed at his sacred equipment. Working steadily, she drew back his foreskin to soap the complete head of his cock and while she was at it, she felt his length with her fingertips, wanting to suck him, to take him deep in her mouth, to feel him touch the back of her throat as he'd promised.

He stepped back. Yes, there was masses of room in the shower. "I'm rinsing off. You might was well stay on your knees, Ginny."

When he returned, water still running down his legs, she forgot the hard tile under her knees as he stroked her cheek with the tip of his cock, and then brushed it over her lips. She didn't need telling to open her mouth. Not taking him in would have been a hardship. She smiled around his cock. Slowly, she eased her lips up his shaft, swallowing him in a little more at a time as her tongue caressed the smooth head and tasted the sweet drop of moisture that rose at her touch, breathing carefully as he filled her mouth with his male power and strength. His hands grasped her head, spray from the still running shower brushed her side, but nothing could distract her from her duty with her lips.

Now Mac took over, setting the rhythm as he held her head steady and fucked her mouth. He came deeper and deeper, slowly to allow her to breathe through her nose, and, yes, he touched the back of her throat, bringing tears of excitement to the corners of her eyes. Tears that ran down her cheeks as he pulled away.

"Sweet Ginny," he said, stroking her now-damp hair as he stepped back and opened the shower door. "Quite impressive. We'll do that again soon, but meanwhile, you need to shower thoroughly. You must be clean all over for the strict physical exam you will receive in a few minutes. When you are clean and dry, come immediately into the bedroom where I will be ready for you."

He was gone. Might as well shower as he'd ordered. No point in giving him an excuse for the over-the-knee spanking he mentioned with such relish.

She shampooed her hair, even using the conditioner. As she stepped out of the spray to reach the soap, she heard a hair dryer. He was still there, taking care of himself while she was here, on the other side of the mottled glass door, alone, horny as can be and convinced a medical exam wasn't what she had in mind when she'd accepted his offer of lunch and hot sex. But she'd agreed to the submissive role, might as way play it through.

She soaped up and rinsed off. Mac was gone. A large blue bath towel lay on the bench waiting and, yes, he'd left out the hair dryer—a rather fancy German model. Mac Brodie appreciated creature comforts.

Dried off and hair soft and fluffy. She looked at herself in the mirror. Not a perfect bod but none too shabby. She hoped he liked it. He had so far, hadn't he?

Smiling to herself to give her courage, she stepped though the door, across the hall and into the bedroom.

Mac was waiting, wearing a white coat, but no doctor had ever walked the wards in anything like this. The front was cut away, a bit like an old-fashioned tailcoat, but the effect was to leave his cock on display. Framed in crisp white cotton, his erection seemed bigger and more demanding than before. She longed to fall to her knees and bring him to climax, to finish what they'd started in the shower but she held back, waiting for his order.

"Ah! Ginny," he said. "Punctual and ready. How nice." He swung the stethoscope round his neck as he spoke and she couldn't fail to notice the end was not the customary round disk for listening to hearts and chests, but a long, narrow smooth...dildo. "Ah, my dear. Come closer. You noticed my little stethie toy did you?"

"Yes."

"Know what this is?" He held it out to her.

"A dildo?"

"No, dear, far too small for that. Your lovely cunt can take much more than this. In fact, it's going to when I put my cock up you. No, dear, this is a rectal plug. You'll feel it soon enough."

Her innards clenched. She dreaded having that cold, gleaming metal up her arsehole. And wanted it more than anything in the world right now.

"Now, my dear, hop up on the examining table. Time to check out your breasts and cunt. I must give them a good examination. Up you go and no complaining. I don't want any carrying on about cold hands. If I choose to fill you with ice cubes, that's my prerogative. I'm the doctor and I know what's best for you."

Ice cubes was where she'd use her safe word! Keeping that thought to herself, she crossed to the folding exam table. He must have pulled it out since she last saw the room. What else was stashed behind the built-in cupboard doors that filled one whole wall?

He'd provided a little stepstool and with that she managed a more or less graceful climb. She sat on the edge and looked at him. At least they were eye to eye. "What now?"

His mouth twitched as he swung that darn butt plug. "Now, my dear, I begin by examining your breasts." He let that damn plug swing free and cupped a breast in each hand, hefting it, squeezing gently and rubbing her nipples with the pad of his thumb. "Had any problems with them, my dear?"

"No." Not in real life and she was not about to invent any.

"Excellent, lie down and let me examine them more." As he spoke, his arm under her knees turned her and his free arm pressed her down so she lay on her back, looking up at the ceiling and a pair of large eyebolts she hadn't noticed earlier.

"What are they for?" She wasn't too sure she really wanted to know, but the words were out before she could bite them back.

"The hooks?" He followed her gaze up as his hand closed over her breast and his fingers pressed into her soft flesh. "That's in case I have a recalcitrant patient and have to resort to restraint."

"Have a lot of patients do you?" She gasped as his fingers pressed and kneaded.

"A few, over time, my dear, but seldom one as promising or cooperative as you." His fingers ground into her breast and she let out a little groan. "Hush, my dear, not a sound, you must accustom yourself to my examination. You'll be receiving them regularly." His hand moved to her other breast, which got the full treatment. She held her breath, hoping he'd finish soon, but wishing he wouldn't. His touch stopped just short of hurting, but it seemed each time he pressed or massaged her breast, her cunt responded with a warm, damp thrill.

By the time her breasts felt thoroughly squashed, he started on her nipples, squeezing them between finger and thumb, pulling gently and then rolling them until she whimpered.

"Does that hurt?" he asked.

"No." Truthfully it didn't. "Feels nice but…"

"But what? Kindly express yourself more clearly, Ginny."

"I like it but I'm scared you'll do more and hurt!" It was out.

His response was a raised eyebrow. "Indeed? You may well be right, Ginny." He ran his hand from between her breasts, over her belly to pause just above her pussy as his finger tapped gently, just missing her clit. "Time I examined your other more sensitive parts, Ginny. Now where to start, your cunt or your tight little arsehole? I must check them both—can't leave an orifice unchecked, can I?" He stroked across her belly in smooth circles as he spoke. "Ever been fucked in the arse, Ginny?"

"Once."

"Did you like it?"

"No!" It had been a case of once and never again.

"What a shame, my love. It can be the most stimulating experience. What didn't you like about it?"

He would have to ask, wouldn't he? "It hurt like hell!"

He tsk-tsked like a reproving teacher. "Unfortunate. It won't hurt when I bugger you, I promise. Now on your side—first I'll examine your cunt then I'll have a little poke in your tight little rose. You will lie completely still for me, my dear, won't you? Whatever I do to you there will be no wiggling. Do you understand?"

"Yes." Her throat was so tight, just one syllable was an effort.

"Over you go, then." His hand, warm on her naked hip eased her, turning and caught her behind her knees, drawing her legs up to her chest, leaving her exposed and vulnerable. His hand rested on her thigh. "Will I need to use lubrication, Ginny, or are you sufficiently aroused to take my examination easily?"

She held back the giggle. This was definitely unlike any physical exam she'd ever experienced. Even the medical student she'd gone out with at Uni hadn't been this inventive. "I'm wet, but perhaps you'd better check that I meet your standards."

He chuckled at that, stroking her thigh. "I agree, Ginny. I think I'd better." He lifted her thigh to get a better view. "Nice! What a lovely, rosy pink cunt and, yes, dear, it is wet, almost glistening. How nice." How red her face! Her cheeks burned. Just as well she did have her back to him. Fingers eased into her. She relaxed, or tried to. It wasn't too easy with his other hand gliding up her rib cage to her breast.

His strong fingers probed, withdrew and came back in. More of them this time, she was sure. She felt filled, stuffed, and as he curled his fingers inside her, she gasped. Her hips wanted to rock but she managed to keep control until he found her G-spot. She couldn't keep still, she bore down on his hand and he was gone! She was empty and bereft, and cried out.

"Settle down!" It was almost a snap. "I told you to keep still. You disobeyed." Her hip stung where he'd slapped.

"I couldn't help it! It felt so good!"

"You had better learn to 'help' it, Ginny. I really don't want to have to tie you down at this point in the proceedings." His hand was gone from her breast, too. She wanted his hands back, on her and in her and... "You lie there, my dear, while I wash my hands. Don't you dare move."

As if she could! The table was so darn narrow, roll the wrong way and she'd be on the carpet. So she waited, breathing slowly to calm her racing pulse but nothing could calm the throbbing in her cunt. He knew just how to arouse her—and leave her hanging. But he had promised her the climax of her life—eventually. All she had to do was hang on.

Chapter Six

§つ

Mac was back, standing right in front of her. His cock only too obvious through the cutaway jacket, and the darn butt plug swinging from his hand. The metal gleamed wickedly at her. "I warmed it," he said, "so you won't have cold metal rammed up you." He held it at her eye level and waved a tube of lubricant in his other hand. "I'm going to lube the probe up then squirt the jelly up you. Jelly always feels cold, so I don't want any complaints. Put up with it. Won't be cold for long, your body will heat it up, then I'll press the plug in slowly. It will be to your advantage to relax, Ginny. Relax and permit me to plug you just as far as I want to push it up you."

"Easier said than done!" Not exactly submissive, but darn it.

"If it was easy, I wouldn't have taken so much time to get you aroused. But you are and it will be easier, trust me." As she opened her lips to answer or maybe gripe, he kissed her. A gentle brush over her mouth she felt deep in her groin. The sigh was involuntary, as was the rush of dampness between her legs. Grief! She could smell herself. How could he miss it? His grin suggested he hadn't.

"All right, dear. I'm ready." He walked around the table to stand behind her. She tensed. "No, no, no, Ginny. That won't do at all." His voice was gentle. "Relax." He stroked her hip. "That's the key, Ginny. Relaxation and arousal. I'm not buggering you yet, just opening up your tight little rose."

The first sensation was cold and sticky but he'd been right—her body soon warmed the jelly. Now she was moist both fore and aft. She relaxed, a little, just in time to feel the hard tip against her ring of muscle. "This, Ginny, is where you decide how much you want to hurt. Relax and press back."

It was easier said than done but she managed to relax a little. Mac waited as slowly she pressed down on the metal tip, stopping as it penetrated her muscle. "Continue, Ginny," he said. "Keep going. The more you press down, the less I have to press up you. A true submissive will take her Dominant's cock with pleasure. Up to the balls. Better practice."

She pressed a little more and hesitated. She was stretched and it was hurting, not much, but she was very much aware that a hard, foreign object was going up where things usually came down. She took several deep breaths — suddenly her sphincter relaxed and she bore down hard. She was filled, stuffed, the metal plug hard within her soft flesh but it felt incredible.

"Oh!" she cried out as a torrent of sensation flooded her and her cunt responded with a persistent throb.

"'Oh!' good or 'Oh!' it's horrible?" Mac asked.

It took her a few seconds to reply. "Oh! Wonderful!"

"What did I tell you?" He bent forward and whispered, his breath warm in her ear. "Where else do you feel it, Ginny? Just in your tight, little arsehole?"

"No! In my cunt, my clit, even my breasts."

"Wonderful!" And pulled it out. At her gasp of shock, he asked, "Want it pushed back in?"

"Please, oh, please!" She was begging for what she'd dreaded, but she needed it back in deep. She cried out as he pushed it back, not easily this time but with a hard shove. Lubricated as she was, it felt fantastic. She was shaking with excitement as he gently pulled out again. "Enough for now, Ginny. There will be more, much more."

She wasn't sure she could take much more. Her hips itched to rock and her clit pulsed. "I want it back," she moaned.

"Certainly not! You are too close to coming and remember you're forbidden to climax until I give permission."

She wanted to cry with frustration, to yell at him, to snarl in her need, but his mouth on hers took away her objections. His lips were pure magic—soothing and arousing her at the same time, making her shudder with pleasure and sigh with need and satisfaction. Short-lived satisfaction, as he broke the kiss and her still raging need burst anew. "Mac," she said, her voice coming raspy and hoarse. "I can't last much longer."

"The longer you wait, the better it will be," he replied. "Trust me in this. I know best, my dear." He brushed her hair off her forehead, dropped a soft kiss above each eye and rolled her onto her back. "You have been brilliant, Ginny, a wonderful patient, and very, very soon we will try out your remaining orifice. Get on your back!"

"You mean..." she began and rolled over. She gasped, Mac was on the table, kneeling astride her, pinning her on her back. She didn't need to ask which orifice he was examining next.

As he loomed over her, still wearing the cutaway white coat, she looked up at his cock, hard and ready, and just inches from her mouth. Wild need raged through her. Damn playing games! She wanted—needed—to close her mouth over his cock and make him vulnerable.

As she parted her lips, he reached into his breast pocket and pulled out a foil packet. Good thing one of them was thinking straight! She contained herself while he eased the thin sheath over his magnificent cock. Tossing the packet aside, he leaned forward, cupping the back of her head in his hands. Her lips parted as his cock brushed her chin, her mouth opened wide at his touch and she circled him with her lips.

Her heart raced, and her mind spiraled with sheer and utter elation. How she loved this, feeling his strength between her lips, knowing she held his cock between her teeth, making him vulnerable in the very act that so pleasured him. She might be on her back, straddled by his admirable thighs but she held the power. It was her lips that drove his desire and her tongue that was teasing him to climax. She smiled around his erection as she worked her mouth along his length then drew back to tease him just a little.

His groan suggested she was succeeding.

She'd chuckle, but every bit of effort that wasn't intent on his cock was focused on holding back her climax. Maybe he was right about delay intensifying pleasure, or maybe he just liked retaining that last shred of power.

His mounting need creased his face and had him throwing back his head as she fluttered her tongue on the underside of his cock.

He froze a moment as he let out a slow gasp. "Ginny," he said, his voice taut, "come whenever you are ready. I'm so close it hurts!"

Now he knew what he'd put her through! But he'd known all along and now she had permission. She worked her mouth harder and faster, her own need burgeoning as she fixated on his cock and the power of her lips. She'd never, ever climaxed like this, just by a lover's cock in her mouth and the power of his will, but as his own climax burst, he leaned close, groaning, "Ginny! Come! Come for me, Ginny!"

She came. In a wild, intense spate of sheer joy that flooded her mind and possessed her body. She was flying, spiraling upward on a vast tide of pleasure and sensation. She screamed with joy, the sound muffled by his cock, until he withdrew and the full volume of her satisfaction echoed off the ceiling. She let out another great cry and sagged back, her body limp and sweaty, and still enclosed in his strong thighs.

"Magnificent!" he said, kissing her breasts, one after the other, before easing off the table and helping her up.

Help was what she needed! Sitting up was difficult and she doubted she'd be able to stand for a while. Her body still thrummed with the after-pleasures of her climax and her clit throbbed with a life of its own. She tried to echo his exuberant "magnificent" but only managed a weak "Mac!" before sagging into his strong arms.

"Don't worry, Ginny. I've got you!" He did. She was swept up in his arms, carried across the room to his bed and settled on the pillows as he pulled the covers over her. "I'll be back in a jiffy," he said kissing her softly and then padded off, still wearing the now-crumpled white doctor's jacket.

Mac could barely contain himself. If his flat was bigger, he'd run, leap and halloo until the walls echoed. He had to content himself with bit of a hop, skip and a jump, and a big grin in the mirror. He'd been inspired! Ginny inspired him! His wild impulse to meet her and invite her over to play had been inspired. Her body was inspired!

He was close to gibbering, but never been happier in his life.

Okay, he'd better settle down. He peeled off the condom and flushed it way.

What in Hades was happening? Things were getting out of hand. He'd played this scenario before, enjoyed it before but never had a submissive partner responded with such ardor and sheer delight in following his lead.

He was tempted to keep her naked forever. To stay naked with her forever. To spend the rest of his life devising sensual torture for her pleasure and— Whoa! Better backpedal a bit here. He washed off, splashed water on his face and pulled on his spare dressing gown. He needed to settle down. Get back in control. Keep things under his control. But something deep in his soul told him things would never be the same again.

Ginny had changed everything.

He was dead scared she didn't feel the same. Did she? Could she? Best ask her. No! That might scare her off. He needed to tread carefully, proceed with caution, woo her slowly. But if he held off, maybe he'd lose her. Heck, London was packed with Dominants dreaming of a submissive like Ginny. He couldn't let her out of his sight.

He had to. He didn't own her. She had a life of her own. What if a wild afternoon of sex was all she wanted. Ever!

That thought all but had his cock shriveling. Surely she hadn't just used him for sex? Why not? That was what he'd invited her over for. He splashed cold water on his face, hoping to calm his racing thoughts. Didn't help.

He had to get his mind straight and focus on convincing Ginny she'd be happy with him for the rest of her life.

Whoa!!

What was that thought?

The truth. Sheer and unadulterated truth. He wanted Ginny forever and ever as his. For life.

A bit of a tall order after an invitation to lunch and play.

But—

"Mac?" The object of his lust and adoration stood naked in the doorway. "Sorry, but I need to wee."

And he'd been fixating on his out of control emotions. Had to be he was just overcome after the best sex he'd ever had. "Sorry, love. Come on in, I'm through. Just a tic." He reached for his toweling dressing gown hanging on the back of the door. "Put this on, and we'll have that dessert I promised. If you want to wash up…" He nodded toward the bidet in the corner. "Go ahead. There's plenty of towels and soap. See you in a few minutes." After he got his mind back into shape.

"Thanks, Mac." She came close and kissed him. "And thank you!"

He was humming to himself as he closed the door and walked back to the kitchen. He took the pudding out of the fridge, set the coffee machine going and reached for two of his grandmother's Meissen dessert plates. Pity he didn't have champagne already chilled. Big oversight on his part that, but how could he have dreamt Ginny would be so magnificent?

As the coffee started to gurgle, he found two mugs, filled a jug with milk and told himself the wild rush inside was just the result of phenomenal sex. Good try! He was too old and too aware of his own body and its reactions to fall for that one. Twenty-four hours ago, he'd have laughed at the notion of love at first sight. Now, he knew better.

He'd been drawn to Ginny at sight—no—before that. When he read those delicious, outrageous stories of hers. When he'd read her darn personal ad. One look at her smile and gleaming copper hair had him transfixed. But now, after being inside her body and touching the core of her submissive soul, he knew.

He had it bad, had fallen in love and if he couldn't keep her, he didn't know how he'd survive.

He wanted her. Needed her. Ached for her.

"Mac?"

He spun around at her voice, crossed the yard or so that separated them, pulled her into a bear hug and swung her around, fastening his mouth on hers, swallowing her gasp of surprise. "I love you," he said, as he set her back on her feet. "Honest, I do, Ginny. I've never felt this way about anyone in my entire life. Will you marry me?"

Chapter Seven

ଅ

The smile on her face faded and the light in her eyes went out as if snuffed. Shit! He'd rushed her. Hell, he'd stampeded her when she was no doubt still sorting out her response and reactions to his dominance. Bugger!

Damage control needed urgently.

He kept hold of her, this time dropping a soft kiss on her forehead. "Don't look so worried, Ginny. I'll still love you even if you say 'no'." His hopeful smile managed to draw a wary one from her. "Coffee and decadent pudding, my love?"

At least he had one "yes".

He really had screwed up. She leaned back in her chair eating slowly and sipping coffee, but avoiding his eyes. He half-suspected she'd have been out the front door and down the road if her clothes weren't still on his bedroom floor.

Ginny licked the whipped cream off her spoon. The pudding was every bit as marvelous as he'd promised. Too bad it was so hard to swallow. Gulping coffee helped but, oh, dammit! Wonderful splendiferous sex—and what did he have to do but kill the moment? At least he wasn't trying to force conversation. Why did men do things like that? Or, more precisely why did Mac? Marriage proposals weren't customary post-coital conversation openers in her experience.

And why did it upset her so? She could have laughed it off as the joke it was. Except something deep inside convinced her he hadn't been kidding.

She stared at the now-empty plate. Pity she hadn't tasted anything while she was scarfing it down. Pity she was going to grab her clothes and run for the wilds of Earl's Court. Pity it—

Damn!

She pushed away the empty plate, picked up her coffee to drain the last mouthful or so, and met Mac's eyes over the rim of her mug.

They were the same eyes she'd met when she opened his front door just a couple of hours ago, but now they looked tortured, strained, worried.

"Meringue all right?" he asked.

"Very nice."

"Good."

Blow it! She was not sitting there, wearing nothing but his dressing gown and exchanging monosyllables. "No, it's not!" At least that got a reaction. Eyebrows rose nicely and a bit of light came back into his dark eyes—puzzled and exasperated light, but a distinct improvement over confusion. Having his attention, she might as well dive in. "Something's wrong. After the best sex I ever had, I end up hurting your feelings. I eat through the most scrumptious dessert imaginable without tasting it, and now feel it's all my fault—which it really isn't—and on top of it, I never did get the velvet manacles you promised."

Not quite what she'd intended but once she'd started it all poured out.

And left him speechless for a good thirty seconds.

But he did smile and the sexy light returned to those gorgeous eyes.

"I see." Surely he could do better than that? He reached across the table and covered her hand with his. "Thank God, you're not one of those women who hisses 'fine' when it's anything but." He paused, his head angled to one side. "I rushed you on the 'marry me' bit, I presume?"

"You bowled me over, as the saying goes, and trampled the breath out of me."

"A bit too sudden. Too soon?"

"Yeah!"

"But it was the best sex you've ever had?"

"So far."

He beamed, his eyes creasing at the corners and his lips all but demanding to be kissed. "So far? You expect more and better? Am I faced with a rapacious submissive? Bit of an oxymoron that."

It was going to be all right! She knew it from the wicked twist of his mouth and the twinkle back in his eyes. She opened her fingers to mesh with his. "Going to do anything about it?" They should probably be talking things out, but darn it, just touching him made her horny and he had promised...

"Definitely." He tightened his hold on her fingers. She'd have to yank her arm to withdraw from his touch—if she ever wanted to. "Just answer me this, was it just sex for you?"

Questions, questions. Thinking was needed and her current brain chemistry wasn't inclined to cognition. But it was a perfectly reasonable question in the circumstances. Better tone down the libido and up the rational part of her brain. Not easy but not a hard question to answer. "No, Mac, it wasn't 'just' sex. It was fantastic, mind-blowing sex. You were incredible but it went deeper. I felt a connection to you and when I came, it was as if I leapt into the heavens with you. I used to think tales of the earth moving and rockets going off were just a bunch of hyperbole but—"

His big, smacky kiss interrupted her. "Sorry to break you off like that," he said, "but, Ginny, I feel the same. I've had…okay, don't take me wrong here, but I've had scores of nice women as play partners. Most of them were just that—fun people to enjoy kinky sex with. A few I really clicked with and we played repeatedly, but you're the first one to stun me out of complacency. My French grandmother would have called it a *coup de tonnerre*—a thunderbolt and she'd have been spot on. It was like a bolt from the heavens. I meant what I said—I'd love to marry you and play with you for the rest of my life, but won't belabor the point. The offer stands—if you want to consider it a day or two, even a few weeks.

"Sorry I ruined the pud for you, I can always get another, but meanwhile I do have those manacles waiting if you're interested."

She went warm, cold, shivery and sweaty all at the same time. No man could be so reasonable, so utterly decent, so kind and so all-around sexy in one package. But Mac was and offering himself to her. Thinking about being manacled sent goose bumps down her spine and a hot rush to her cunt.

Amid the wash of hormones and horniness, reason still stirred. "The safe word still applies?"

"Always, Ginny, always." He stood. "Remember it?"

"Virginia Amy Elizabeth Wallace."

He gave her hand a little tug. "Come on then."

They practically ran down the corridor, Mac pulling her along. Once back in his room, he spun her to face him and he kissed hard then untied the belt, easing the dressing gown off her shoulders. It felt so right to be naked again. His mouth pressed on hers, pushing her lips apart before his tongue invaded with heat and passion. She tried to meet his kiss, pressing her tongue on his, exploring his mouth, but she couldn't match his power and strength. There was no question who led the kiss and who followed, and her heart fluttered with happiness.

She whimpered with disappointment when he lifted his mouth to break the kiss. "Hush," he chided tapping her lips with his finger. "Don't you dare complain, Ginny. That's not one of your options. Unless you want to safe word out."

Not a chance! "Play" he might call it, but there was nothing frivolous about his purpose. "I don't want to safe word out."

"Good. Prove your sincerity by kneeling and sucking my cock. Take it as deep as you can. Show me how much you want to please me." His hands on her shoulders pressed gently. She could easily have resisted the pressure, just stepped back and walked away. But she wasn't loony!

She knelt.

The carpet was soft under her knees, the hair on his legs brushing her breasts as she leaned in. She raised a hand to stroke his beautiful cock, but his fingers closed over her wrist.

"No," he said, "no hands. I want to see what you can do with your mouth alone. Clasp you hands behind your back."

It made balancing up on her knees a little harder but if worse came to worse and she toppled forward, she'd fall smack into his legs and that could hardly be bad. Finding his cock wasn't going to be difficult—his silk dressing gown tented over his erection.

Once steady, she leaned in and grasped the colored silk in her teeth pulling it a little aside so his cock sprang out, hard, and aimed right at her. She kissed the tip, caressing the smooth, rounded flesh with her lips and licking gently to savor the sweet bead of moisture, before opening her lips and taking the rounded head into her mouth. She worked her lips up and over the smooth, rounded knob, fluttering her tongue over his ridge and frenulum before moving her head and taking him in deep.

His cock was the perfect size—strong and lusciously firm, but not so long as to choke her or wide enough to gag her. It could have been made to measure to suit her needs and wants.

Was Mac right? Were they made for each other? Had the thunderbolt hit her, too? Now was not the time to worry over that. Not with his wondrous cock in her mouth and her lips working up and down the hard rod of muscle. Her mind blanked out, her reason lost in the vast tide of longing, need and heat. On her knees, worshiping his cock, peace flooded her. This felt so right, to be there, naked for Mac—to show her willingness and prove her worthiness.

His hands tunneled in her hair, clasping her head as he gently eased her mouth up and down his cock. With Mac controlling, Ginny concentrated on using her tongue. Licking round him, flicking the head of his cock with soft, large movements then whirling around with faster, lighter darts circling his ridge and teasing the sensitive spot underneath. She longed—itched—to stroke his balls, but kept her hands clasped as ordered, confident he'd let her worship his balls in his own good time.

She looked up and met his eyes. His smile and the dazed but ecstatic look on his face was all she needed to increase her efforts. This was sheer and utter joy and feminine power—she reveled in it.

Until he eased her head off him—gently but firmly. "Enough, Ginny. Enough. You've convinced me. You are completely sincere in your desire to submit to me. You delight me with what you offer." He grasped her upper arms and raised her to her feet. Seeing his mouth smiling down at her, she parted her lips, ready for his kiss, but it never came. "Time now, Ginny, for you to prove you meant it about rending yourself helpless. Are you sure you want to go on? Once I have you bound, you cannot escape me. You will be helpless, vulnerable, utterly in my power. I can do anything to you I choose and you can do nothing but accept. Can you take it?"

She was beginning to doubt herself, but no… "I don't know if I can, Mac. I know I want to. It's always been a secret fantasy. Just listening to what you offer has me ready. I don't know, but I'll try."

"No, sweet Ginny. I'll try you." He ran his hand down the side of her face, caressing her chin with his fingers and tilting her face. His touch was soft and gentle, but if she resisted would it be so tender? "Get on the bed, Ginny. Face down. Now."

The sharp tone of that last word sent a shiver down to her cunt. She was facedown in seconds, head on the soft down pillow and arms by her sides.

"Good, very good." It was almost a whisper but all the more forceful for the quiet confidence in his voice. His fingertips trailed down the bumps of her spine sending goose bumps skittering across her skin. A slow kiss on her shoulder elicited a little moan before she bit it back. Had he told her to be silent this time? Did the order from last time carry over?

Darn it, she needed to know. "Mac?"

He stopped stroking her and rested the flat of his hand in the middle of her back. "You want to use your safe word?"

"No, I want to ask a question."

"Ask!"

Okay. Deep breath. "Do I have to remain silent?" Part of her recoiled at the thought she even had to ask, and a deeper, wilder part of her mind reveled in needing to ask—having to do whatever he decreed.

"Do you have to remain silent?" he echoed. "Mmm, let me think. It would be good discipline for you to have to restrain yourself, but on the other hand, you made such a sterling effort earlier, this time—and mind you, Ginny, just this time—you may express pleasure and contentment. If, and only if, you do so quietly. No rambunctious yelling or shouting. We will have sedate, controlled expressions of passion only." Sedate, controlled and passion in the same sentence was an oxymoron. But she knew enough to keep that to herself. "Thank you, Mac."

"My pleasure," he replied. "Now, if you are through with interruptions, I will continue."

"Please!"

She sensed him move away then return and lean over her. Warmth pooled between her shoulder blades then slowly trickled down her back. She had her mouth open to ask what he was doing when she realized the smooth, warm liquid was massage oil. Virgin olive oil from his sister's father-in-law? Now was not the time to worry about its provenance, but just enjoy the warmth on her skin. Moments later the mattress shifted as Mac climbed on the bed and knelt astride her, his thighs brushing her hips. His hand settled on her shoulders and began to knead her flesh.

A massage! As he worked her shoulders, she let out a long sigh of pleasure.

"Like that, Ginny?"

"Oh, yes!"

"Good, you're tense. I want you thoroughly relaxed before I restrain you."

And that comment was supposed to help? No, just the opposite, he wanted her on edge. He was going to get it. Perhaps. His hands did work magic. She'd thought herself relaxed after that rather stupendous climax, but he was finding tight muscles she never knew existed. Finishing her shoulders, he moved lower. Now straddling her thighs, he worked her lower back and hips. She gave into his touch, closed her eyes and sank into the mattress. He could do this all day and into the night. To lie there, limp on his bed while his hands worked her flesh was a pleasure she'd never turn down.

Damn! Mac wasn't just a marvelous lover. He was a marvel worker. She let out another sigh of pleasure and he eased back up her shoulders and worked her right arm, stroking and kneading the muscles as he lifted her arm and fastened a strip of cloth around her wrist and tightened it with the soft scritch sound of Velcro.

She looked up and pulled at her wrist as he grabbed her left hand and fastened that down, too.

She was bound, flat on her belly and... She bit back the protest that rose by instinct. This was what she'd wanted, dreamed of and asked for. She was helpless—

"Completely," Mac said, as if reading her mind. "Utterly helpless now, Ginny." He rested his hand on her bum, pressing a little as if to emphasize exactly where he had her. "At my mercy."

A wonderfully slow shiver rippled down her body and settled deep in her cunt. She wanted so much to sit up and reach for him but her arms were tied securely to the bed head. Even rolling over would be a gymnastic feat.

All she could do was lie there. Her body thrilled at the reality. This was her fantasy to be helpless while a lover pleasured her and Mac's massage was pleasure indeed. So was his hand on her bum. She'd always felt it was too big, blamed it on the hours she'd spent riding as a schoolgirl, but apparently he was entranced by hers, stroking, brushing his fingertips over her curves and cupping her bum cheeks from the underside and jiggling.

She almost left the mattress when he planted a kiss on her right cheek then her left. "You have such a perfect arse, Ginny," he said. "It's beautiful." He ran his hand over her flesh, a gentle caress that teased and promised. She lay still, relishing his touch and waiting for more.

Chapter Eight

ஐ

Needing more—which never came.

She bit back the demand that rose by instinct. She needed more, ached for more, but she'd agreed. Not a sound unless of pleasure. Damn! This being submissive was harder than she'd imagined. He could tease her the rest of the afternoon and into the night. Arouse her and then pull back. That, no doubt, was exactly what he planned. She took a deep breath and lay still, waiting, and yelped as he bit her bum!

She pulled herself up by lifting her shoulders, and turned scowling at him, but strong hands forced her back down.

"No noise, Ginny, no yelling. Didn't you agree, and what was that?"

"I yelled because you hurt me!"

"I know I did. Time for you to experience a different sensation. If you hadn't made such a noise, I'd have kissed it better. You'd have enjoyed that, you like my kisses don't you, Ginny?"

"Yes."

"And for now you'll have to do without. Shame about that, but, my love, you have to learn to do exactly as you are told. In my bed, you obey. I had hoped you'd obey just by being asked, but seems you are one of those women who need discipline to learn."

A shiver that wasn't pleasure crossed her soul. Discipline! Mac had promised he wouldn't spank her this time, but was that conditional on her obedience? She was trying to word her question, so it wouldn't sound like more complaining when she felt Mac move off the bed, and from the corner of her eye she saw him move out of her line of vision. A hand grasped her right ankle, pulled it to the side and in seconds it was restrained. It took even less time to tie down her left ankle.

She was spread-eagled, flat on her belly and unable to move. She tensed, expecting a slap or even a series of spanks, but nothing. Not a word, not a touch. A few moments later he returned to the head of the bed, a small kitchen timer in his hand.

"Ginny, I'm giving you ten minutes to show me you fully understand what 'lie still, and be silent' means. I'll put the timer here so you know exactly how much longer you have left. It won't be easy, but I have every confidence in you. I expect you to make every effort, and I expect you to succeed. If you fail, I will be thoroughly disappointed."

Darn! He sounded like the headmaster of her old school. Probably Mac's intention. "I'll try."

"You'd better, my dear. Very hard." She bit back that response, too. Now was not the time for wisecracks. "Not a sound, Ginny, not a movement, whatever I do to you."

Feeling the tension build in her back, she made herself relax. She'd go limp and lie there unmoving…she hoped. More than anything she wanted to obey, to do exactly what Mac wanted, to prove her sincerity.

His fingertips trailed up her spine. Slowly. She bit back the sigh of pleasure and another as he stroked down from the nape of her neck. She loved his touch, wished for more, but he'd moved away again. She lay there, breathing slowly, waiting. Hoping.

Seemed ages before he touched her again. This time his hand rested on her bum, and openhanded he circled her arse cheek. Pleasant, but she could hold back the appreciative moan. But it couldn't all be this easy could it?

Seconds later, he parted her bum cheeks, cold gel shot inside her arsehole followed almost immediately by the pressure of cold metal. Biting her lip kept sound back. She held her breath, waiting to feel the intrusion of the plug. This time she got what she expected but without any gentle easing. One moment the tip of the plug pressed against her tight muscle and the next it was inside her, filling her narrow passage and she tasted blood where she'd bitten her lip.

She gasped in the silence. Trying to relax and not fight the hard intrusion.

It was damn difficult, but eventually she managed it. Her tight muscles relaxed around the plug and the strange pleasure of being so invaded eased away her hurt and shock. She smiled into the pillow.

"Brilliant, Ginny!"

She positively grinned at his pleasure. She'd done exactly what he wanted and a glance sideways at the timer showed she had eight and a half minutes to go.

He could come up with a lot in eight and a half minutes, and she bet every single touch was intended to make her cry out. She'd show him!

Or, to judge by the past few moments, he might show her. Better not disappoint him. She pressed her lips together, just before something soft and warm slid up the inside of her left leg, stroking the soft skin on the inside of her thigh, skimming her cunt and then sliding down her right leg before coming back, brushing her arse and swirling over her back and shoulders. It felt so frightfully wonderful, it took her a few seconds to realize he was using one of her silk scarves. Nothing else was so warm, so soft and so— She had to bite back the sigh as he brushed the scarf along her crack, catching the edge of the plug and moving it just enough to set her nerve endings humming.

And he knew exactly what it did to her, she bet! Back and forth he pulled it, and steadily she breathed, willing her body not to let her down. Just as it seemed she was relaxed and controlled enough to enjoy the sensation but stay quiet, he whisked the scarf away and she let out a slow, silent shudder. It had been so good and now it was over…until his next tease.

"Arch your back and put your arse up in the air!"

Not too hard but entailed a good bit of ungainly wiggling, which he no doubt enjoyed to the full. Once she was up, he pushed a pillow under her belly. Not uncomfortable—maybe even comfortable—once the pillow settled around her body, but talk about exposing her even more!

"Perfect!" He slapped her gently, right where she was most prominent. "Just how I want you. All around available. I can see your rosy, wet cunt, your lovely arsehole and your delectable thighs." Her opposite cheek received another gentle slap. The noise echoed in the quiet room, and a warm flush covered her rear. From the slaps or downright embarrassment, or both, who knew—or really cared at this point? Seemed the sensation faded to a wonderful glow that seeped into her bones. Shutting her eyes, she focused on the joy in her body and relaxed in anticipation of whatever Mac planned next.

"How do you like being helpless?" he asked. "You may speak."

She turned her head to his voice and opened her eyes. He was just inches from her, his lips so close she could almost touch them with hers. Almost but not quite.

"It's incredible, wonderful and scary all at once. Thank you, Mac."

"Don't thank me yet, we're nowhere near finished. Any special requests?"

"To kiss you."

"I see." He angled his head to one side, creasing his forehead as if considering the pros and cons. "I think we can permit that, Ginny, don't you? A reward for your effort so far." As he spoke, his face came closer, his hand steadied her neck as she turned her head and his lips touched hers. She opened to accept his kiss, her mind, heart and soul responding to his touch. Helpless, naked, she reveled in the physical contact with Mac, her lover, her Dominant. Nothing else in the world mattered but this room and the pleasure they shared. As he pressed his lips harder, his tongue found hers and her mind zapped. She was past thought or reason, every fiber of her being fixed on the pleasure of his mouth and the comfort of their intimacy.

She whimpered as he broke the kiss, but quickly stifled it. "Sorry!"

"You are pardoned, Ginny, but look, we have another four minutes. Now your silence begins again. Understood?"

She nodded. That had to have been the longest six minutes in history—given a good two of them had been taken up in that kiss.

She gasped but bit it back in time. He'd pulled out the plug and made not the slightest effort to be gentle, but as her muscles eased back, a sense of emptiness engulfed her.

"I'll give it back to you another time," he promised. "For now, let's try this for size." It was his finger, warmer and much softer than the plug. He penetrated her in a gentle, spiral motion that had her biting back groans of delight. If this was how his finger felt, how more fantastic would his cock be? Except it was three times the size!

His other hand came between her shoulder blades, holding her down so her bottom rose higher and stretched her thigh muscles. She'd be hurting—was hurting—but the wild awareness in her arse overshadowed any possible discomfort in her thigh muscles. Wild sensations built, not only in her tight arse, but deep in her cunt, which mirrored the simulation and magnified the pleasure.

"Splendid!" Mac said. "Next time, I'll push into your lovely tight rose with my big cock and watch my prick disappear as I fuck you right deep here!" He poked in and out as he spoke.

The overwhelming stimulation and the prospect of a buggering were close to too much. She was wound so tightly her hips rocked of their own volition and he immediately withdrew his finger. "Naughty! Naughty! Didn't I tell you too keep still?" She braced for the slap, but it never came. Nothing did. "Just compose yourself, Ginny, or I might change my mind about spanking you your first time!"

That threat had her creaming. Again she tasted blood as she bit her lip and every muscle tensed under the effort to keep still. She ached to rock her hips, hump the bedclothes, anything to ease the building need and heat in her cunt and the raging hurt throbbing her clit. This was torture! Bliss! Submission! The fabric of her dreams. Even her breasts ached where they rubbed the sheets. Her belly hurt, her legs were stretched and her stinging cunt begged for release.

And she had to lie there and wait until Mac chose to take pity on her or…tease her again with the damn silk scarves.

He was right behind her, leaning over, rubbing her back with the scarf, one little spot at a time and kissing before he moved on up her spine. Reaching her neck, he tossed away the scarf. From the corner of her yes, she watched it flutter to the ground, but before it landed, he raked his nails down her back. Once again, she bit her lip. Somehow, the hurt transferred to her cunt as pleasure built into great roaring waves as Mac held her hips steady and plunged his cock in deep. At last she could move something! Her cunt muscles closed around his hard flesh. It didn't help much. She wanted—needed—more and more and more, and when he started moving in and out with long, steady strokes, Ginny closed her eyes and gritted her teeth as the buzzer went off.

Released, she threw back her head and let out a long cry of sheer pleasure. Mac pulled out and drove back deep. At this angle, every sensation intensified. She let out her pleasure in great whoops and groans.

"God! Ginny, you are incredible!" Mac said, his voice as loud as hers. "Wonderful. Such a fantastic fuck!" Faster he came and faster, pistoning into her with all his male power and strength. Bound and restrained, all she could do was soar on the pleasure he gave her. His hand came down, a finger touched her swollen and burning clit, seeing her face as her climax peaked, he whispered, "Come for me, Ginny, Come!" She obeyed, climaxing with a shout. She'd have collapsed but he didn't permit it. Holding her steady, he drove on and on. Deeper and faster as her body peaked again and again. With each climax, she screamed, and he still continued. She was dizzy, caught in a great crescendo of ever-growing pleasure until she felt him tense and pause before he came with loud grunts and cries. As his climax eased, she came again, screaming until the room went hazy and quiet. She came to moments later. She was untied, lying on her side with Mac's arms around her. "All right?" he asked. "I think you fainted a moment. Do you do that often after multiple climaxes?"

"I've no idea. I've never had so many climaxes. I think I drowned in them."

"I love you, Ginny, don't ever forget that. Sudden I know, but I'm old enough to know my own mind and I love you."

"I know." She meant to say something else. She should at least thank him for the best sex of her life. Sex that surpassed her admittedly wild dreams. Her mind was too fogged and sated to shape the right words. She settled for snuggling into him and shutting her eyes—just for a minute.

Chapter Nine

ॐ

She woke to an empty bed, the sheet beside her cold. Ginny rolled over and squinted at the alarm clock. She'd been asleep nearly two hours. Multiple climaxes really did one in. That — and fucking — and being fucked by Mac Brodie. She ached in certain strategic muscles — her cunt and arse still throbbed gently. Her body remembered.

And was not likely to forget in a hurry.

Mac had been wonderful — incredible! If she could clone him and bottle him up, there wouldn't be a discontented or unsatisfied woman in London. No! She did not want to share him with anyone. She found him and she wanted to keep him.

But keep him in holy matrimony?

That was another matter entirely. Damn! It was far too soon and far too fast. Yes, Mac was a superlative lover but, heck, marriage meant more than mind-shattering sex, didn't it? The niggling voice in her brain insisted incredible sex was a good place to start and she wouldn't argue with that but...

She sat up, deciding this was not a question to debate lying on her back and noticed her clothes neatly folded in a heap at the foot of the bed. Seemed a lifetime ago Mac had stripped her of her clothes and inhibitions during an afternoon of glorious submission.

On top of the clothes was a note. *I love you, Ginny. Take your time showering and dressing. When you're ready, we can have dinner and talk about next time.*

So her reluctance to commit hadn't ruined her chances. The more she thought about Mac, the more he did seem like a dream come true.

She padded down to the bathroom, clothes and shoes in her arms. He'd left out two lovely thick towels and a bottle of scented shower gel. She helped herself to that and his shampoo, letting the warm water ease the lingering aches in her body.

She dried her hair, ran her fingers through it to settle the curls and glanced in the mirror.

The face of a well-satisfied woman beamed back at her. So, this was what was meant by a glow after lovemaking. She rather liked the look.

"Ginny!" His call from down the corridor interrupted her self-admiration.

"Coming!" Something she'd done plenty of this afternoon.

Mac was in the kitchen, wearing a chef's apron as he put a frying pan on the stove. "Thought we'd have omelets. They're one of the few things I cook well. Have a seat, Ginny. Your wine's there." He nodded to the already poured glass on the countertop. "Tell me, do you want ham, cheese, mushroom or all three?"

"Mushroom, please." She sat down and sipped the wine—slowly. Marvelous. She should have guessed he wouldn't buy plonk! She took a second taste and watched Mac move around the kitchen, beating eggs with a fork and heating butter in a copper-bottomed pan.

The omelets were ready in minutes. Mac slipped them onto two warm plates. "Here you are, madam," he said, with a grin and a little bow. "*Bon appétit!*"

He sat opposite her at the table and raised his glass. "Will you drink to 'us', Ginny?"

"Of course. Did you think I wouldn't?"

"Not after this afternoon. Coming back next weekend?"

"Please."

"All weekend?"

Was she ready for that? Only one way to find out. "Yes, Mac. All weekend."

He smiled and clinked glasses. "Good. You do realize, don't you, that I'm going to do all I can to convince you to marry me?"

She should have expected that. He really was dead-on serious here. Was the prospect so bad? She took a sip of wine, eying him over the rim of her glass. "I might take a lot of convincing," she said, setting the glass down.

"I have lots of time, plenty of patience and a whole repertoire of sensual play. Want to play and come again and again and again?"

"Yes, please!"

About the Author

&

Email: books@madeleineoh.com

And visit Madeleine's website at www.madeleineoh.com

Madeleine welcomes mail from readers. You can write to her c/o Ellora's Cave Publishing at 1056 Home Avenue, Akron, OH 44310-3502.

Also by Madeleine Oh

&

Party Favors (*anthology*)
Power Exchange
R.S.V.P. (*anthology*)
Tied With a Bow (*anthology*)

Must Love Music

Jennifer Dunne

෩

Dedication

ॐ

To Sister Jane Theresa Murphy ~ you taught me how to make my song take flight. Thank you. You're surrounded by the music of God's angels now, but I still think of you every time I sing.

Trademarks Acknowledgement

~

The author acknowledges the trademarked status and trademark owners of the following wordmarks mentioned in this work of fiction:

Google: Google, Inc.

Chapter One

Let me help your spirit to sing. Leather-loving dominant seeks submissive for scene play, potential relationship. Must love music. Reply to voicemail box 665.

Gayle bought a newspaper along with her customary strawberry cream cheese-covered bagel and grande chai, and unfolded it on the spindly café table to peruse while she cooled down from her morning run. Ignoring the news, she flipped immediately to the classifieds.

The Thursday paper was the Arts and Entertainment edition. A special supplement listed all of the activities available for the weekend. More importantly, it also listed all of the auditions for the coming week.

She'd been in this city for a month now, and had yet to form any friendships with the people in the local branch office where she worked. They were all either in sales or management, and had nothing in common with her, their designated technical support person. Oh, they were polite and friendly, in an impersonal way—especially the ones in sales. But it was like she spoke a different language from them, or something.

So she was turning to her hobbies. She had a good voice, and had enjoyed doing community theatre before her unpredictable work schedule had forced her to give it up. Now that she had a standard work-week again, she could connect with the local theatre scene. She'd be bound to find friends there. Or, at any rate, find out where all the good bars, clubs and other hot spots were in this city.

She ran her gaze down the column of auditions, looking for musicals. The local opera company was casting bit parts for *Faust*, with the possibility of joining the company after the production ended.

Gayle shook her head. She was good, but not that good.

The high school honors theatre program was staging a production of *Grease*. Even if she got one of the adult parts, she'd be surrounded by children. Hardly a likely source of friends to go clubbing with.

The Gilbert and Sullivan operetta was a possibility. A lot of work to spit those patter songs out, but definitely for adults.

Then she spotted a notice for Sondheim's *Into the Woods*. Perfect! A challenging but not impossible score. A large enough cast to get to know a bunch of people. She'd need to bring music to the audition. Next Tuesday at 7:00 p.m.

She ripped out the audition notice, and tucked it into the zippered pocket of her jogging set's jacket.

Just having a plan already improved her spirits. Nibbling at her bagel, she glanced at the section of the paper revealed by the missing audition notice. The personals.

Smiling, she flipped the page and started to read the ads. There was more than one way to find a friend in a new city. Maybe a new boyfriend was what she should be looking for.

The first few ads were predictably from losers.

"'Discreet afternoon fun'? He's a married guy, looking for a little on the side. 'Not interested in head games, players, or women who can't commit'? That's a guy who still has issues with his last girlfriend. 'Single father of three who do not live with him'? Sounds like a guy who can't be bothered to wear a condom."

The rest were similarly mock-worthy, or sounded as dry and uninteresting as an all-day meeting. Then she came to a new headline.

"Alternative lifestyle personals? What's that?"

Her eyes widened at the first entry. "Skilled master seeks slave for 24/7 D/s lifestyle. I'll whip and beat you until you cry, then make you beg for more."

Gayle shook her head. She'd tried a little bondage with her last boyfriend. It had been fun. Okay, more than fun, it had been a huge turn-on for her. But that guy sounded more like a psychopath than a sexual partner.

Her breath caught at the next ad.

"Let me help your spirit to sing. Leather-loving dominant seeks submissive for scene play, potential relationship. Must love music."

Heat pooled low in her groin, her panties growing damp as the blood pulsed between her legs. She didn't know why the words affected her so deeply. But she knew she couldn't let this opportunity get away from her. Fingers trembling, she tore out the ad.

* * * * *

Later that morning, showered and dressed in a neatly professional skirt and blouse, Gayle was still thinking about the ad while working at her computer. She kicked off a database compaction, then leaned back in her desk chair and stretched her arms high above her head. It would be fifteen minutes at least before she could do the next task on her list.

A smile teased her lips. There was a voicemail box associated with the ad. Fifteen minutes was plenty of time to call and leave a message.

She dug the ad out of her wallet and nervously dialed the paper's personals number, then carefully entered the extension at the prompt. The system clicked, transferring her to the voicemail box she'd chosen. And then the man who'd placed the ad spoke.

"Thank you for your interest in my ad," he said, his rich and resonant voice reaching through the phone line to wrap around her lungs and squeeze. Her heart hammered. God, she could come just by listening to him talk. His words slid across her skin like a velvet caress, and her body arched, aching to bring him closer.

"Leave a message, and a way to reach you. If I like the sound of your message, I'll contact you."

"No pressure," Gayle muttered, her fingers tightening around the handset. Instinctively, she straightened her back, lifting her head to relax her throat and breathing deep into her diaphragm. This was just as much an audition as the Sondheim production would be.

The phone beeped, cueing her message.

"Your ad intrigued me," she began, pitching her voice to be as clear and carrying as if she was onstage. "I love to sing, and tremble at the thought of putting myself in your hands. If you would be interested in making music with me, call me. My name is Gayle."

Then she rattled off the phone number for the unassigned extension in her office that she used to test the marketing team's modems. It had an old, analog phone plugged in to it. His would be the only incoming call on that line.

She ate her lunch at her desk, mocking her own foolishness. He probably wouldn't even check his voicemail messages until the evening, when he got home from work. And if he liked her message enough to call her, he'd call back when she didn't answer. But she couldn't take the chance that he wouldn't. So she grabbed a microwavable bowl of macaroni and cheese from the vending machines and a diet cola, her ears straining to hear the distinctive ring of the analog phone.

She was completely absorbed in debugging a glitch with one of the manager's email accounts when the clanging bell of the phone startled her. Taking a deep breath, she sat up straight and relaxed her throat, then answered the phone.

"Hello, this is Gayle."

"Hello, Gayle. This is Rikard. I got your response to my ad."

A wave of warmth curled through her as his voice stroked and caressed her. The soft, slightly husky tone welcomed her to an intimate conversation, and suggested he might have been as moved by her response as she was by his initial ad.

Or, she might be reading way too much into the whole thing, and the poor man was getting over a cold.

She chuckled, half in nervousness and half at her own overblown imagination. "So, I guess you liked the sound of it, since you called back."

"Yes, I did. Are you a musician?"

"Programmer. But I do some community theatre on the side."

"Ah. I thought you sounded like you'd had training."

"Sister Jane would be pleased to know some of her lessons stuck. How about you? Are you a musician?"

He hesitated just a moment before saying, "Composer."

"Really? What do you write?"

"A little of everything. Jazz. Pop songs. Jingles."

"Jingles?"

"It pays the rent." He laughed, the sound spearing to her core as if he'd suddenly appeared in her office, thrown her onto her desk, spread her legs and thrust deep inside her.

Gayle smothered a moan. Her breasts were tight and tingling, aching for his fingers to squeeze the pebbled nipples, or for his hot mouth to cover the tips and suck deeply. Her stomach quivered. And the flesh between her legs pulsed with every heartbeat, wet and steaming, ready for his fingers, his mouth, or his long, hard cock to push deep, again and again, until she screamed her release. Or shrilled it over and over like a demented Mozart aria.

"If you're a programmer, you're probably at work."

Gayle answered with an affirmative noise.

"I won't keep you long, then. Would you like to get together to talk more in person?"

"I'd love to," she answered immediately. Then thoughts of all the horror stories about blind dates prompted her to caution. "How about Saturday? We could meet for lunch or coffee at the café on the corner of Washington and Twelfth."

"Coffee. Say, two o'clock?"

"Sounds great. How will I recognize you?"

"I'm tall, shoulder-length blond hair, and will be wearing green sunglasses and a black leather jacket. You?"

"My hair's dark brown, in a kind of pageboy, although my stylist had a more expensive name for it. I'll probably be wearing a denim barn jacket with black velvet trim."

"Sounds like you're very sensual."

"Wait until Saturday, and you can see for yourself."

He chuckled, a dark rumble of sound that wasn't quite as intense as his earlier laugh had been—more like he was leaning over her for some intense French kissing, while his hand fondled beneath her skirt.

"I'll count the hours."

"Me too."

After he hung up, Gayle remained clutching the handset, panting for breath, while her clit throbbed, begging for his touch. If he was half as scrumptious in person as he sounded over the phone, she was a goner. She hung up, and furtively pinched her nipples. The sharp pain triggered a wave of heat that rolled over her. It wasn't as good as an orgasm, but it was some relief.

She'd treat herself to a long, hot bubble bath tonight when she got home, soaping herself all over and pretending it was Rikard's hands sliding over her slick skin, imagining Rikard's mouth on hers, dreaming of his cock thrusting in and out, harder and faster, until she came beneath him in a sobbing, screaming rush.

She groaned, already aching and swollen with desire. It was going to be a long afternoon.

* * * * *

Saturday afternoon, Gayle abandoned the pile of rejected clothes on her bed, and headed for her date wearing a chic black leather miniskirt and pink angora sweater under her denim coat. After all, Rikard's ad said he liked leather. And she recalled reading somewhere that pink was a good color to wear to a first date, because it sent signals saying you were gentle and feminine. Fuzzy textures implied you were soft and invited thoughts of touching.

Plus, she knew pink looked good with her skin tone. She'd actually bothered with full makeup, as if she was going to a customer site, instead of just her usual tinted moisturizer and lip gloss, and knew she looked good.

Her cell phone was tucked into her black and pink purse, with her friend Carrie on the speed dial. Carrie was more than willing to act as her safety net for the date, provided she got all the juicy details in return.

As the blocks melted away beneath Gayle's determined stride, the nervous quiver in her stomach grew progressively stronger. What if he was a complete troll? Or had some odious personal habit? What if he was drop-dead gorgeous, with the elegant and sophisticated manners of a James Bond? She took a deep breath, straightened her spine, and forced herself to smile cheerily. Just another audition.

She turned the corner to the café three minutes before two o'clock. A tall, blond man in a fitted black leather jacket was bending his head to talk to the hostess. Was that him?

He straightened and turned to scan the tables on the sidewalk, revealing his rectangular sunglasses of pale green, and a strong profile of high cheekbones, firm jaw, and well-shaped nose. His blond hair was artfully styled to give a rumpled, just out of bed look, falling across his forehead in graceful arcs, covering his ears and brushing his neck and shoulders.

Gayle hurried up to the hostess stand. "Rikard?"

He smiled, his gaze flicking down and up her body, lingering for just a moment on her leather skirt. "Gayle."

A shiver rippled across her skin at the sound of her name being said in his rich voice. The false sexual purr of the hostess startled her out of her reverie.

"This way, please."

She followed the hostess' swinging hips, the woman working her clinging Hawaiian print silk sarong to full effect. Gayle was aware of Rikard's presence behind her, and casually shrugged off her barn coat while she walked. She was rewarded with a soft intake of breath, and felt the heat of his gaze on her formfitting fuzzy sweater. Oddly, the hostess's blatant attempt to hijack his attention made Gayle feel better. She wasn't the only one to fall under the spell of Rikard's voice.

When they reached the table, Rikard held out a chair for her, giving her the better seat, with a view overlooking the sidewalk. He took the facing chair, looking back at the café.

The hostess handed them their menus, lingered a moment longer, then returned to her station. Rikard and Gayle stared at each other in silence, then both began speaking.

"So, what do you — ?"

"Is this your first — ?"

They both broke off, chuckling, and any lingering nervousness dissipated.

"You first," he offered, gesturing her on with one gloved hand.

He wore black leather driving gloves, the supple leather clinging to his hands like a second skin. Gayle's heart sped up as she pictured those gloved fingers stroking her body, circling gently around her ear, slipping along the edge of her jaw, and finally dipping down to fondle and caress her breasts.

"Thanks. I was just wondering how many responses you'd followed up with so far."

"Judging the competition?" Rikard smiled, although something seemed vaguely wrong with his expression. The green lenses of his glasses made it difficult to read the look in his eyes, and even though the sun was behind him, he hadn't removed them.

She shrugged, inexplicably nervous again. "Just curious."

"Yours is the first message I returned," he admitted. "I have a musician's ear, and the other respondents' voices were frankly painful to listen to. Whereas yours is a pleasure."

"Well, I am always the first one asked to make phone recordings at work."

"You said you were a programmer. Of telecom equipment?"

The waiter interrupted them before she could answer. She ordered a grande chai, with whipped cream. Rikard ordered a tall cinnamon coffee. They turned in their menus, then he indicated she should continue with a wave of his gloved hand and another of those oddly off smiles.

"No, I'm a general purpose programmer. I do tech support for a marketing branch office, keep the sales people's laptops running, clear the viruses off the manager's system, and do back office databases and demo code off the server." She paused, then laughed and shook her head. "That probably made no sense to you whatsoever."

The corner of his mouth crooked up. "I was with you until back office databases. What are those?"

Gayle launched into an explanation of the difference between the front office systems used by the sales people, and the back office systems which ran automatically, collecting and compiling data and taking appropriate actions, such as issuing bills or prompting follow-up work. She kept the front office systems patched and running, holding the sales people's hands and talking them through the various screens when they had to do anything unfamiliar. But to the back office systems, she was a god.

"And do you like being a god?" Rikard asked.

A joking reply was on the tip of her tongue, when she realized he was asking a serious question. Fortunately, the waiter delivered their drinks, and she bought some time to think by stirring the whipped cream into her chai, licking the spoon, cradling the mug in her hands, blowing on it, then taking her first sip.

"No, I don't think so," she finally answered. "I like not having to clean up other people's messes, or waste my time redoing something because a sales guy with a one-week database class behind him thought he could 'improve' the system. But that's not the same."

"Good. Because if we decide to go forward with this, there's only room for one god, and it'll be me."

She trembled at the dark promise in his voice, her stomach bouncing like she'd swallowed rubber balls instead of silky chai. "Okay," she whispered.

"You have whipped cream on your lip."

She licked it off, feeling his eyes tracking the movement of her tongue behind the green shield of his sunglasses. Suddenly her lips felt parched, and she nervously wet them.

Rikard lifted his coffee and took a hasty sip.

"Speaking of going forward, I've never done this before. What would we do next?"

"You've never been in a BDSM relationship, or you've never started one via a personal ad?"

"A little of both, I think. I tried some bondage games with my old boyfriend, after we'd been lovers for a while, and really enjoyed them. But that was on top of an existing relationship. I never had it *be* the relationship."

"We wouldn't jump straight into our first scene. There needs to be trust on both sides—you trusting that I have your best interests at heart, and me trusting that you'll tell me how you're really feeling during a scene. So I'd start by asking you to do things, little things, like wear a certain item of clothing, or sit a certain way. I'd touch you, non-sexually, and learn your reactions to things. And we'd talk, about what you wanted, what you feared. Then, when we felt comfortable with each other, we'd move on to scene work, where I'd force you to face your fears and desires. Again, starting small, with things like binding your body but leaving your breasts exposed, and tickling your nipples with feathers, furs, and other things, until you came from the pleasure." The corner of his mouth quirked in his lopsided grin again. "It would take a very long time."

Gayle's breasts tightened, the nipples hardening and stretching her clinging sweater, as if he was already teasing them. She imagined ghostly caresses—wisps of feathers, soft strokes of fur, a quick rasp of something rough like sandpaper, a sharp nip of teeth.

She gasped, her panties growing not just damp but actually wet. "No, I don't think it would take long at all."

Rikard's smile broadened into smug self-satisfaction as he leaned back in his chair and studied her through lidded eyes. She felt like a partially devoured bowl of cream being examined by a not-yet-sated cat.

Yet somehow, the blatantly sexual expression didn't trouble her the way his earlier smiles had. With a jolt of surprise, she recognized what had bothered her previously. Now that his eyes were half-closed, they were even. When he smiled with amusement, one was slightly wider than the other. That was why his crooked grin didn't disturb her. She expected one eye to close more when he only moved one side of his mouth.

Her logical nature immediately kicked in, tossing out hypotheses as fast as she could test them. Coupled with the sunglasses, and the way he sat with the light behind him, she suspected he'd had some sort of eye treatment recently. Maybe he'd gotten laser eye surgery to cure his nearsightedness, or been given some sort of drops that affected his eye muscles for an infection.

As if recognizing her change of mood, he straightened and returned to his previous easygoing manner. "There are a few other things. I mentioned my fondness for leather in my ad."

"Yes. But I wasn't sure what you meant by that."

"When I touch you, I'll be wearing gloves." He extended his hand, displaying the soft leather driving glove that encased his skin. "And I also have a mask of black leather that covers most of my face. Without the mask, I'm just Rikard, your equal and, hopefully, your friend. In the mask, however, I'm Master Rikard, and expect your complete and total obedience."

His voice darkened and deepened, hinting at dire consequences should she fail to obey Master Rikard. He made no movement, other than returning his outstretched hand to wrap around his coffee mug, which could hardly be considered threatening. Yet she trembled in fear. And excitement.

"Obedience like we talked about. Little things until we trust each other."

"Yes." He paused, then added, "Since this is the first time you've entered a relationship with someone unknown to you, you'd probably feel safer the first time if you set up a safe call with a friend. Every hour or so, check in with someone you trust who knows where you've gone and who you are with, and can inform the police if you don't respond to her calls."

Gayle blushed. "I already did that. My friend Carrie will be calling in about ten more minutes."

The crooked grin tugged at his lips again. "I hope you anticipate all of my other suggestions as well."

Reaching into his jacket's inside chest pocket, he withdrew a business card which he placed on the table in front of her.

Rikard Sorenson, Composer. Below that, in smaller print, was listed his phone number and address, a semi-rural area to the west of the city that was in transition from farms to housing developments. She'd looked at houses there when she'd moved down, but they were executive homes well outside of her price range.

"Those jingles must pay really well to afford the rent out there."

He shrugged. "There's my phone number. Take the night to think it over, then call me with your answer. If you want to go ahead, I'll expect you at my house tomorrow at one o'clock."

Her hand closed around the card, the blood pulsing through her fingers making the card seem to throb beneath her touch.

"That's it? Just show up at one o'clock?"

"I'll give you more instructions when you call. *If* you call. You may change your mind once you're alone and have a chance to think things over."

He tipped back his head and downed the rest of his coffee, effectively ending the discussion. Setting the empty mug on the table, the tip of his tongue darted out to lick the stray droplets of coffee from his lips.

Gayle swallowed a hasty gulp of her chai, fighting the urge to lean across the table and taste his coffee-flavored mouth. But she couldn't tear her gaze from the gleaming track of wetness.

"Oh! The coffee must have been too hot. Your lip is peeling."

Rikard stiffened, his gloved hand rising to pat his lips. "You're right. Fortunately I have a tube of lip balm in my car. But I should take care of it as soon as possible."

He stood, pulling out his wallet and dropping a ten-dollar bill on the table.

"That should cover the drinks. It was a pleasure meeting you. I look forward to receiving your call tomorrow."

He bent his head in a gesture reminiscent of a bow, turned, and walked away from the café without a backwards glance.

Gayle sat at the table, stunned by his sudden departure. There was something strange about him, no doubt about it.

Smiling, she leaned back in her chair and sipped her chai, the spicy warmth heating her mouth as thoughts of what tomorrow might hold heated her blood. Her heart pounded. Rikard had been quite clear that they wouldn't have sex until they trusted each other. But how long would it take to build that trust? Not long, she hoped.

Although, if he planned on talking to her to build trust, she'd probably be orgasming anyway. The man's voice could charm the panties off a nun. And despite six years of Catholic school, Gayle was most definitely not a nun.

Picking up his business card, she memorized his phone number and address. She was taking no chances that it might get lost before she could call him. Sunday afternoon, she fully intended to have her first session with Master Rikard.

Chapter Two

ℬ

Recounting her date with Rikard to her friend Carrie, Gayle was at a loss to explain her reaction to him. Her willingness to blindly accept his comments with no question seemed, in retrospect, strangely suspicious.

Yet, he obviously recognized the effect he had on her, or else why would he tell her to take the night to think it over rather than asking for her answer then and there?

"So, what are you going to tell him?"

Gayle rolled over on her bed, the cell phone tucked against her cheek, and braced her stocking feet against the beige wall that she hadn't yet found time to decorate.

"I'm going to say yes, of course."

"Even though he's giving off these weird vibes?"

"God, Carrie! He's giving off sex-on-a-stick vibes. The man could have had any woman in the café just by opening his mouth and asking."

Just remembering the warm darkness of his voice made her hot all over again. Idly, she stroked her fingertips across her nipples, wishing it was Rikard's hand caressing her.

"Did I mention his gloves?"

"No."

"He was wearing black leather driving gloves. They hugged his hands like they'd been painted on. And they were incredibly sexy."

"Driving gloves were sexy? Next you'll say you get turned on by those woolen crosses between baseball hats and berets that British guys wear to drive around the countryside."

Gayle laughed with her friend. "Don't worry. I'm not that far gone."

"Uh-huh. Only because Rikard the Super Stud hasn't worn one yet."

They giggled like schoolgirls.

"So what are you planning on wearing tomorrow?"

"I don't know. I kind of figured he'd tell me what he wanted me to wear."

"And you're okay with that?"

"Yeah. It's one of the first steps for establishing trust. I show I'm willing to do what he tells me, and he shows he won't tell me to do something stupid, like wear high heels, a matching bra and panty set, and nothing else."

Carrie's next question was filled with awkward hesitation. "Gayle? How, uh, far are you willing to go? I mean, if he asks you, or tells you, to do something. You can still say no. But would you?"

Gayle stared at her toes, wiggling restlessly against the wall. "I...don't know. It's like he's some sort of Svengali, his voice leading me wherever he wants me to go, and I just follow like a little sheep. That's one of the reasons we need to build trust."

"So you can follow him even more blindly?"

"No, so I can be comfortable that he won't lead me astray."

"But what about until you build that trust? What about tomorrow?"

"Will you be my safety net again? Call my cell every hour. If I don't pick up, call again in fifteen minutes. If I still don't pick up, call the cops."

"I hope you know what you're doing."

Gayle sighed, her vision drifting back to the remembered sight of Rikard lounging in his chair, gazing lazily at her through his green-tinted sunglasses, while a smug smile pulled at his lips. A languorous warmth slowly uncurled deep within her. Would he touch her tomorrow the way she ached to be touched? Leave her hungry for his possession? Or transport her to a rapturous state she'd never even dreamed existed?

"I hope I know what I'm doing, too."

* * * * *

Gayle spent the rest of the night working on her audition number. She wasn't foolish enough to try and learn something new only three days before the tryout, but there were plenty of songs she'd sung in previous productions that she could brush up on with just a little practice.

Since Sondheim songs were notorious for their difficulty, the vocal line just one of many in the instrumentation, she'd win major bonus points from the casting director if she could prove that she'd already mastered one. Back in college, she'd played the role of Beth in a production of *Merrily We Roll Along*. It was one of Sondheim's lesser known works, having lasted all of sixteen performances on Broadway. That was why her school had been able to afford to perform it. But the musical included the fabulous number "Not a Day Goes By", which Carly Simon had later turned into a hit. The song just happened to be sung by the character of Beth.

She found the marked-up music in her stack from past shows. The recorded accompaniment for her numbers was buried at the bottom of her box of cassette tapes.

Over and over again, she practiced the song, working until she got the tricky shifts in meter to flow smoothly, and started jumbling the words because she was so tired. But she'd successfully kept herself from thinking about her upcoming date with Rikard.

In the morning, she busied herself with laundry and other household chores until ten o'clock, when she judged it was late enough to call Rikard without risk of waking him. She paced back and forth across the kitchen while she waited for him to pick up. He answered on the second ring.

"Good morning, Gayle." His velvety voice wrapped around her, making her shiver.

"How did you know it was me?"

"Caller ID. It's a local number I don't recognize, so I guessed it was you."

Gayle laughed self-consciously, leaning back against the counter. She'd expected to hear him say he was psychic, or confess to some other bizarre power. His voice seemed to drive all rational thoughts from her brain.

"I'm glad you called," he continued. "I've planned a late lunch for us, to get to know each other better. Do you have any food allergies I need to be aware of?"

"No. Well, I'm not allergic to them, but avocados make my lips go numb."

He chuckled. "Most people would call that an allergy."

Her knees went weak, and she collapsed into one of the chairs at her kitchen table. His voice should be registered with the FBI as a lethal weapon.

"So what did you do when you left the café yesterday?" he asked.

"I had a long talk with my friend, Carrie. She's the one who will be doing the safe calls today, too."

Rikard's voice was noticeably cooler when he asked, "What did you tell her?"

Gayle blinked in confusion. "Just what you told me. I thought you wanted me to set up safe calls."

"Yes, I did. That's fine. I'm sorry. I thought you meant you'd discussed me."

"Well, but we did. I mean, that was part of the deal for her doing the safe calls, that I had to dish about how my date went. I didn't say anything bad, though. Just about how good-looking you were, and how your voice made my stomach do back flips, and—"

"Back flips, hmm?"

"At least. Possibly an Olympic floor routine."

"What about after your call?"

"I worked on the song for my audition next week. I'm trying out for *Into the Woods*."

"What song are you singing?"

"I thought I'd sing 'Not a Day Goes By' from—"

"*Merrily We Roll Along*. Good choice."

Gail sat upright in surprise. "You know it?"

"A cautionary tale about a composer who gives up everything that matters in a fruitless pursuit of meaningless fame and fortune, by one of the greats of American musical theatre? It would be surprising if I didn't know it."

"Oh, right. Because you're a composer."

"Bring your music with you. I'd like you to sing for me."

Her cheeks heated. "I'm not that good."

"I'm not expecting a concert. And it will be good practice for obeying me even when my orders make you a little uncomfortable, and push you outside your comfort zone."

"Oh. When you put it that way…"

He chuckled, sending another shiver quivering through her. "And speaking of pushing you outside your comfort zone, I'd like you to wear that leather miniskirt again, but no panties, and no pantyhose. So that if I wanted to, at any moment, I could reach up under it and put my fingers inside you, teasing you until you trembled and came on my hand."

Gayle's breath caught, her breasts tightening and heat pooling between her legs at his suggestive words.

"Did you hear me, Gayle?"

"Yes," she breathed. "I heard you."

He chuckled again. "Ah. Imagining my fingers inside you already, are you? Stroking in and out, sliding between your slick folds, then pressing deep, my thumb rubbing your clit—"

She gasped, her legs falling open and her head lolling back as waves of warmth crested within her. She shuddered, and cupped her pulsing flesh through the heavy interference of her jeans.

"Yes," she whimpered.

"I'm the only one allowed to touch you," he cautioned, as if he knew where her hand was and what she was doing.

"But I'm—"

"That's an order, Gayle."

Reluctantly, she lifted her hand away from her hot, throbbing crotch. "Yes, Master Rikard."

"Don't sound so sad. Think of the anticipation, the constant state of arousal as you wonder when I'll finally touch you and give you the climax you deserve."

"Soon, I hope."

"Oh, no. You're going to have to work for that reward. When you get here, we'll start with our light lunch. Then you'll sing for me. And then, maybe, if you've been good, I'll give you what you want."

"I'll be good. I'll be very, very good."

"That's what I wanted to hear. I'll expect you at one o'clock. Don't be late."

"Wait! You didn't tell me what top you wanted me to wear."

"Something clingy, so I can see how tight and hard your nipples are. And no bra."

Gayle moaned softly, the idea of displaying herself before Rikard's avid gaze making her insides clench. Her breasts were already tingling, the nipples tightening as if he was looking at them right now.

She shifted, trying to get comfortable on the hard wooden chair. But what she really wanted was to straddle the curved arm, riding the wood and crushing it against her clit until she came, screaming Rikard's name.

"I'm going to be in agony for the next three hours," she protested.

"I have it on the best authority that suffering is good for the soul."

"Then I'm going to be damn near angelic by the time I get to your house."

"I look forward to helping you fall. One o'clock. Bring your music. Don't be late."

* * * * *

Once again, the sensual haze consuming her faded once Rikard was no longer speaking to her. After some time spent staring into her closet, Gayle dressed in a bright blue exercise top that hugged her curves, clearly outlining her nipples. It also showed the slight pudginess in her upper arms, and a thickness around her waist that she'd rather not reveal. She needed to start wearing wrist weights when she jogged.

She pulled on the leather miniskirt, the leather cupping her bare ass like a pair of hands. Like Rikard's hands.

Forcing the image away, she concentrated on finding a pair of sandals to match the skirt. She wouldn't think about Rikard's long, graceful fingers, sheathed in leather, stroking and caressing her sensitive skin.

"Oh, hell."

She leaned against the closet door, eyes closed, and let her imagination run riot. She pictured him doing her against the wall as soon as she entered his home. Or maybe stripping her and serving the late lunch he'd mentioned on her quivering body, licking and nibbling his way through a three-course meal that included her for dessert. Or setting her down, legs spread, on the keyboard of a piano, while he coaxed melodious cries of passion from her.

"No." She shoved away from the door, stalking out of her room to the computer set up in the living room. Quickly logging on, she surfed over to an online mapping site and printed out driving directions to Rikard's home. She wanted to trust him, but found herself filling in his name in the Google search box, just to be sure he was who he said he was. Nothing. She frowned, and tried R. Sorenson. Some lyric sites popped up, attributing various songs she didn't recognize to R. Sorenson, as well as listings for diatribes from a political activist in California and genealogical information on the Sorenson clan. But no news articles, and no home page. She wasn't sure if that was a good or bad thing. Then she checked her email and surfed the news sites, killing time with distractions until she needed to leave her house.

She'd allowed an extra ten minutes for traffic downtown, and cruised into the suburbs with a comfortable cushion of time, allowing her to arrive with leisurely grace. Rikard's home was a two-story modern design of angled cedar planks and plate glass windows. It appeared to be situated to maximize the view of the sprawling apple and pear orchards behind the house, as well as the distant green hills. A stone wall, high enough to keep out animals but easily scaled by a determined person, surrounded his property, or as much of it as she could see before it faded into the distance. The black scrollwork gates at the end of his crushed stone drive stood open, and didn't appear to have been moved since the last time the drive was graded.

The gravel crunched beneath her tires as she rolled slowly up the drive, stopping next to the flagstone path that curved gracefully to his front door. After giving herself one last once-over in the rearview mirror, Gayle grabbed her purse and sheet music, and exited the car. It chirped as she engaged the locks, but her attention was already focused on the path beneath her feet, and the man awaiting her inside. A decorative wall fountain burbled happily beside a stone bench, the feet carved to resemble two squirrels. Their cheerful welcome counteracted the subdued menace of the wrought iron safety door that matched the gates at the end of the drive.

The inner door swung open before she could ring the bell. Rikard must have been watching for her. Then he stepped around the door to open the safety door, letting her see him for the first time.

His features were hidden behind a black mask of boiled leather that covered his face from just above his jaw to mid-forehead. His eyes—a medium blue, she could see now that he'd gotten rid of his green sunglasses—looked through cutouts their precise size and shape, and the lower edge of the mask curved up to reveal his lips but no more. The mask had clearly been designed specifically for him.

If the mask had left her in any doubt, the rest of his outfit showed his fondness for leather. Black riding boots encased his narrow feet in elegance. Tight black leather pants clung to his legs, laced up the sides rather than zipping in front. They were tight enough that she could appreciate his endowments, a moderate bulge between his legs promising that he had enough to satisfy her, without being uncomfortably overlarge.

He wore his black leather driving gloves, the cuffs hidden beneath the flowing sleeves of a white poet shirt, the only thing he was wearing that was neither black nor leather. She wondered if that meant he planned on taking it off, later, and found the thought made her throat dry with anticipation.

His gaze slid up and down her body, checking her out with all the thoroughness she'd given him. He smiled, his attention lingering on her pebbled nipples, clearly visible beneath the clinging exercise top.

"Very obedient. Good."

Gayle felt her nipples tighten in response, and her breath quickened. "Thank you, Master Rikard."

Her fingers clenched, rustling her music. Rikard's gaze focused on the sheet music clutched in her hand.

"May I?" he asked, already reaching for it.

She handed the pages over without a word. Odd, that he felt he could order her to dress in a certain way, speaking casually of touching her body as if it was his right, but had to ask for permission to touch her music.

He stepped back, inviting her to enter the spacious two-story foyer with a casual wave of his gloved hand, even as he eagerly studied the fanfold of pages. More wrought iron decorated the sweeping stairway to the second floor, and lined the upstairs balconies overlooking the flagstone entryway. He closed the doors without looking, his attention on the papers in his hands. His foot tapped softly, unconsciously keeping the beat as he scanned the music.

Reaching the end of the piece, he shook himself out of his fugue state. He folded the music and tucked it under his arm, then took her hand and lifted it to his lips, brushing the lightest of kisses across the backs of her fingers.

"Welcome to my home."

Gayle shivered, the drumbeat of desire beginning to pulse in her ears. "It's lovely."

"The first floor holds the kitchen, living room, music room and home theater. Upstairs are the bedrooms, playroom, and my studio. We'll be visiting the playroom later." His fingers tightened on hers with relentless promise, then he turned and led her through an arch into the music room.

A grand piano claimed pride of place in the room, the mahogany gleaming in the sunlight that streamed through windows covered by rich gold sheers. Gold satin padded the walls above mahogany wainscoting, and she realized the room was designed to soak up sound, so the music of the piano would not echo off the walls and windows.

A neatly folded, padded drape sat on the chair nearest the piano. The instrument was normally covered, then. Rikard had removed the drape in preparation for her visit.

Cold chills collected in her stomach, and she stopped dead in her tracks. "I can't do this."

"You can, and you will. While I wear this mask, I am your master, and you are mine to command." Rikard's voice was cold and implacable, then gentled as he brushed a gloved finger across her cheek. "Come, we will make a game of it. You will sit with me at the piano, and I will pick out the tune with one hand. See if you can sing along with me."

Swallowing against the lump in her throat, she nodded. "Yes, Master Rikard." He wasn't expecting perfection. It was just a game.

He pushed the piano bench to the left, so that he could sit on the end and still be centered in front of the keyboard. Placing the score on the music rest, he accidentally hit the corner with the trailing sleeve of his poet shirt, sending the pages flying.

Gayle bent and grabbed the music, then arranged it before him, no longer worried about needing to be perfect. She suspected he might have fumbled the pages on purpose, to put her at her ease. If so, it had worked. Rikard took his position on the bench, shifting bench and music slightly until everything was aligned as he desired. Then he patted the bench beside him.

"Join me."

She slipped onto the bench, her leather skirt sliding smoothly across the glossy mahogany. Rikard wrapped his left arm around her shoulders, holding her close, then proceeded to "pick out the tune" with his right hand.

He played the melody line flawlessly, interspersing it with accent notes from the accompaniment, his fingers dancing across the keys. She frowned. If he was this good, he should be playing professionally, not composing music for other people to play.

"Now sing," he ordered, as he began the piece again.

Gayle breathed deeply, cleared her mind of everything except the music, and sang. When she finished, she turned to face him, eagerly anticipating his reaction. She'd nailed it.

Rikard's head was bent, his hand curled loosely in his lap.

"You sang every note as written, no easy task in a Sondheim piece."

"So why do you sound disappointed?"

"Music is not about getting the notes right, any more than poetry is about spelling the words correctly. It's about freeing your soul."

"I don't understand."

"Listen."

He began the piece again, his voice light and wistful as he described a love who was with him every single day. Then his voice broke on a ragged inhalation, and shook with agony as he cried, "And you *won't* go away!"

His love would not leave him alone, no matter how much he wished she would. Gayle's heart ached for his pain. Then his voice shifted again, turning flat and toneless as he revealed if she ever did leave, it would kill him. Dull and hollow with hopelessness, he whispered, "Dying day after day after day, as the days go by."

Gayle blinked her blurry eyes, focusing on Rikard's bent head, the fall of his blond hair screening his black mask from her sight. His right hand was fisted on the keyboard, the leather of his glove stretched taut across his knuckles.

"Did you love her so very much?" she whispered.

"With all my heart and soul."

"What happened?"

"A car accident. Four years ago. A truck's tire blew, and the driver swerved out of control, jackknifed and skidded across the highway. A minute later or a minute earlier, and the road would have been deserted. Instead, I got there just as he crossed into the oncoming traffic lane. The truck's fuel line ruptured. The dragging chassis struck a spark. My windshield blew out, glass everywhere. The doctors were afraid I was going to be blind. I wish I had been, rather than—"

His jaw clenched, his entire body going rigid as he fought the demons in his memory. He breathed deeply, then again, and slowly relaxed. His fist uncurled.

"I'm sorry," she whispered.

"I'm alive, even if it's not the life I intended." He turned to face her, then smiled sadly as he wiped her cheeks with his gloved thumb. "It's I who should apologize to you. I've made you cry."

She bit her lip, good manners warring with turbulent emotions. Emotion won. "Would it be too hard for you to play it once more? I'd like to try it again."

Rikard straightened, his fingers returning to the keyboard. After a deep breath, he began playing the song from the beginning, although this time, he played only the melody line, without any of the embellishments.

Gayle couldn't match the strength of his loving and losing, but she'd experienced her own losses over the years. Her beloved aunt, dying of a lung infection. Her dog, Tiger, who had been her inseparable childhood companion. Even the slow corporate death of spending more and more time on the road, until her life became a series of disconnected hotel rooms with no goal beyond reaching the next assignment, the next contract, and her hobbies, interests, and existence outside of her job faded away.

She put all of that emotion into the song. And when it ended, she sat, stunned, as the last notes faded. She'd heard the difference. It was unbelievable.

Rikard brushed his gloved fingers across the keys in a caress too light to sound them, then closed the piano with a snap. The music fluttered to the floor.

"Yes. That time you let me hear your soul."

He stood, gracefully sliding off the bench in a well-practiced move. Offering his hand to her, he said, "Come. It is time for that lunch I promised you."

Gayle slipped her hand into his, and allowed him to pull her off the bench and out of the music room. She felt somehow lighter than she had before, yet at the same time, her heart was weighted by what she'd learned of him. It explained how come such a dishy guy wasn't already taken. Another woman had won his heart, a woman he'd loved so fiercely that it had taken him four years after her death before he was able to reenter the dating scene. No wonder he was only interested in scene play, at first, rather than a relationship.

That was okay. They'd go slow. It would be better for both of them that way.

Chapter Three

ᔕᕋ

The eat-in kitchen boasted a glass-walled breakfast nook that overlooked the back deck with a panoramic view of the well established orchards. The round table and chairs were of white-painted wrought iron, the table topped by a thick piece of beveled glass and the chairs cushioned with pale blue and white striped pillows.

Blue- and white-striped placemats were already set kitty-corner on the table, the matching linen napkins folded in graceful fans beside them. Condensation frosted the chilled white china plates resting on top of pale blue chargers. Swirls of blue glass patterned the water goblets, already filled with ice water and a thin slice of lemon. Condensation frosted their sides as well.

Gayle shook her head. This was not what she was expecting.

"I was just filling the water glasses when you arrived," Rikard told her. He released her hand and walked over to the stainless-steel refrigerator, opening it and withdrawing a pale blue salad bowl. From what she could see over his shoulder, the refrigerator was well stocked, but neatly, rather than filled with things stuffed haphazardly where there was room.

"It's more Martha than Marquis de Sade."

Rikard laughed, the sound wrapping her in warmth that made her stomach flutter. "But I told you, the goal for today was to get to know each other better, and establish trust. There's plenty of time to torture you with food later."

She stood awkwardly next to one of the chairs. "Do you want me to serve you?"

"No. I'm not one of those dominants who equates submission with household service."

He held out a chair for her, giving her the better view of the apple trees to the south, and leaving the eastern view of the deck and kitchen for himself. Once she was seated, he grabbed salad tongs and served the mix of field greens, sliced strawberries, and a balsamic vinaigrette dressing onto her plate.

After helping himself, he returned the bowl to the refrigerator. Then he set a covered platter, no doubt the second course, on the counter to warm up to room temperature. Finally, he returned to the table and claimed his seat.

He snapped his napkin open with a sharp crack, making Gayle jump. A hint of a smile played about his lips, although his mask made it difficult to read his expression.

She spread her own napkin, waiting until he picked up his salad fork before reaching for her own. "What kind of a dominant are you, then?"

"I enjoy caring for my submissives, surrounding them with elegance and comfort, so that they may give themselves completely to the moment, with no petty worries to distract them. Skin that has grown accustomed to fine silks and velvet, redolent perfumes and exotic oils, will feel the contrast of a loving lash far more than one dulled and deadened by overwork and uncomfortable clothing."

Gayle stopped with the first forkful of salad halfway to her mouth. She could almost feel his gloved hands stroking and caressing her body, smoothing massage oil into her skin, and trailing wisps of silk across her sensitive breasts and between her legs.

She jumped, certain she'd felt a light swat against her ass. But that was impossible. She was sitting in a padded chair. Unless he'd hidden some sort of spanking device under the cushion?

Rikard's low chuckle swirled around her. "You're very responsive. Are you that responsive in bed, too? Are you a moaner or a shouter?"

Gayle licked her lips, her gaze locking on his blue eyes glimmering in the depths of the black leather mask. "I like to beg."

He closed his eyes and inhaled sharply, as if she was a fine wine and he was sampling her bouquet.

"Eat your salad."

Obediently, she slipped the forgotten forkful of greens into her mouth. Her eyes widened in surprise. It was unexpectedly good, with a hint of…was that ginger? And something sweet besides just the strawberries—brown sugar or maybe honey.

"This is great!" She forked up another mouthful.

Rikard had already regained his composure after her confession, and turned his attention to his own plate. "Thank you. It pleases me to know you enjoy it."

They ate in silence for a brief interval, giving the delicious salad the attention it deserved. Then he asked, "What things give you pleasure?"

"You mean, in bed?"

"In bed or out. What warms your soul?"

She considered. "Well, I like performing, singing onstage."

"What exactly about performing do you enjoy? The adulation of a crowd? Making a public act out of your private emotions? Touching their hearts and minds?"

She blinked. "I never really thought about it. Are those some of the reasons the performers you know like performing?"

"Don't dodge the question."

"Yes, Master Rikard." She bent her head, staring at the half-eaten salad while she puzzled out what she enjoyed about singing onstage. "I think it's the challenge. I like working hard to get it right, and the audience reaction is like a grade, telling me how close I came to doing it."

"Ah. So as your Master, I should set challenging tasks for you, and provide feedback so you know whether or not you succeeded."

The flesh between her legs began to pulse, hot and wet with arousal. Her breasts tingled, the nipples tightening, and her breath came in short, quick gasps. She loved to learn new things. The constant training was the best part of her job. But it had never occurred to her that a skilled Master would want to train her.

"Oh, yes," she whispered. "Please, Master."

"Very well, then. Here is your first task. Finish your salad."

A muffled sigh escaped her lips as Gayle picked up her fork.

"You don't think it's a challenge? Perhaps if I tell you, you aren't allowed to make any noise while you eat?"

She looked up at him, her mouth opening to ask what he meant before she realized that would be disobeying his instruction. Instead, she shook her head.

"I'll just have to make it more challenging, then. You eat, and I'll tell you all the things I plan on teaching you."

He began with the simple things, that he would teach her how to speak to him with proper deference yet still giving him all the information he needed to care for her, and how to sit beside him so that he could touch her at his leisure. He would teach her how to remove her clothes so that each item stroking across her flesh enflamed her desire. He would teach her how to position herself so that she was completely open to him, her hot, wet pussy his for the taking, and how she would beg him to take it.

Gayle felt the moisture growing between her legs, instinctively spreading her legs as wide as her tight leather skirt would allow. She wriggled against the cushion, struggling for relief. At least, if she'd been wearing underwear, the friction of the cotton or lace against her swollen clit and wet lips would have offered some pleasure. But she was bare beneath her skirt, with nothing to rub against.

A soft whimper broke from her lips.

Rikard's hand slapped the glass tabletop, making the plates bounce. "No!"

She jumped, her wide-eyed gaze locking on his face. Was he angry? No, he was smiling.

"You made a noise," he said. "Perhaps this is a challenging task after all?"

She nodded vigorously.

"Finish your salad. We will begin again. And since the task is more challenging than you expected, I think you deserve a reward if you complete it. What reward shall I give you?"

His blue eyes glittered with desire, and the ambrosia of power, as he pondered his answer out loud.

"You seem to be having trouble sitting. Perhaps I should investigate, and do a thorough probing between your legs to determine what is causing the problem."

Gayle bit her lip to keep from moaning. Hot liquid ran down the inside crease of her thigh, to pool beneath her ass on the supple leather of her skirt. She wriggled her hips, imagining his gloved fingers pressing between her folds, slipping inside her, stretching her opening as he slowly added fingers, until his entire hand forced its way over the ridge of muscle into her vagina.

Her vision was blurring, her breath coming sharp and fast. Her nipples were so tight they hurt. And all she could do was shovel strawberries and lettuce into her mouth as fast as possible, to end this torture.

"You're not savoring your food," Rikard warned her. "If I think you're not appreciating it, I'll have to give you a second helping."

Gayle wanted to scream in frustration, but she didn't make a sound. She slowed the pace of her eating, her trembling hand making it difficult to carry the salad to her mouth, and slowing her even further.

She'd never felt so turned on in her life.

"Very good."

She glowed, warmed by his praise. All she wanted was to please him, to make him happy. Then he would reward her. But pleasing him was its own reward. He'd gone to so much trouble to put together a nice lunch for her. The least she could do was enjoy it properly.

Her tongue swept out, licking the dressing from her lips. Looking deep into his eyes, she opened her mouth and sucked the dressing from the tines of her fork.

His eyes darkened, and she could hear his labored breathing in the silence of the kitchen.

"You seem to enjoy that salad dressing," he said, a rough huskiness marring the smooth fluidity of his voice. "Perhaps I should anoint you with it, drizzle it on your breasts, let it drip onto your thighs. Then I could lick it off you."

Gayle fisted her free hand, her nails digging into her palm. The sharp pain distracted her from phantom sensations of liquid running across her skin, followed by a warm, wet tongue.

Triumphantly, she popped the last slice of strawberry into her mouth, and laid her fork down with a clatter.

"Excellent," Rikard purred. "You have done very well. And that was a challenge, indeed. Come here."

He held out his hand. Gayle rose, unsteady on quivering legs, and tottered over to his side. He drew her onto his lap, her leather skirt squeaking softly as it slid across his leather pants. His gloved hand cupped her hip, anchoring her yet burning her with the heat of his banked passion.

His velvety voice was low and strained as he asked, "I know I said I would not touch you sexually until we'd established trust, but am I right in thinking that's what you want me to do now?"

She nodded.

"You may speak now. Your challenge is completed."

"Yes, Master. Please. Touch me."

"Where?"

"Put your fingers inside me. Make me come in your hand."

He smiled tightly, recognizing his own words. Then he reached beneath her skirt, his gloved fingers trailing lightly up the inside of her thigh. They were soft, and warm, and everything she'd dreamed of.

Gayle's head tipped back and she moaned, arching against his supporting arm behind her back, lifting her hips and spreading her legs. His fingers brushed her clit, and she gasped, jolted by a sharp rush of pleasure. He worked his way between her folds by touch, guided by her breathy moans. Then his fingers slid over the edge of her opening, and she cried out, "Master!"

He pressed two fingers inside her, thrusting up to the second knuckle.

"Yes! Yes! More!"

A third finger joined the other two on the next thrust, stretching her to the edge of pain. His thumb worked her clit, sliding over and around it, his glove wet with her fluids, as his fingers stroked in and out. He found her nerves and pressed them against the bone, wrenching a scream of ecstasy from her.

"Beg me," he rasped, his breath hot against her neck. "Beg."

"Please, Master. Please. That feels so good. Touch me. Deep. Deeper. Ahhh." A rush of pleasure blanked all thought for a moment.

"Beg!" he growled.

In a flash of insight, she knew what he needed her to say. He wanted to fist her, the way she'd imagined earlier, but he wouldn't risk hurting her unless she gave her permission. "I want you. All of you. I need your whole hand inside me. Please, Master. I'm yours. Take me. Take me now. Please. Make me scream for you. Only for you."

His shuddering breath told her she'd guessed correctly. Gently, he stretched her opening even wider, until the muscle burned. All four of his fingers slipped inside her, to the first joint. The second. And still he stretched her, wider and wider, until his knuckles thrust past her opening.

She gasped, the brief pain swirling streamers of red and black through her vision.

Then his hand was inside her, filling her as she'd never been filled. His fingers stroked the walls of her vagina, rubbing and circling, as slowly, slowly, he reached deeper and deeper. Her muscles clenched his fist, seizing and releasing him again and again. Each time, he moved just a little bit further inside her.

She was going to go insane from the pleasure. He was killing her. She never wanted it to end.

"Please, Master. Please. Please."

She didn't know what she was begging for, to have him put her out of her agony now or to keep her writhing in his lap for hours.

Then the tip of his middle finger brushed her cervix, and she exploded. She screamed, a wordless howl of ecstasy, as she bent back over his arm, lifting her hips in a final thrust against his fist. The force of her shudders pushed his hand out of her in a wet rush, as if she was in the final stages of giving birth, and she screamed again as his hand stretched her opening on the way out.

He held her, cradled against his soft poet shirt, as she sobbed into the warm cotton. And continued sobbing, helpless to stop the tears. She felt the tension that rippled through him as he realized this was more than a simple release.

He brushed the hair away from her face, tipping her head back to look at him.

"Gayle, look at me. Did I hurt you?"

The fear in his voice only made her cry harder.

"Gayle."

She shook her head no. Then yes. "Just a little. It was worth it."

"Then why are you crying?"

"Because I'm twenty-six years old, and I never knew an orgasm could feel like that. If it hadn't been for you, I never would have known. I'd have grown old and died, thinking I knew what good sex felt like. And I would have been wrong!"

Rikard chuckled in relief. "Oh, is that all?"

A giggle slipped out between sobs, then another, and soon she was laughing instead of crying. She slapped weakly at his chest, until he caught her hand and stopped her. Slowly, her laughter faded.

She wiped roughly at her eyes.

"God, I probably look a fright."

"I think you're beautiful."

She stared up into his incredibly blue eyes, shining through the black leather of his mask. The moment stretched out like a note held impossibly long at the end of an aria.

Then her cell phone rang.

"Oh! Where's my purse?"

Rikard pulled it from the back of the chair she'd been sitting in and handed it to her. She fumbled for the cell phone, flipping it open and pressing the button to answer the incoming call.

"Sorry it took so long. I couldn't find my phone."

"I was starting to get worried," her friend Carrie answered.

"No, everything's fine here." Gayle covered the phone with her hand and whispered to Rikard, "My safety call."

"Take the call. I have to prepare the next course, anyway," he murmured.

Deftly, he slid out from beneath her. He cleared the table of the salad plates and forks, and carried them to the sink. She heard the clink of plates and a rush of water, followed by the throaty whoosh of a gas range, and the soft opening and closing of kitchen cabinets.

"Gayle?" Carrie asked. "You sound kind of funny. Are you sure you're all right?"

"I have just had the most amazing orgasm of my life," Gayle whispered.

There was a moment of silence. "I thought you were having lunch."

"We are. The orgasm came after the strawberry salad. It was to die for." She turned and looked over her shoulder into the kitchen. Rikard was spraying oil onto a griddle pan. He'd taken the cover off the platter he'd placed on the counter earlier, revealing two red slabs of meat, liberally coated with seasonings. "I think we're having steak for the entrée."

"You had sex right there among the salad plates?"

"No, it wasn't like that."

"You did it on the floor? Up against the wall?"

"On a kitchen chair, actually."

"Gayle, honey, are you listening to yourself? You aren't a 'sex on the first date' kind of girl."

"Technically, this is our second date."

"And you slept with him less than an hour into it! The man is messing with your head somehow. Maybe calling him a Svengali wasn't so far off the mark."

Vigorous sizzles came from the kitchen, along with a heavenly aroma blending Asian spices and seafood. Gayle moaned, her mouth watering, and closed her eyes to better focus on the delicious smell.

"Good grief! Is he touching you now?" Carrie demanded.

"No. He just put the steaks on the grill. I think they're tuna steaks. They smell so good."

Rikard called, "Two minutes."

"I've got to go. The food's almost done."

"I'll call you back in an hour."

"There's no need. I'll be fine with him."

"Uh-huh. Then you won't mind me calling back in an hour."

"Okay, but if I don't answer right away, it's not because something's wrong. It's because we're having incredibly hot sex and I don't want to stop to answer the damned phone."

"Hey, *you* asked *me* to do this for you. Don't get all snotty with me just because I'm doing what you asked me to."

"Oh, Carrie, I'm sorry. I know, you're just trying to help. But that's what I'm telling you. I don't need your help on this anymore."

"Humor me. Okay?"

"You're wasting your time. But if it'll make you feel better, fine. Call back in an hour. I have to go now. Lunch is almost ready."

"All right. But tonight, after you get home, you're giving me the whole story about what went on during this date."

"Deal."

Gayle closed the phone and stuffed it back into her purse. She hadn't realized Carrie was such a worrywart.

Although usually Carrie was incredibly laidback, unless it involved a shoe sale. Maybe there was something to her concern. Now that Gayle thought about it, she *was* acting out of character. She normally took forever to make important decisions, preferring to thoroughly research all the aspects of whatever she was deciding. She should have spent hours debating the pros and cons of having sex with Rikard, instead of just opening her legs and melting beneath his touch.

And letting him fist her! Never mind that it had been the most mind-blowing experience ever. The point is, she hadn't even kissed him yet. She'd jumped right in to the kinky sex, with no thought other than satisfying the raging need churning within her. That definitely wasn't like her.

The sizzling stopped, and she heard the rapid strike of a knife against a cutting board. Then Rikard carried two plates to the table.

"Take your seat," he prompted.

She blushed, realizing she was still in his chair. Hanging her purse over her chair back, she switched seats.

He set her plate down on her charger, then put down his own plate and sat. She'd guessed correctly. A slab of tuna steak, coated in red, brown, black and white spices, rested on a colorful bed of sliced cucumbers and radishes. The tuna was sliced in ten narrow pieces, each one shading from gray through pink to a hint of red, then back to gray. A golden brown sauce was drizzled decoratively back and forth across the entire plate.

Gayle closed her eyes and inhaled the sharp aroma. Her eyes watered, and she blinked rapidly.

"Does this have a lot of pepper in it?"

"Wasabi."

"Pardon me?"

"Wasabi paste. It's Japanese. And very strong. Really opens up the sinuses." He smiled. "If hot foods aren't to your taste, just avoid the sauce. But you ordered chai at the café, so I figured you'd like it."

A warm glow suffused her. He'd paid attention to what she'd ordered at the café, and used that to decide what kind of lunch she'd like. He really meant it when he'd said he wanted to care and cosset any woman who became his submissive.

Carefully, she separated one of the slices of tuna. Feeling his eyes upon her, she lifted the fork up and slid the fish into her mouth.

Flavors burst to life on her tongue. The sauce held a hint of acidity—soy sauce or vinegar—and heat, which must be the wasabi. But the tuna itself was seasoned with warm spices like cinnamon and ginger, and the unexpected taste of licorice, as well as the more prosaic salt, pepper, onion and garlic.

Gayle groaned. "Oh God, that's good."

"Try the vegetables."

The radishes and cucumbers were crisp and crunchy, perfect counterpoints to the sharp sauce. "Fabulous."

Rikard relaxed and picked up his own fork. "I hope you'll have room for dessert."

She gulped and swallowed her mouthful of tuna and cucumber. "There's more?"

When she'd fantasized about him serving a three-course meal on her body, it had been just a fantasy. She hadn't seriously expected such a lavish lunch.

"Of course. But if you'd prefer, I can show you the rest of the house first, then we can come back for dessert later."

"After I've worked up more of an appetite?" she teased.

He laughed. "I'll show you the playroom. Then you can decide if you'd like to work up an appetite or not."

His molten gaze scorched the skin of her neck and chest, her nipples tingling and tightening as his attention slipped lower. Her pulse beat, slow and heavy between her thighs.

"I want to play," she whispered.

Chapter Four

છ

Rikard smiled at Gayle's admission. "We can play after lunch. But we're supposed to be learning about each other. Tell me about some of the productions you've been in."

He listened attentively, asking pointed and intelligent questions, as she described her theatrical background. She'd had lead roles in a slate of standard musicals — *Annie Get Your Gun*, *Oklahoma!*, *Fiddler on the Roof*, *My Fair Lady*, and *Camelot* — as well as innovative and experimental works like *Merrily We Roll Along*, which started at the end and went backwards to the beginning, and *archy and mehitabel*, the story of Don Marquis' literary cockroach and the cat who befriended him.

Rikard didn't seem to care all that much about the staging or dance details, although he did listen politely. But when she described the songs, he came alive.

All too soon, the delicious lunch was consumed. She set her fork down, and drank the last of her water.

"But I've been going on and on about me. What about you? What are some of the things you've worked on?"

Gently, he sang, "Everything's sweeter in the dark of night. Dark desire. Dark chocolate."

"Earworm!" she shouted. "I'm going to have that stuck in my head for days, now."

"I told you the jingles paid the rent."

"Do you have any idea how many bars of Desire chocolate I scarfed down because of that damn jingle? I'd be in the store, see the candy, the tune would start running through my head, and next thing I knew, I had half a pound of chocolate in my cart."

His warm gaze stroked her body with admiration. "It couldn't have been too many bars."

"That's why I have to go jogging every morning."

"Every morning?" Horizontal creases formed across his forehead, even though his raised eyebrows were hidden behind the mask.

"Yeah. The office only opens at nine o'clock. The last place I worked started earlier, and I had a longer commute, so I'm used to getting up at six. I have a nice jog and leisurely breakfast, then shower and dress for work."

"I never worked a regular schedule," he admitted. "Sometimes I'd spend all day slaving over a single phrase, twisting and turning it every way possible until it sounded like how I wanted it to sound. And sometimes everything would flow so perfectly, I was done in two hours. That was for home days. During tours, the schedule was more regimented, although still not what anyone would call regular."

"Tours? I didn't know composers went on tour."

"I did." He stood, and cleared the table. "Speaking of tours, are you ready for your tour of the house, now?"

A shiver rippled over her skin. "Yes."

Taking her hand in his gloved one, Rikard led her out of the kitchen.

"Hey, your glove's all wet."

"Damp, not wet. I washed my hands earlier, before cooking the tuna steaks."

"With your gloves on? Can you do that?" She hadn't been paying attention, since she was on the phone at the time, but she'd just assumed he'd taken the gloves off while cooking, then put them back on when it was time to serve the meal.

"They're deerskin. It's washable." They returned to the open entryway, and he led her through the arch opposite the music room. "This is the home theater."

A huge flat-screen television that was at least four feet across was mounted on the wall. A modular reclining sofa with built-in cup holders and snack tables faced the television. Trim black speakers were mounted in the corners of the room and bolted to the floor. The only other furniture was a wrought iron cabinet, filled two-thirds of the way full with DVDs.

"Do you watch a lot of movies?"

"Not so much now. For a while that was pretty much all I did."

She nodded. That would be after his car accident, while he was recovering from the injuries that had nearly blinded him. He probably had broken bones, too, and wasn't supposed to move much.

He turned and led her out of the room, back to the foyer. She followed him up the stairs to the spacious landing. Four doors radiated off it, two before them and two to the sides.

"My bedroom and the master bathroom," he indicated, pointing to the left-hand door before them. Then he pointed to the right. "The guest bedroom. It shares a bathroom with my recording studio."

Gayle tensed with anticipation, knowing where the remaining door must lead. Rikard turned her to face the door, and gave her a gentle push forward.

"The playroom. Open the door."

Unlike the other doors, this one had a heavy silver lock, with an antique key in it. She tested the doorknob, and when the door didn't move, turned the key. The lock snapped open with a loud click of its tumblers, and the door swung outward.

"I warn you, it was decorated in a fit of self-indulgence," Rikard cautioned.

She stepped inside, her eyes going wide. Any windows the room had once possessed had been blocked up. The walls were covered, floor to ceiling, with *trompe l'oeil* paintings that gave the appearance of being in a rocky cave, softened by sweeps of burgundy velvet. She glanced upward. The ceiling was painted, too. Flickering torches were mounted on the walls, and branches of lit candelabra were scattered around the room. Despite knowing that she was on the second floor of a modern house, her mind insisted she was standing in a cave belowground. Even the air seemed different, cool and damp.

"Isn't all this open flame a fire safety violation?" she asked, the mundane question the only thing she could think of to say in response to the bizarre setting.

"They're not real candles or torches. The candles are a flickering bulb designed to simulate candlelight. And the torches are just orange satin, blown by a fan."

She glanced over her shoulder and saw his gloved hand resting beside the doorway, where a light switch would normally be. Where a light switch no doubt actually was, camouflaged by paint, to control the candles and torches.

She nodded, allowing her eyes to focus on the contents of the room. Black padded benches in different heights, with triangular leather pillow wedges, occupied much of the floor space. A wrought iron wine table had been repurposed to hold a collection of floggers instead of stemware and paddles instead of wine bottles, with two black woven baskets hiding their contents from view inside the base cupboard of the unit. And a number of heavy eyebolts had been screwed into the wall and ceiling. Some had chains dangling from them, while others were bare.

"I feel like I've stepped back in time," she whispered.

"To a time when a man was truly the lord of his castle, and had the power to enforce his desires?"

She nodded, her legs beginning to tremble. "You said you were interested in scene play. What scenes play out in here?"

He stepped up behind her, hands wrapping loosely around her waist to pull her against him. His masked cheek rested against her hair.

"What scenes would you like to play?"

"I don't know. I told you, I'd only ever done a little bondage before. And that was straightforward, let's-tie-you-to-the-bedposts sex."

"Then perhaps you are a lovely Victorian maid, innocently sailing to Spain, when your ship is attacked by pirates. The pirate captain is captivated by your beauty." Rikard reached up and stroked her cheek with the back of one gloved finger. "And so, rather than killing you, he takes you back to his hideout. He will spare your life, if you can convince him that it is worth his while to keep you as a slave. A slave to service all of his sexual needs."

She shivered, leaning against Rikard's warmth. In his black mask, laced leather pants and poet shirt, he looked like a pirate. Her imagination ran wild, inspired by his words, until she smelled the cordite, and squinted against the fog of gunsmoke that blurred her vision. Distantly, she heard the cries of men fighting and dying.

"And if I am unable to convince you, Captain?"

"Then I will give you to my men. They deserve a treat." He trailed his finger between her breasts, down to her pussy. "I'm afraid you wouldn't survive the experience."

Fear flushed her body, even though she knew Rikard was not a pirate, that there was no crew waiting to ravish her to death if she failed to satisfy him. Her heart pounded, and her palms sweated, as if the scene he'd described was real.

He stroked her cheek again, turning her face so that he could read her expression.

"So, my sweet pirate prize. Do you want to play?"

"Yes, Master Rikard. I want to play."

"Pirate booty does not wear clothing. Take it off."

He released her, stepping back so that he was out of her way. Quickly, Gayle pulled off the clinging top, then unzipped the leather skirt and stepped out of it. She dropped her clothing to the floor, and stood naked before Rikard.

His blue eyes gleamed within his mask as he approached her. Softly, slowly, he reached out and glided his gloved fingers over her shoulders, down her arms, around her breasts, across her nipples, down her stomach, over her hips, and around her ass. Closing her eyes, she tilted her head back and sighed with pleasure.

Something warm and wet touched her shoulder, and her eyes flew open. Rikard was kissing her, with a gentle openmouthed kiss that was barely firmer than a breath. He licked her shoulder, then traced the line of her muscles and vein with his tongue, placing another soft kiss in the hollow of her neck.

"From now until the end of the scene, you will address me as Captain. If you need to stop the scene for any reason, refer to me as Master Rikard."

"Yes, Captain."

"The first thing I must do is make sure you can't jump ship and try to swim to safety." He opened the wine cabinet and dug in one of the baskets. Triumphantly, he turned to her holding a pair of black leather wrist restraints and a rough length of hemp rope.

"Turn around, and put your hands behind your back."

Quivering, Gayle did as he instructed. She was giving him her trust and belief in addition to her obedience. With her hands bound behind her, she'd be unable to fight him off if he decided to try something she didn't want him to do. But she had no doubt that she could stop him with a word.

Getting into the game, she pleaded, "Please, Captain. Don't tie me up. I promise I'll do everything you ask. *Everything*."

He chuckled. "Saucy wench."

The length of rope flicked out, rasping lightly across her ass cheeks. She gasped, more surprised than pained.

"You'll do everything I demand anyhow, or I'll see you walk the plank."

A delightful tendril of fear skittered up her spine, her skin turning icy. Her nipples tightened into hard buds, from the cold, her growing excitement, or both.

Rikard's gentle hands placed the restraints around her wrists, testing the fit and ensuring that her shoulders were not pulled too severely. Then he wrapped the length of rope around the restraints, not tying it, but letting the rough hemp brush against her wrists and forearms. Her mind transformed the padded restraints into heavy loops of rough rope.

He circled around her, admiring her naked body. Gayle held up her head and stood rigidly beneath his examination.

"Yes, you're a proper lady. I can tell. But you're my prisoner now. I'll break you of that soon enough, and have you begging and moaning like the commonest of gutter trash."

She tipped up her chin in defiance. "Never! I am a lady, Captain. And nothing you do to me will make me less of one."

He sucked in a deep breath, a slow grin lighting his face. "I do love a challenge. But I can't have you disagreeing with me. This is my ship, and what I say goes. If one of my crew dared to contradict me as you've done, it would be twenty lashes of the cat, until he learned to keep a civil tongue."

Rikard stalked closer, his gloved hand shooting out and gripping her chin in a firm hold. She couldn't pull away or twist out of his grasp, but his fingers merely rested against her skin rather than digging into her flesh.

"But I'll forgive you this time, if you beg. Get down on your knees and beg me not to whip you."

Gayle stiffened her back, completely lost in character. "A lady does not beg, Captain."

He laughed, deep and low in his throat. "Right. It's the cat for you, then."

Grabbing her by her upper arm, he dragged her over to a waist-high bench, and bent her across it. He loosed the rope and unlinked the wrist restraints, then pulled her arms out to the side, clipping the restraints to rings at the top and bottom of the bench. Gayle tried to lift her upper body, and found herself unable to move. She had never felt so completely helpless.

Hot fluid gathered between her legs. When Rikard slipped his booted foot between hers and kicked her ankles apart with a gentle nudge, flattening her completely against the bench, a trickle of fluid coursed down the inside of her thigh.

He moved away, returning a moment later swishing something back and forth through the air with ominous snaps. Narrow strips of leather trailed across her shoulder blades.

"This is the cat. Twenty strips of leather, each with an edge sharp enough to rip open that delicate skin. And you're getting twenty lashes with it. You'll be nothing but a bloody wreck from your graceful neck to your sweet, tight ass. Sure you don't want to beg?"

Gayle trembled. Rikard wouldn't really slice her back open. She remembered his desperate panic in the kitchen when she feared he'd hurt her. But stretched across the bench, the lashes of the cat sweeping back and forth across her quivering skin in teasing caresses, she had trouble believing she was not at the mercy of a bloodthirsty pirate.

"Never," she whispered.

"One." The whip rose and fell, the tips of the lashes flicking across her shoulder blade before the body of the cat smacked her upper back.

Gayle cried out in shock and surprise. She hadn't expected he'd hit her with no warning. But it hadn't hurt.

"Two." The lash tips flicked across her other shoulder blade, followed by the heavy smack of the body.

"Eighteen more to go. Are you certain you don't want to beg?"

"Do your worst!"

Rikard laughed again, the low sound chillingly unlike his normal melodic laughter. The cat smacked her shoulders over and over, as Rikard counted his strokes.

"That makes ten." He trailed the whip's lashes down her sensitive spine. "Halfway there."

"You'll never break me, Captain."

"Your skin is a lovely shade of pink, blushing like a virgin bride's. Where else could my whip touch you? Where else are you a virgin?"

The lashes stroked down, feathering across her ass, and tickling her crack.

"Are you a virgin here?" he whispered, one leather-clad finger following the path of the whip to press lightly at her hole.

Gayle moaned, her ass clenching tightly in reaction to his invading finger. What would it feel like to have him press his finger not just against the entrance, but actually inside? Two fingers? His cock, slicking in and out of her ass?

"Captain, please."

"Please stop? Or please continue?"

"You're right. I am a virgin, there."

"And…?"

"You're a pirate. I'm a lady."

"No, I'm a pirate and you're my prisoner. If I wanted to slide inside that tight hole, pumping in and out until you screamed, I could do it, and no one would stop me. I'm the captain of this ship. My word is law."

His fingertip tapped lightly on her sensitive nerves. Gayle gasped, her muscles tightening and contracting. More fluid trickled down her leg.

"But you didn't finish whipping me. Or do you want to leave my challenge to your authority unmet?"

"I answer every challenge."

The cat tickled and struck the firm globes of her ass, once on each side. She didn't think he'd hit her harder than he had before, but what had felt like a weird kind of massage on her shoulders felt mildly painful on her ass.

"Thirteen." The whip hit her first ass cheek exactly where it had struck before, wringing a soft whimper from her. It didn't hurt, so much as burn.

"Fourteen." He slapped the cat against her other ass cheek, again in the exact same spot as his first strike.

Gayle moaned low in her throat.

"Fifteen." Another smack, falling on her already tender skin, then again on the opposite side.

"Sixteen. Are you ready to beg yet?"

"Never," she panted.

Rikard slapped her with his gloved hand. She clenched her ass muscles, determined to resist him, even as her breath grew short, and her body trembled, eager for him to claim her.

"I said I was giving you twenty strokes with the cat." His leather-clad palm smacked her ass with short, sharp strokes, rocking her against the bench. "If I hit you with something else, it doesn't count."

"Vile pirate! I might have known you wouldn't keep your word."

His right hand continued to fall rhythmically on her ass cheeks, his left pressing lightly at the top of her ass, covering the base of her spine, while his thumb gently spread her cheeks. Her ass burned, each stroke a brief sting, followed by a glorious heat that spread down her thighs, and pooled deep in her sex like a hot spring just waiting to burst forth into a steaming geyser.

"Master…" she moaned.

Rikard's next slap never fell. "Master…?"

Belatedly, she remembered she was to call him Captain, and to call him Master Rikard would end the scene. She had not used his full name, so he wasn't sure if she wanted him to stop or not.

"Captain. I mean Captain. You can spank me and whip me until the deck of your ship runs with blood, I will never beg!"

"Oh, you will beg, my pretty slave."

His fingertips smoothed across her stinging ass, cool upon her heated flesh. She shivered beneath his soft caress, desire flaring hot and wet, even as fear rippled through her, tensing her muscles.

"You will beg for me to let you come, for me to end your torture. You will beg for me to hit you, again and again, until you explode from the ecstasy. And if you beg sweetly enough, I just might give you what you need."

He slapped her ass, hard enough to hurt instead of just sting. Gayle's knees buckled, and all of her weight rested on her chest and stomach, stretched across the bench. Warmth trickled down her inner thigh. She moaned, crushed beneath a landslide of fear and desire.

"No. Never," she whispered.

"Have I not warned you not to contradict me? That merits another twenty lashes with the cat."

Gayle whimpered. He teased her with the body of lashes, stroking them over her hot and swollen ass. Was he going to whip her there?

He lifted the hand holding her down. Oh, God, he was.

The cat smacked her ass, wrenching a cry from her. She couldn't endure twenty of those. She couldn't.

"Seventeen. Eighteen." The cat smacked the other side of her ass, pulling another cry from her lips. "We never finished the first set."

She moaned. She was going to die. Her entire body was on fire, rivers of flame coursing through her veins with every pulse, driven by the beating tempo of his strokes.

"Nineteen. Twenty." He paused, and this time, it was the cessation of blows that made her give a pained cry of helpless need.

Rikard inhaled deeply, his shuddering breath hinting that he was growing as excited as she.

"Yes," he whispered. "You begin to understand."

The cat's lashes landed on her shoulder blade, harder than the previous blows, and spreading further. The tips swept outward from her spine, then outward from her spine on the other side, as if Rikard was tracing giant figure eights. Sometimes harder, sometimes softer, sometimes faster and sometimes slower, he varied the whip's caress so that she never knew what to expect. Then she stopped trying, and just allowed herself to feel.

Sting. Smack. Pain. Heat. Pleasure, thick and heady, coiling deep within. She began to grunt, low and guttural, with each blow.

Rikard paused, his gentle fingers stroking soft caresses over her ass, reminding her that she was still delightfully sensitive there.

"Do not grunt like a pig," he admonished. "God gave you a voice. Use it. Sing for me."

"I don't understand." She nearly cried, devastated that she might not be able to please him.

"Relax your throat. Open your mouth. Hold in your mind the sound of a perfect high C."

The whip fell on her ass, and she released a high, shrill note of pain and pleasure.

"That was more like an E-flat. But much better."

She was being ravished by a pirate with perfect pitch.

Then his whip landed on her shoulder blades, and she cried out in joy, careful to lower her tone a minor third. Again and again, the whip stroked her with flaming lashes, and she sang out in need and hunger.

She waited, trembling in anticipation, but the whip did not fall.

"That was twenty," he said softly.

"No. Please. Don't stop. I'm so close. Please. Don't stop."

"Are you begging?"

"Yes. Please. Whip me again. Please. I'm begging you."

Rikard stroked her shoulders with trembling fingers, then smoothed her skin with his gloved palms. Gayle was certain that he molded her body anew out of sheets of living flame, holding her untouched in the center of the blaze.

"Please, Captain. Please. Let me come. Don't stop."

"I can refuse you nothing when you sing."

The whip fell again, and she sang. Slowly, relentlessly, she climbed the scale, a quarter-step at a time like some strange Indian modulation. Each blow drove her higher, deeper into the heat and flames, surrounded by music that pulsed and rippled like nothing she'd ever heard before. Finally, with a long, drawn-out A above high C, she climaxed, shuddering and shaking as the orgasm thundered through her body like a surging series of arpeggios.

And then the music claimed her, and she was gone.

* * * * *

Rikard smiled at the limp, sweat-soaked woman sprawled across the whipping bench. He felt sated with power, relaxed and replete. Her charming insistence that she would never beg had made him as hard as the leather-wrapped handle of his whip, eager to prove her wrong. And her voice as she came! Perfection.

His lips twisted, self-mockery spoiling the moment. His proficiency in playing the human body had grown over the past two years, after he realized the scar tissue in his left hand would never allow him to play the piano again. Like a blind man whose hearing grows acute to compensate, he'd been given another instrument to assuage his loss. Sometimes it helped.

Now, though, his ears were filled with Gayle's slow rise to that final, drawn-out note. His mind stacked chord progressions beneath, with a series of descending sevenths in staccato triplets as counterpoints.

He freed her arms from the restraints, then lifted her up to lay her on her side on the bench. Popping the recessed latch on the concealed closet, he retrieved a thick white robe in soft French terry. The logo of some hotel he no longer remembered was embroidered on the breast in gold thread.

Carefully, he wrapped her in the fluffy embrace of the robe. She gave no sign of awareness, letting him dress her as if she was a rag doll.

Another thrill of power surged through him, stiffening his cock. He'd well and thoroughly pleased her, his touch shooting her deep into whatever place subs went when their minds left their bodies. If all went well, when she woke, she'd be eager for sex. He didn't always want sex with his submissives. Often, the rush of dominating them was enough. But he wanted sex with Gayle.

He'd take her from behind, the reddened marks of his whipping visible on her pale, perfect skin as he thrust into her, again and again, driving him into a frenzy until she came in a crying symphony of delight.

But first, she needed to rest in warmth and safety. Swinging her up into his arms, he carried her from the room.

He was almost at the doorway to the home theater when an annoyingly chirped rendition of an old Motown classic stopped him in his tracks. What the hell was that?

"Shit!" Gayle's cell phone.

Chapter Five

80

Rikard hurried into the kitchen. Placing Gayle's limp body in one of the chairs, he held her steady with one hand while he dumped her purse out on the table. There!

Grabbing the chirping phone, he flipped it open and took the call.

"Hello. Gayle can't come to the phone right now."

There was a moment of silence, followed by a woman's accusing voice demanding, "Where is she, and what have you done to her?"

"She's right here, but she's asleep. And as for what I did, I'll say she enjoyed it, and leave it at that."

"I don't believe you. Put Gayle on the phone."

Rikard took a deep breath, and flipped the switch in his mind that engaged the other new instrument he'd been gifted with after his accident. He'd studied self-hypnosis as a way to manage the agonizing pain of the third-degree burns, working with the visualizations his therapists suggested. It hadn't been very effective until he'd tried recording himself, and playing back his spoken suggestions. Then it was surprisingly successful. Even more surprisingly, he developed the ability to hypnotize others into sharing his visualizations—or any other belief he wanted them to hold.

"Gayle is asleep," he repeated, his voice vibrating with hidden emphasis. "She is safe, and you have no cause for fear. Call back in an hour, and she'll speak to you then."

"Well, if she's really asleep, I suppose you shouldn't wake her. I'll call back in an hour. But if I still can't talk to her then, I'm calling the cops!"

"You are a good friend to her. She will thank you for your concern when she wakes."

"She'd better."

The phone went dead in his hand.

He dropped it onto the table, ignoring the scattered debris from Gayle's purse, and lifted her into his arms again. That had been close. He'd sworn that she'd told her friend all was well and not to call again. Then again, he hadn't heard her entire conversation, just snippets between the sizzles of the tuna steaks. It's possible her friend had convinced her to continue the calls. Or else, her friend had called back despite Gayle's request to leave them alone.

Carrying her into the home theater, he sighed. He wasn't sure how long she'd sleep, but it would probably be long enough that any sex would have to wait until after her friend's damnable follow-up call.

He kicked out the recliner, then settled into it with Gayle cradled in his arms. She snuggled closer, her cheek resting just above his heart. One-handed, he flipped the top of the built-in table, exposing the storage area beneath housing his remote controls, as well as one of his ever-present notepads of staff paper. After all, inspiration could strike anywhere.

The DVD in the player spun up. *Amadeus*. Damn, he had been feeling melancholy the last time he'd watched a movie, hadn't he? Well, he wasn't about to get up and disturb Gayle's sleep again. And you couldn't argue with the beauty of Mozart's music. He'd just fast-forward through the bits with Salieri falling into a suicidal depression because he'd been given the desire to create music but not the ability.

He was smiling, nodding in time with the music, until he reached the scene where Mozart attended a party, and was asked to play a piece of music in the style of Bach. When that triumph was not enough, the party guests flipped him on his back and demanded he play that way, reaching behind his head to the keyboard. He did, gloriously, until his father's ominous displeasure ruined everything.

Rikard thumbed the DVD off, his throat tight and his eyes burning. He'd once tried that trick at a party. Had it been the tour in Munich? Although not on a par with Mozart's movie performance, he'd done a credible job.

He'd had a gift, and he'd wasted it, playing tricks at parties. What he wouldn't give to just once be able to play the piano again, to let his soul fly free on the waves of sound, and carry the audience with him to heights they'd never dreamed existed. Hell, he'd play in a deserted basement, as long as the piano was in tune. But that would never happen. The scarring on his left hand had damaged his extensor tendons. He could hit the notes just fine, but he couldn't lift his fingers away from the keys, not at anything approaching the right speed.

Softly, he began singing the Sondheim melody he'd played for Beth earlier. Not a day went by that he didn't think of the music he could no longer play. It had been his life, his heart and his soul. Sometimes, he thought it would be easier if he could just forget. But that way lay madness and death. If he ever lost the memories as well as the music, he knew it would kill him. A man may be able to live with a blade of ice imbedded in his heart, but he could not withstand the removal of his soul.

* * * * *

Gayle woke slowly, aware of warmth and a soft thudding drumbeat. And music. Rikard was humming softly to himself, occasionally punctuated by "No, that's not right", or "Yes, that's it". A pencil scratched frantically across paper.

Awareness returned to her body. She was sitting curled on his lap, wearing something heavy yet soft, her cheek pressed to his chest. His left hand was cupped loosely around her hip. Her ass throbbed in time with her pulse, still sensitive from the thorough whipping and spanking he'd given her.

Experimentally, she rolled her shoulders. No stiffness there, although she could feel the muscles, like the burn of pressing a stretch when working out.

Rikard's humming stopped.

"I didn't mean to disturb you."

"No, that's all right. I was just waiting for you to wake up."

Gayle sat up, hissing as her weight rolled onto her ass. The brief flash of pain was followed by a delicious warmth, spreading out over her skin while at the same time spiraling deep to ignite the slumbering desire within her. She wriggled on his lap, stoking the flames.

He inhaled sharply, and tightened his grip on her hip, holding her still. She recognized the firm pressure against the back of her thigh as his suddenly hard cock.

"I don't have any condoms in this room. And if you keep that up, I'm not going to remember why I need to go get them."

She froze at the low threat in his voice, more than the words he used. When she remained still, his hold loosened and he released his breath in a soft gust.

"Thank you."

Careful to move only her head, she glanced around the room. They were no longer in the playroom. He'd carried her downstairs, to the reclining couch in the home theater.

Her glance dipped down to the fluffy white robe she was wearing. The breast was embroidered in gold thread with a fat bird. A bird wearing antennae. At least that's what it looked like upside down. She struggled to read the scrolling print beneath. *L' Perdrix*. That didn't help.

She flicked her gaze upwards to Rikard, meaning to ask him about the logo. His blue eyes watched her from within the dark depths of his black mask.

"You're still wearing your mask."

"Yes."

"Then you're still Master Rikard, and not just Rikard?" She couldn't explain the sadness this caused. After all, Master Rikard was the one who had given her the best orgasm of her life in the kitchen, then topped that with the full-body meltdown of ecstasy in the playroom.

Maybe that was it. Master Rikard was about the sex. Held close in his arms, cuddled and cared for, she wanted an emotional connection. If it had been Rikard holding her, she'd have thought that's what he wanted, too. But it wasn't Rikard. It was Master Rikard who held her on his lap while his cock pressed hard and solid against her thigh. Master Rikard who wasn't done with her yet.

Her breath quickened, her breasts tensing and tightening despite herself. He was watching her reaction carefully. When her breathing shifted, he slipped his gloved hand between the folds of her robe, the black leather dramatic against the fluffy white terry.

His warm hand cupped one of her breasts, his thumb rubbing gently across the nipple. Gayle arched into his touch with a sigh, her eyes closing to focus all her attention on the feel of his hand upon her. Her nipple tightened even further, to a hard point.

He tugged lightly with his thumb and forefinger, ripping a gasp from her lips. Her hips bounced without conscious volition, pulling an equally sharp gasp from him. His cock dug into the soft flesh of her thigh.

"Where are those condoms?" she asked.

"Upstairs, in the guest bedroom. But we can't go up just yet. Your friend will be calling soon, and she'll be distressed if you don't answer the phone."

Gayle blinked. "How did you know…?"

"She already called once, while you were asleep."

The blood drained from her face. "Oh my God! What did you say? What did she say?"

"It's fine. I told her you were sleeping, and she promised to call back in an hour."

"An hour? How long was I out?"

"Forty, forty-five minutes. Something like that."

"Wow."

He tugged on her nipple again, soothing and inflaming her at the same time. Gently, he untied the belt on her robe, and pushed the collar off her shoulders, exposing her body to his gaze. His hand stroked her thigh and hip beneath the robe, then glided up her rib cage to once again cup her breast, while his head bent, and he pressed a soft kiss to the pulse point in her neck.

She shivered and moaned. Reaching up, she thrust her fingers into his thick blond hair, clutching his head and pressing his mouth against her neck.

Rikard stiffened, just long enough for her to fear she'd done something wrong, before he relaxed and resumed kissing and licking her neck. His hand dropped away from her breast, making her whimper softly in disappointment. He chuckled softly, the sound rolling through her like a wave of pure delight.

"I'm not stopping," he whispered. "Just moving us to the kitchen, so we're not unduly interrupted by your friend's call."

He slipped his arm beneath her thighs. Then, with a fluid surge of graceful power, he rose with Gayle in his arms. He carried her through the house, into the kitchen, and sat down at the table. Her purse was upended, with the contents strewn across the glass tabletop. She had a brief spike of worry. Was there anything in her purse she'd have preferred him not to see? Although, since her cell phone was sitting on top of the pile, she doubted he'd looked at anything else.

Then he lowered his head, this time covering her breast with his mouth. His tongue swirled around the tight nipple, then he tugged lightly on it with his teeth. She groaned, already hot and wet for him.

His fingers stroked up her thigh, making soft circles that drove her insane with need. Then he slipped his hand higher, slicking his fingers between her folds.

She moaned, letting her legs fall open, encouraging him to touch her deeper.

"Are you going to fist me again?" she asked breathlessly.

"Would you like that?"

"Oh, yes. Please."

"Then I will. But you must take your friend's call when it comes. Even if my hand is all the way inside you, and you're writhing with pleasure, you must take the call. Can you do that?"

"Yes, Master Rikard." She'd promise anything to feel him inside her again.

He stroked the circle of her opening with his fingers, probing with first one, then two. "You're not ready, yet."

The leg supporting her jiggled, bouncing her up and down, awakening her sensitive ass. Gayle moaned, and felt the change in his touch as his gloved fingers became coated in her fluids. He found her clit with his thumb, and worked her, swirling around the thickening bud, then brushing back and forth across the tip, and finally pressing against it.

She gasped, and his fingers slid inside her.

"Now you're ready," he whispered.

Licking and kissing the tender tip of one breast, he built her to a frenzy of need, then scraped his teeth across her nipple. When the wave rippled through her, he slipped a third finger inside her. Shifting position slightly, he turned his attention to her other breast, and repeated the process. This time when the wave broke, he slid a fourth finger through her opening.

He moved on to kiss and lick her neck, sensitizing her pulse points with openmouthed kisses then blowing lightly across the damp skin to make her shiver with need. Each time, his fingers pressed ever so slightly further into her. His fingers were in her up to the second joint, his thumb stroking her opening preparatory to joining them. Then the phone rang.

She didn't recognize the cheerful chirping at first, focused on the feelings coursing through her body.

"Answer it," Rikard ordered.

Gayle fumbled for the phone and flipped it open. "Hello?"

"Gayle! Are you okay? Is everything all right?"

"Everything's fine." She gasped as Rikard's thumb joined his fingers, stretching her even further. He wasn't planning on stopping his assault while she was on the phone.

A rush of wet warmth filled her, at how completely he controlled her body and its response. His hand slipped further inside, almost up to the knuckles, and Gayle moaned with pleasure.

"What's going on? Are you sure you're okay?" Carrie demanded. She sounded ready to hop on a plane and check out the situation in person if Gayle didn't give her the answers she was looking for.

"What's going on is we're having sex, okay? Hot, sweaty, kinky sex. And your call came right in the middle of it. Stop calling me. I'll phone you when I get home, and we can talk then."

Carrie was silent for so long, Gayle was afraid they'd lost the connection, then Carrie said softly, "I'm sorry. I was worried about you. I didn't mean to interrupt."

"Oh, Carrie, I'm the one who's sorry. You're the best friend ever, and I know I asked you to call. But your timing stinks! I'm halfway out of my head with what Master Rikard is doing to me. I can't talk now."

Rikard bit lightly on her neck, making her whimper, and murmured, "Only halfway?"

"But you are okay, right?" Carrie pressed.

"Never better in my life."

"Okay. I'll wait for your call tonight. But if I don't hear from you by nine, I'm still calling the cops."

"Great. Wonderful. Call by nine. Got it. Bye."

She shut the phone and tossed it onto the table.

"Open for me," Rikard whispered. "Open as wide as you can go."

His hand spread her opening the last fraction of an inch, then he slid fully inside her, up to his wrist. Her muscles clenched and gripped his hand, as she shivered and moaned.

Unlike the first time, when he'd reached deep inside her, this time, he immediately started to pull his hand out. The wide part of his hand pressed her vaginal muscle, stretching her fully open again, before he pushed his fist deep inside her once more.

She gasped, bucking against his hand.

"Shh," he said softly. "Let me do all the moving."

"Yes, Master." Gayle spread her legs wide, tipped her hips, and leaned back against his other arm. She was his to control.

His fist pumped slowly in and out, eliciting soft groans of pleasure with each stroke. Then he began speaking, softly, gently, in time with his hand movements.

"You're so hot. So wet. It's like putting my hand into a steam bath. A paraffin dip. Warm and wet and closing tight around me. So tight. Tighter."

She clenched her inner muscles, wrapping them around his fist. He filled her completely, pressing back against her with his sheer size. His knuckles rubbed the wall of her vagina as he slid back and forth. She gasped, her hand once more thrusting into his hair and clenching tightly.

"Please, Master. Please."

"What do you want, Gayle? You were very good, and followed my orders about the phone. You deserve a reward."

"Please. Do me faster."

His fist stroked steadily in and out, building speed, while his hand on her hip kept her where he wanted her to be. Her gasps and groans became short, sharp cries at the apex of each stroke.

"Sing for me, Gayle. Sing."

Her next cry was a warbled note.

"That's it. Sing."

His fist pumped harder, faster, driving her cries of passion higher and higher up the scale. With a series of high notes worthy of Mozart's "Queen of the Night", Gayle gave a final shriek and came in a shuddering rush. Rikard's hand spurted clear of her body.

His mouth closed over hers, his lips tender and gentle as he pulled her lower lip into his mouth to suckle. Slowly, he soothed her down from the heights where he'd taken her. Her trembles subsided, leaving her filled with warm lethargy.

"I think you need to build your energy up after that performance," he said. "We should have dessert now."

"Dessert?" Gayle opened blurred eyes, then closed them again when it was too much effort to resolve the wavering images into a scene that made any sense. "I couldn't possibly eat dessert. I can barely keep my eyes open."

"I'll just have to feed you, then."

A ripple of anticipation coursed through the sluggish circulation of her body. He would care for her. Completely.

"First you dressed me. Now you're going to feed me. When do I do something for you?"

"I told you, I believe my role as dominant is to ensure you're surrounded by luxury, and have all your needs met."

"I thought your role as dominant was to blow my mind with incredible sex."

He laughed, the sound washing over her in benediction, filling her with joy. "That's one of your needs, isn't it? You can satisfy my desires later."

Gayle frowned. "Have you had…any…?"

"Satisfaction?"

She nodded.

He lifted his hand from her hip and stroked her cheek with the backs of his fingers. "Yes. There's more to satisfaction than simply coming. Helping you with your music was satisfying. Watching you enjoy the meal I prepared for you was satisfying. Having my touch send you into orbit was extremely satisfying."

She closed her eyes and relaxed into his gentle caress.

"That being said, I would like you to make me come, hard and long."

"Yes, Master Rikard." She swallowed, inexplicably nervous. "What do you want me to do?"

"I want you to let me make love to you."

She blinked. "That's it?"

"That's it. Ready for your dessert now?"

He lifted her off his lap, and set her down in her previous chair. While she stuffed her belongings back into her purse, he washed his gloved hands, then dished the dessert out onto two plates.

Gayle's eyes widened at the confection he placed before her. A half pear glistened in a coating of thick golden syrup, topped by a scoop of French vanilla ice cream, the whole thing drizzled with swirling loops of caramel and garnished with chopped pistachio nuts. "It almost looks too good to eat."

"It's just poached pears."

"Just poached pears. Like you have them for dessert all the time?"

"Actually, I had one for dessert last night, and will have one for dessert tomorrow night. The recipe is for two pears, and it'll keep for two days."

"So what do you have the rest of the time? Crème Brûlée?" she mocked.

Rikard's eyes narrowed. "What is your problem, Gayle?"

She threw her spoon onto the table, and buried her face in her hands. "I don't know!"

Instantly, he pulled her into his lap, tucking her head against his shoulder and rubbing soothing strokes up and down her arm. "Shush, now. Forget the dessert. What's bothering you?"

She sniffed. "I don't understand this. I thought it was an even trade. But you're doing everything for me. And then you don't even want me to do anything to get you off, just have sex!"

"So you'd be happier if I wanted you to kneel and suck my cock until I came?"

Despite the confused tone of his voice, she nodded. She could taste his smooth length filling her mouth, hot and hard, thrusting deep into her throat almost farther than it was possible to take him. She swallowed, her throat suddenly thick.

"At least that would make sense."

He sighed, and trailed damp fingertips along her jawline. "I wasn't going to mention this until you were ready to go to bed with me, but I do have a request. I want to take you from behind, so I can see the marks of my whip and my hand on your skin as I'm plunging into you. I want to claim you completely, and know every inch of your body belongs to me, to do with as I will."

Beneath her thighs, his cock rose and pressed against her, illustrating just how much he wanted that.

His fingers trembled as he stroked them down her throat, then reached inside her bathrobe to skim her breast. "You are my instrument. I will play you, and create beautiful music with you. Through you, my soul will take flight. And in return I will give you all the care a musician lavishes upon his most valued possession. You will want for nothing. But only if you will be completely mine."

Gayle shivered beneath his touch, aching to erase the note of desperate isolation in his voice. It was almost as though he expected her to refuse him.

"Yes."

His hand stilled. "Yes?"

"Yes. I will be yours."

For a moment, he clutched her tightly, burying his masked face in her hair. Then he stood abruptly, setting her on her feet and stepping away from her.

"You don't know what you're agreeing to. I'll ask you again once you understand what I'm asking."

Pain lanced through her. "Are you rejecting me?"

"No! Never that." He thrust both hands through his hair, the thick elastic band holding his mask catching in his fingers and snapping loudly. He winced at the blow. "Forget dessert. Come upstairs with me. Now."

"Yes, Master Rikard."

Taking her hand in his gloved one, he led her from the kitchen, shaking his head. "You want to serve me? I'll show you how to serve."

Chapter Six

∽

Rikard hauled her up the stairs to the second floor, then dragged her into the guest bedroom. Gayle had only a moment to note the décor — a dresser and nightstand of natural oak with wrought iron accents, a wrought iron bed with swirling spires topping each corner post, and matching curtain rods covered with black and white sheers — before he ripped off her robe and pushed her onto the bed.

"Is this what you wanted?" he spat.

Gayle scrambled into the center of the bed and turned to face him, crouched ready to spring to freedom if he gave her a chance. "No."

He ignored her protest. This was not going down the way she'd expected, and she braced herself to fight if he tried to take more than she was prepared to give.

"So eager to serve, you don't care what will be asked of you."

He untied the laces of his leather pants with sharp, savage jerks. His pants fell to the floor, tangling with his boots. He kicked them off, his motions full of anger rather than his usual grace. One boot flew across the room to strike the dresser with a solid thud. He wrenched off his poet shirt next, flinging it aside to stand naked before her in only his leather mask and gloves.

His rampant erection jutted forcefully at her, red and angry-looking.

She tried one last time to get through to him. "Please, Rikard, what did I say?"

"That's Master Rikard. I still wear the mask."

"Master Rikard. I'm sorry. I didn't mean to make you angry. Only tell me what I said, and I'll never say it again."

Terror choked her voice. Carrie had been right. She didn't know enough about Rikard to trust him. What insanity had possessed her to spend the whole day having sex with him? They were just supposed to be getting to know one another.

"First you vow you'll belong only and ever to me, now you promise to never give yourself to me again? I find I'm having trouble believing you."

Okay. That's what had set him off. She could think this through logically. That's what she was good at. Given a problem to solve, she forced the fear to keep at bay. It helped that he wasn't advancing on her, merely clutching the nearest bedpost in a death grip and glaring at her.

"I didn't vow to belong only and ever to you. All I said was that I wanted to be yours. I wanted to be your submissive."

He hesitated, his voice losing its strident tone. "My submissive only."

"All right. I'll give you the only. But not the ever. I wasn't talking a lifetime arrangement. I was thinking of right now."

A shudder rippled through him, his eyes closing as his head bent. He released the bedpost, and took a step backwards. Then another. She noted with relief that his cock had softened to semi-erect. Sighing, he bent to pick up her fallen robe and his discarded clothing. Gayle started to relax. He folded the robe and placed it on the bed beside her, then turned away to set his folded clothing on top of the dresser.

Softly, he whispered, "Nothing lasts forever. Not even when you want it to."

"The accident."

She hadn't realized she'd spoken until he whipped around to face her. "What did you say?"

"The woman you loved and lost in the accident. She'd vowed to be with you forever, hadn't she?"

"Actually, I'd vowed to devote my life to her." His lips twitched, as if he was trying to smile, but the effort was beyond him. "I would still, if fate hadn't taken that choice from me."

The raw pain in his voice reminded her of the lyrics he'd sung earlier, overwhelming her fear with shared suffering and understanding. He hadn't wanted to attack her just now. He'd been trying to drive her away. Whether he did so because he was afraid of being hurt again, or from some twisted loyalty to his dead love was unimportant. All that mattered was that her first impression of him had been correct.

Gayle shifted position, from a crouch to a cross-legged seat, and patted the bedspread. "Why don't you come sit over here?"

Rikard's brow furrowed. "Don't you want to get dressed and leave?"

"No. I want to talk to you. And I don't want to do it from across the room."

Hesitantly, he crossed the room to the bed. He lingered a long moment beside it, then slowly climbed on top and crawled over to where she sat. She watched him with avid appreciation. No longer terrified, the adrenaline flooding her bloodstream had made her incredibly horny. All she wanted right now was to get laid.

"I still want to be your submissive. I still want you to make love to me, whatever way gives you pleasure. But I can't say it's forever. I don't know. Maybe we'll discover we're so good together, we want to make this a permanent relationship. Maybe we'll find out we get on each other's nerves and go our separate ways. The only way to find out is to try."

He reached toward her, checking his gesture when his hand was still half an inch from her face. "You want to try?"

She leaned forward, pressing her cheek to his gloved palm. "Yes."

His breath caught. Then he pulled her into his arms and kissed her.

He clutched her to him, stroking his cool, damp gloves over her heated back in a frenzied effort to press her body closer to his. His mouth devoured hers, his tongue plunging deeply to capture her every soft whimper and moan. His cock rose between them, but he didn't break the kiss until she was growing lightheaded from lack of oxygen.

When he finally lifted his head, his breathing was harsh and ragged, as he struggled to pull air into his lungs.

"Say you're mine," he rasped. "At least for now."

"I'm yours."

He plunged into another kiss, the warm leather of his gloves gliding across the thin sheen of sweat on her back. Gone was the slow and careful buildup of passion that had characterized their earlier loveplay. He used no games or skillful tricks to whet her appetite. There was only crushing need, threatening to engulf them both in a firestorm that would burn them to cinders if they didn't find a way to express it.

This was not a Master, controlling his submissive's actions and reactions. This was a man, driven past his ability for self-restraint. This was Rikard.

She reached for his mask, wanting to remove the symbol of his mastery, freeing them both to be nothing more than a man and a woman, making love. He chose that moment to lift his head again, out of her reach, as he dragged in another gasping breath.

"Let me make love to you," he whispered.

"Yes."

"Let me see my marks on your skin while I love you."

"Yes." She could refuse him nothing.

Gently, with hands that trembled, he lowered her to the bedspread, then rolled her onto her stomach.

"Kneel," he whispered, his hands on her hips guiding her ass into the air as she pulled her knees up, her head pillowed on her crossed arms. Reverently, he kissed the swollen results of his earlier scene play.

Gayle shuddered, his soft lips reawakening the painful pleasure of his hand and whip striking her ass. Her folds parted, plump and wet, ready for his possession.

The bed shook as he clambered over to the nightstand and the supply of condoms in the drawer. She heard the packet tear, then his soft groan as he rolled the condom onto his engorged cock. A moment later, he was kneeling between her legs, one hand on her hip, holding her steady, while his other guided his cock to her entrance.

The tip slid between her folds, then found her opening and thrust deep. They both groaned in pleasure.

The angle was unlike anything she'd experienced before, his cock pressing hard against her vaginal muscles with every deep stroke. He thrust twice, then groaned low in his throat and folded himself over her, his chest pressed to her back. He kissed the lines of the cat across her shoulders, trailing his tongue over the faint welts and swellings.

She moaned. "Yes. Please, yes."

Sheets of fire cascaded over her skin from where his lips touched her, all that she had felt earlier and then some. She felt her fluids pouring forth, coating his cock and running down both of their legs.

Rikard reached around to caress her swollen, aching breasts. His blind fingers found the nipples, first stroking, then squeezing them.

She gasped, her hips jerking in response.

"Like that," he groaned. "Again."

They found their rhythm, her hips bucking beneath him as he pumped in and out, squeezing her nipples with every thrust. Kisses landed scattershot on her shoulders, his mouth finding new territory each time he lunged forward.

He moaned, a note of utter purity that nearly stopped her breath with its beauty. Twice more, he thrust in time with his cries. Then he thrust deep and exploded, shaking as his body covered hers.

Her hips continued to rock, and he fumbled between her slick folds, his fingers questing for her clit. When he found it, two quick squeezes were all she needed before she shrilled her own release and collapsed, her knees no longer able to support her. The heavy weight of his body pinned her to the bed, as his knees gave out too.

His arms still around her, he rolled them to their sides so they'd be able to breathe. His limp cock slid free, wringing one last shaking moan of pleasure from her.

He tightened his hold, nearly crushing her lungs despite freeing her from his weight. His arms shook, his ragged breathing rasping hot and damp across the back of her neck where his face was pressed tight against the hollow of her shoulder.

She froze, her brain refusing her interpretation of what she was feeling. She cataloged the sensations again, feeling moisture trickle down the back of her neck, and hearing his wet gulps of air as his chest shook with the effort of breathing.

He was crying.

"Rikard? Master?"

He drew a deep, shuddering breath, then a second with more control. His arms loosened, and he lifted his head. Brushing one last kiss across her shoulder, he whispered, "Thank you."

"I enjoyed it, too."

He chuckled softly, the sound vibrating through her ribs where her back pressed against his chest. "That, too. But I meant for being willing to try. It's been...a while."

"I'd think women would be throwing themselves at you, for the hot sex and fabulous food."

He bolted upright. "Shit! Dessert. It's probably melted all over the kitchen table by now. I've got to go clean that up before it runs onto the floor."

Rolling out of bed, he hurried to take care of the culinary disaster, grabbing his leather pants off the dresser as he passed. Gayle heard his footsteps pound down the staircase, and a cry of horror when he entered the kitchen.

She shook her head. "And, he cleans."

Figuring he'd be a while—he seemed the type to clean each individual swirl of wrought iron with a cotton swab— she put on the robe and walked back to the playroom to get her clothes. She got dressed, then headed downstairs.

Rikard had shoved the table and chairs aside, and had built a levee of paper towels surrounding the vanilla lake on the kitchen floor to keep it from spreading. He was busy mopping the glass top of the table with yet more paper towels when Gayle poked her head in the doorway.

"Is there anything I can do to help?"

"No. Thanks. I just have to get it all up before it crystallizes. The ice cream's not so bad, it's the caramel." He paused to toss out his sodden towels and rip new ones off the roll. "This isn't how I planned on ending our date, but there's no point in you hanging around to watch me clean. I'll be another half hour at this."

"Half an hour just to wipe up a spill?"

"It's the table and chairs. I love the look of the wrought iron, but it's a bitch to clean. And with a milk-based spill, if I miss anything, pretty soon it'll be stinking worse than a dead skunk."

She winced in sympathy, remembering the misplaced creamer for the coffee at work that had cleared half her floor with its stench. "Okay. You want me to call you?"

He tossed out another handful of towels, and smiled over his shoulder at her. "Give me a call Tuesday night, and let me know how your audition went. We can set up our next date then."

She hesitated, wanting to kiss him goodbye, or at least give him a hug. But he was already scrubbing at the table top with his newest handful of paper towels, and she wasn't sure how to safely cross the lake of melted ice cream to reach him. "Bye, then."

"Bye. Have a safe drive home."

She waited a moment longer, then turned and walked away. A detour through the music room to pick up her music, then on to the front door. She paused again after pulling it open, but he didn't call out to her. Pushing through the safety door with more force than was necessary, she wished the hydraulics would let it slam behind her. Instead, it closed with a soft *snick*.

"That was anticlimactic," she muttered, throwing her purse and music on the front seat of her car. Then, thinking of her last sight of Rikard, she started to laugh. Low-slung black leather pants, high black leather gloves, a black leather mask … and a pile of sopping wet paper towels dripping vanilla ice cream over everything. She could hardly wait to tell Carrie. Her friend would really appreciate the irony.

Chapter Seven

ନ

Gayle picked up a pizza for dinner on her way home. All that vigorous exercise had made her ravenous. As she devoured the perfect balance of tomato sauce, crisp crust, and gooey cheese, she couldn't help contrasting the meal with the gourmet fare Rikard had served her. One wasn't better than the other, but they were definitely different.

Once her hunger was satisfied, she called her friend Carrie for the promised gossip session. She sat down on her couch, kicked off her shoes, and put her feet up on the coffee table, ready for a lengthy call. True to her word, she told her friend everything, starting with Rikard answering the door dressed like a pirate, to the way he'd helped her with her audition piece, the fabulous lunch…and the sex. When she explained that Rikard had fisted her between the salad and entrée courses of their lunch, Carrie dropped her phone with a painfully loud clatter.

Gayle held the phone away from her ear. "Ow."

"Sorry. I can't believe you let him… Didn't it hurt?"

"God, no! It was…it was… I can't describe what it was like. But it was the best orgasm I'd ever had. Up 'til then, at least. It got even better, later." She sprawled across her couch, the familiar hot pulse beginning between her legs. "I'm getting wet just thinking about it."

"But I still don't understand how it happened. I know you, Gayle. You don't usually even kiss a guy on the first date. How'd he get you to agree to…that?"

She hesitated, thinking back to their lunch. The memory was strangely blurry. She remembered the taste of the strawberry salad, the blue and white dishes and white wrought iron table and chairs. She clearly remembered the beginning of her conversation with Rikard. But then it all got fuzzy.

"We were talking, about what I expected from a Dominant/submissive relationship, and he gave me a challenge, to finish eating my salad without making a sound. The fisting was my reward for completing the challenge. But I'm not really sure how it happened... I was so turned on by then, I wasn't really thinking clearly."

"Maybe he put something in your salad."

"No. He doesn't need any help. He's sexalicious."

"He's certainly persuasive. I still can't believe I let him talk me into hanging up without speaking to you when I called the second time."

Gayle smiled. So that's why Carrie was fixating on how Gayle let herself be talked into sex. She was feeling guilty. Gayle hurried to set her friend's mind at ease.

"Well, I'd already told you I expected to be having sex, and not to disturb me when you called back. He was just reiterating that."

"I guess. So what happened after I called and you had tuna steaks?"

"After lunch we went upstairs and played pirate."

"You hoisted his mainsail?"

Gayle laughed. "No. He spun this wicked fantasy, about my being a proper Victorian lady captured by pirates. If I wanted to live, I had to become the pirate captain's sex slave. He vowed he'd make me beg for his attention, and I vowed that as a proper Englishwoman, I would never beg."

"And...?" Carrie breathed.

"And I begged. Oh, God, I begged. And then passed out because it was so good." Her back and ass burned with remembered pleasure.

"You passed out?"

"Well, it's not like I was unconscious. I was just flying, off in the stratosphere somewhere. If he'd tried hard enough, he could have roused me."

"That must've been the second time I called."

"Right. I woke up cradled in his lap while he composed music. He fisted me again, which is when you called the last time, then we went upstairs and had sex in his guest room. And then I came home."

"You can't just skip over all the details!"

So Gayle recounted all the details that she could remember, and was willing to admit to. She explained what Rikard had been doing, exactly where his hand had been, and why she'd been so impatient when Carrie had called. She skipped their strange argument, and her resulting fear, and just described how they made love, the way he'd kissed her with such reverence before finally coming inside her. Then how it ended when he ran off to clean up the melting ice cream.

"You'll get a kick out of this. My last sight of him was in the kitchen, barefoot, his black leather pants slung low on his hips and barely laced, black leather mask, and his black leather gloves full of wadded-up paper towels dripping vanilla ice cream everywhere." Gayle laughed merrily at the memory, but stopped when she realized Carrie wasn't joining in. "Don't you think that's funny?"

"He wore the mask the whole time?"

"Well, yeah. It's his Master mask. When he wears it, he's Master Rikard. Without it, he's just Rikard."

"You've seen what he looks like without it, right? He's not hiding anything."

"When we met for coffee. He's a total hunk."

"He cooks, he cleans, he gives you half a dozen orgasms before getting his own, and he's a total hunk. What's wrong with this picture?"

"Uh...nothing?"

"How old is he?"

"I don't know...late twenties, early thirties."

"Why isn't he already taken? Someone that good doesn't stay on the market unless there's a serious problem with him."

"Oh. Well, he was. His girlfriend was killed in a car accident four years ago. I think he's only just beginning to date again."

"So you're competing with a ghost? Is he still in love with her?"

Gayle thought back to Rikard's agonized confession. "Yeah. Big time."

"Oh, honey, I'm sorry. Enjoy the sex, because that's all you're getting from this guy."

"Maybe." Remembering that moment on the couch when she'd realized she was still with Master Rikard instead of just Rikard, she was inclined to agree. But then there was their final lovemaking. "Or maybe not. He cried when we made love."

"He cried? Really? How come?"

"I don't know. But that's got to mean he's emotionally involved, doesn't it?"

"Or else it reminded him of his dead girlfriend, and how much he loved her."

Gayle sighed. That was also a possibility. "I guess I'll have to wait and find out if he can have a relationship, or if it'll just be about the sex. But the sex was so good…"

"A relationship would be better."

"You're right. As usual. Guess that's why I keep you around, huh?"

"Nah, you keep me around because I know where all the bodies are buried."

Together, they said, "In the graveyard," then laughed at the familiar refrain that had amused them since they were college roommates.

"But Gayle, if he does the Bluebeard thing and tells you there's a locked room in his house you can't go into, for God's sake don't check to see if it's a shrine to his ex. Just get out, while you can."

* * * * *

When Tuesday night rolled around, Gayle arrived early at the theater. She took her time filling out the audition form, and ended up assigned the fifth spot. Close enough to the beginning that she didn't have too much time for nerves to tighten her throat, but with a few other songs first to get a feel for how the accompanist played. He was good, but nowhere near as talented as Rikard.

Gayle handed her sheet music to the accompanist, and took her place at center stage. Closing her eyes briefly, she imagined Rikard sitting in the darkness at the back of the theater, hidden in the shadows underneath the overhanging balcony.

She sang to him, letting her voice fill with all of her emotions, the way he'd shown her during their date. He was the one whom she couldn't get out of her head, thinking of him constantly. And now that he'd brought her body to life, she'd die without his masterful touch.

There was a moment of silence when she finished her song, and she inclined her head in the slightest of grateful bows. Her competition had stopped talking and humming in preparation of their own auditions to listen to her, the best compliment they could give her.

She darted a glance at the director as she walked back to the piano. He was nodding, a faint smile on his face. The accompanist was also smiling, holding out her music to her.

"Good job."

"Thanks."

He traded a look with the director, then added, "You should probably stick around to the end of the auditions."

"Okay."

She walked off stage, her knees starting to wobble as she descended the steps. She managed to stagger back to the eighth row before she collapsed into a seat. Then the delayed reaction of her audition hit, and she began to shake, her heart pounding and every breath a struggle through her tight throat. She couldn't have left the theater if she'd wanted to.

By the time the eighteenth auditionee had performed, her reaction had run its course. She settled back to watch the remaining candidates, idly critiquing their performances and judging which she would choose if she was casting the show.

A pair of young women who auditioned one after the other had sweet voices, but couldn't project past the third row without microphones. A young man allowed his nerves to throw him out of tune, growing worse as he realized his mistake, until the dissonance between his voice and the piano made her cringe. A blonde woman sang Rizzo's solo from *Grease*, her stylized movements and perfect delivery indicating she'd performed the role many times in the past.

Finally, the last candidate completed his audition, and the director stood to address the two-dozen people who'd been asked to remain.

"Steve has some handouts for you. I'd like to hear you read them, please. Number five. The witch's speech."

Gayle returned to the stage, picking up the paper from the pianist. It contained five short paragraphs, from different characters. She read over the witch's speech to the baker, settled her body to mimic the witch's stance, and read it for real.

"Thank you. Number nine. The baker's wife."

Gayle walked off stage as the next woman came up, returning to her seat in the audience.

The director and pianist conferred briefly after the last person had given their reading, then the director announced his choices.

"The baker, number fourteen. The baker's wife, number thirty-two. The witch, number five."

Gayle didn't hear the rest of the casting announcements. All she could think of was that she'd scored her favorite part in the show. And that she couldn't wait to tell Rikard.

As soon as she got home, she called him.

"Hello, Gayle. How'd it go?"

"I got the part! The witch. I got it!"

"That's fabulous."

"I'm so excited. I'm sure it's because you helped me with the audition song. Would you like to go out and celebrate?"

Rikard paused. "Now?"

"Well, no, it doesn't have to be now. It's late, and tomorrow's a workday. But later this week."

"Okay. You can come here tomorrow night, and I'll make you a celebratory dinner. Then we can have a…private celebration. Unless you have rehearsal tomorrow?"

"No, rehearsals don't start until next week."

"Fine, then. I'll see you tomorrow for dinner." His voice dropped to a low, seductive purr. "Congratulations, Gayle. I knew you could do it."

* * * * *

Wednesday night, Gayle went straight from work to Rikard's house. She didn't wear anything special, since her tropical-print circle skirt and teal blue microfiber blouse were both comfortable and flattering, and she'd thought this would be more of a friendly celebration than a sex date. So she was surprised when Rikard answered the door wearing his leather mask and pants again, although this time coupled with a black tunic top that laced up the chest.

"Did I misunderstand? I thought it was going to be just Rikard tonight, not Master Rikard," Gayle asked.

"But it was Master Rikard who helped you with your song." Rikard captured her hand in his gloved one and drew her into the house. "Besides, you deserve to be spoiled and pampered for your success, and Master Rikard is far better at that than just Rikard."

His lips curved, and good humor laced his voice, as though he found speaking of himself as two separate people extremely amusing. Then he led her into the kitchen, and all thoughts of protest evaporated.

Tray after tray of tapas covered the glass tabletop. Some fillings were pinkish, some golden brown, some a deep russet. Then there were the small bowls filled with hot sauces in every shade from bright red to dark brown, sour cream, and a green chili paste.

"You must have spent all day cooking!"

"It was for a worthy cause." Smiling, he held out a chair for her.

She sat. He offered her a crisp damask napkin, snapping it open and holding it out for her. Disappearing behind her, he returned carrying two goblets and a bottle of white wine. Then he took his own chair, opened his own napkin, and gestured to the expanse of food on the table.

"What would you like to try first? Seafood? Beef? Chicken? Vegetarian?"

Gayle shook her head, overwhelmed by all the possibilities. "You choose."

He selected a neatly rolled white-and-pink offering, and held it to her lips. "Try this. Crabmeat."

She relaxed and let him feed her, enjoying the complete pampering of delicious food and exquisite service. All of the tapas were good, but some prompted her to close her eyes and groan with pleasure as she savored their flavor. She worried at first that she was taking advantage of Rikard's generosity, but his soft smile and the gleam in his blue eyes proved he was enjoying the meal as much as she was. The final offerings, combining cinnamon and a rich chocolate sauce, were positively heavenly.

"That was wonderful. You're a marvelous cook."

"Thank you. It's good to have an appreciative audience."

"Have you always enjoyed cooking?"

"No, it's a recent hobby. I used to have the typical bachelor diet of takeout food and pizza. But I spent far too long drinking all my meals from a straw, and began to obsess about all the foods I couldn't have. I vowed that once I could eat solid food again, I would make all my future meals memorable ones."

"I'm sorry you had to suffer, but I appreciate the result."

"I think you'll appreciate the rest of what I have planned for you, too. Finish your wine, and we'll go upstairs."

Her heart and lungs picked up a rapid rhythm, and her panties grew damp. "To the playroom?"

"Yes."

She tossed back her wine, then shoved her chair away from the table and jumped to her feet. "I'm ready."

Rikard's gaze slid down to her breasts, and her pebbled nipples, before skimming down to her pussy. "I bet you are."

Heat flamed her cheeks, but she couldn't protest, because he was right. She was ready for him to take her right here and now. Waiting was going to be an exquisite torture.

Placing her hand in his gloved grasp, she allowed him to lead her upstairs. The first thing she saw upon entering the playroom was a scarlet fandango dress draped across one of the tables.

"Put on the dress."

Gayle obediently stripped down to her underwear, then hesitated, looking a question at Master Rikard.

"Only the dress," he clarified.

She pulled off the bra and panties, as well, then lifted the layers of satin ruffles over her head and slithered into the dress. It clung to her chest, then flared out over her hips to cascade in a ruffled fall down past her knees.

Rikard picked up a black cloak that had been laid out beside the dress, and swirled it around his shoulders.

"I am Zorro, the masked avenger of the oppressed people of Los Angeles. You are the lovely and spirited Consuela, owner of the taverna. You are cooperating with the evil Don Rafael, to try and trap Zorro, and now Zorro has trapped you."

"But I'm not evil, right? Don Rafael has something on me to force me to cooperate with him."

Rikard's slow smile promised a wealth of torturous delights. "That is what Zorro needs to determine, using all the skills at his disposal."

He uncoiled a huge bullwhip, and cracked it three times — tracing two horizontal slashes and a diagonal slash connecting them in the air. Gayle shivered, picturing the whip connecting with her flesh and carving the trademark Z into her skin. Or perhaps he'd take a page from Antonio Banderas' Zorro and use the whip to strip away her gown, leaving her bare before him.

Instead, he lunged forward, grabbing her wrists. He cracked the whip, coiling the tail of it around the wooden frame that had been mounted to the wall since her last visit, then used the remaining length to lash her wrists together, binding her to the frame. Gayle gave a halfhearted tug against the restraint, not at all eager to escape. Her rapid breathing threatened to spill her breasts out of the low-cut dress, and she felt the first beads of moisture pooling between her legs.

Rikard crushed his body against hers, his hard thighs forcing her legs apart, while his gloved hands skimmed from her bound wrists down her arms to her flattened breasts.

"I'll scream," she whispered. "Don Rafael's men will come running to investigate."

"Not if I silence you first."

His mouth captured hers, his kiss hard and merciless. But she didn't scream. She could barely breathe.

She returned his kiss, opening her mouth to draw his tongue inside as she tipped her hips, straining to press her throbbing pussy against the solid bulge in his leather pants.

Rikard's kiss softened, his lips nibbling hers instead of grinding against them. One of his hands glided up to cradle the back of her neck, supporting her head as he tilted it to deepen his kiss. His other hand drifted down to her hip. Tugging on her thigh, he lifted her leg up to his waist.

He reached beneath her billowing skirt and cupped her ass. The smooth leather of his glove caressed her skin, and she moaned into his mouth. Hot fluid dripped down her standing leg. She rolled her hips, wide open and pressed against him.

It wasn't enough. She wanted him out of those pants and inside her. Whimpering a protest, she struggled against the whip restraining her hands, writhing against him.

Rikard broke the kiss and lifted his head, even as he dropped his other hand to her thigh and lifted her remaining leg to his waist, pinning her to the wooden frame with his hips. "Trying to escape, Consuela? Do you plan to run to Don Rafael as soon as I give you a chance?"

"No, Zorro. I have no love for Don Rafael. He forced me to help him. If I did not cooperate, he would destroy my tavern. I would lose everything."

He kneaded her ass with both hands, rolling his hips to stroke his cock against her throbbing clit. "If he catches me, I will lose my head."

"But he won't catch you. You are too clever to fall into his traps."

"Then he will destroy your tavern."

"Not if I can convince him I did as he asked. It won't be my fault if his guards fail to catch you."

"And what did Don Rafael ask you to do?"

"Lure you here. Signal the soldiers. And then distract you with my feminine wiles until they could respond."

"What is the signal?"

"I was to blow out the candle in the window."

"Then I shall have to keep you away from the window."

He unwrapped the whip from around her wrists, and she immediately put her arms around his neck. Easily bearing her weight, he carried her across the room to one of the padded tables. He set her down, then untangled himself from her grasp and stepped back to study her.

Her skirt was rucked up, exposing her legs to the thighs, and her bodice had twisted to one side, one shoulder strap slipping down her arm while the other dug into her neck. One nipple peeked out over the skewed neckline. She sat without moving, enduring his scrutiny.

"What can I do to prove I'm telling you the truth? I will not betray you to Don Rafael."

Rikard reached beneath the table and withdrew a wicked curved knife with a forked tip, like the kind that would be used for gutting hunted animals. Gayle sucked in a sharp breath, and cringed away from it, even as the fear flooded between her legs with wet desire.

"I could mark you with my Z. Carve my symbol into your soft flesh. Here." His gloved fingertips traced the letter on the rapidly rising and falling curve of her breast. Then he pushed her skirt aside and traced a Z on her damp inner thigh. "Or here."

"No. Please," she whispered. "Don't cut me."

He rested the flat of the blade against her exposed nipple. The cold shock stabbed straight to her groin, making her gasp from the pleasure, even as she froze and stared in terror at the deadly blade pressed against her vulnerable breast.

He twisted the knife, sliding the blade beneath her bodice strap. Gayle didn't dare to breathe as the knife stroked upward, over the curve of her breast and up to her shoulder.

With a savage wrench, Rikard sliced through the strap. It fluttered down against her breast and folded down her back.

Her breath gusted out, and she sobbed in relief. She barely noticed when he lifted the other strap away from her skin and sliced through that one as well.

Rikard put down the knife and cupped both of her exposed breasts in his gloved hands, his thumbs flicking back and forth across her pebbled nipples.

"I had to be sure of you," he whispered huskily. "You could have screamed."

"I will never betray you," she choked out through her tears.

He grabbed her savaged dress and pulled it over her head, tossing it aside as soon as the heavy skirt cleared her face. Her legs were spread, exposing her pulsing need for him. He cupped her pussy, and she groaned in agonized pleasure. Her entire body throbbed in time to her heartbeat, from her tingling breasts all the way down to her toes. He slipped two fingers inside her soaking wet channel.

"Please," she sobbed. "Please. I need you inside me."

"Enough games," he growled. "Let Zorro have Consuela. Master Rikard wants to make love to Gayle."

"Yes! Please."

"And I want to do it in a comfortable bed."

Swinging her up into his arms, he carried her into the guest room. A moment later, his pants were down, a condom sheathed his cock, and he was kneeling between her widespread legs.

"Please, Rikard. Don't make me wait any longer."

He thrust, hard and sure, filling her with one strong stroke. Gayle arched up off the bed, screaming her fulfillment as the orgasm ripped through her. Rikard just held her, letting her shake and shudder with his cock buried deep inside her. When she finally began to breathe normally, he started to move slowly in and out, quickly whipping her into another frenzy. His pace accelerated, faster and harder, until they were slamming together in mindless need, both straining desperately toward release.

Rikard stiffened, his arms locking and his spine bowing as he trembled, then came in a powerful explosion. Gayle writhed against him, then arched upward, coming in a shuddering rush. They collapsed onto the bed, hot, sweaty and tangled in each other, but neither willing to move.

"God," she breathed. "I had no idea being scared out of my mind was such a turn-on."

"As was scaring you. I think we'd better back off on that scenario for a while."

"Why? It was great!"

"Because I need to be able to remain in control during a scene. And now that I know what fear of knives does to you, I don't think I could. That makes it too dangerous. I won't risk you getting hurt, no matter how great the sex is."

Gayle smiled, a warm glow of contentment settling deep within her chest. He might not know what he was saying, but she did. He wasn't just interested in sex. He wanted a real relationship.

Chapter Eight

ဆာ

Gayle woke disoriented and alone. Amazingly soft sheets scented lightly with citrus caressed her naked body, and a pillow so fluffy it had to be one-hundred percent goose down cradled her head. Light streamed into the room from the wrong direction, allowing her to recognize the furniture in Rikard's guest room. She stretched, feeling the stiffness of last night's vigorous lovemaking in her hips and thighs. No jogging this morning for her.

She glanced around the room, until she located a small clock on the dresser. Quarter after six. She had plenty of time to drive back home, shower, dress, and still get to work. But only if she got a move on.

Tossing back the covers, she encountered heavy resistance. Rikard had left the bathrobe she'd used before draped across the bottom of the bed. She shrugged into it, then went looking for him.

She checked the attached bathroom and studio first. Both dark and empty, although she took the time to admire the décor of the bathroom. Black and white tiles set off towels, fixtures, and shower curtain patterned with swirls of musical notes and flowing staves, and black-framed prints of pianists graced the walls. It was the first obvious nod to his career she'd seen, other than the music room and studio, and those had been purely practical. Idly, she wondered if the bathroom decorations had been Rikard's idea, or simply a way to use up music-themed gifts he'd accumulated from friends and family over the years.

She frowned. She assumed he had friends and family. But he'd never spoken about them. Oh, he'd made general references, like saying his family was from New York, which had made it easy for him to attend Columbia. But nothing recent. She didn't even know if his parents were still living, or if he had any brothers or sisters.

Her next stop was the playroom. It was empty, except for her neatly folded clothes on one of the tables. As she was getting dressed, she heard water running on the other side of the wall in the master bathroom.

She went back out into the upstairs foyer, and politely knocked on the doorframe before poking her head inside the open door of Rikard's bedroom. It shared the same oak-and-iron furniture as the guest room, but the walls and linens were all soothing blues and greens, shading from dark to light as they swirled upward. It felt like she was standing at the bottom of the ocean looking up through the water toward the light of the surface.

"Rikard?"

"In here," he called from the bathroom.

She followed his voice, and found him leaning against a cream and white marble countertop, wearing only black silk pajama bottoms. Droplets of water clung to his broad back, and his wet blond hair was slicked back into a ponytail. In the mirror, she could see that shaving foam coated his face from eyes to halfway down his neck, except for a stripe the width of his razor on the right cheek and jaw.

He glanced over his shoulder at her. "I'll be another few minutes shaving. But if you're willing to wait, I can make you breakfast. How do blueberry pancakes sound?"

Gayle grinned. She loved a man who was so willing to cook for her. "It sounds heavenly. But I'm afraid I can't wait. I've got to get home, or I'll be late for work."

"No jogging this morning?"

"I got enough exercise last night."

He grinned, the shaving foam puffing up on his cheeks. A slight dimple was visible in the thin strip of shaved skin, where it would be covered by his Master's mask. She hadn't noticed the dimple when they met for coffee, and thought it was a sign that he was more relaxed around her now. His eyelids were much more even when he smiled now, too, the faint offset no more than most people's side-to-side discrepancies.

He dropped his razor onto the counter and turned to face her, leaning back against the edge of the counter and stuffing his hands into the pockets of his pajamas.

"If you want to bring some clothes over next time, go ahead. Then you won't have to run away in the morning." He tossed out the suggestion with a studiously neutral tone that implied he didn't care if she did or not. Recalling his reactions the first time they'd made love, she suspected he cared, and cared deeply, about her answer.

"I'd like that. A lot." She shook her head. "But I don't know when I'll see you again."

"Friday?"

"Works for me. And then I can spend Saturday with you, too."

He stiffened, his eyes widening, the right opening wider than the left. "I won't be available during the day. I have a previous obligation. But I can see you Saturday night."

"Oh." He didn't have to look so panicked at the thought of spending the day with her. "Are you busy Sunday, too?"

"Afraid so."

Gayle pursed her lips, trying to give him the benefit of the doubt. "What are you doing?"

"I have to meet with someone about a song. It's a four-hour drive."

Her eyes widened. "And you're driving there and back in the same day?"

"I've done it before. It's no big deal."

"Well, would you like company for the drive?"

He shook his head, bits of foam flying off to spatter on the thick blue carpet. "No. I won't be good company. I will, in fact, be the stereotypical neurotic artist, obsessed with what they think of the song."

He hesitated, then asked, "Would you like to hear it?"

"I'd love to." She was going to be late for work. Maybe she could skip the shower, and just do a quick rinse-and-go. She knew an olive branch when she saw one, and she wasn't about to refuse.

"Come on. It's already cued up in the deck."

He bounded out the door, making her run to catch up with him. He crossed directly to his studio, bypassing the guest room and bath, and fired up the banks of electronic equipment. After a few minor adjustments to various switches and dials whose purpose escaped her, he punched a button and the opening power chords of a pop ballad thundered through the room.

It started like so many other songs, extolling the virtues of the bad boy who stole the singer's heart. Hearing Rikard's voice singing lyrics obviously meant for a woman was a little strange, but his knife-like delivery didn't give her room to think about it, cutting straight to her heart with his pain and anger.

"I thought it was forever. You thought it was one night. Now I'm hotter than hot, and you're sniffing at my heels like you never went away. Gonna buy me a lover, make him big and strong and dumb. Gonna buy me a lover, one who's never gonna run. Gonna buy me a lover, and we'll have all kinds of fun. Gonna buy me a lover, and he'll love me until the money's all gone."

Tears streamed down her cheeks as verse after verse hammered her with Rikard's pain and desperation. Despite the upbeat, perky music that practically begged her feet to dance, the lyrics spoke of a bleak, meaningless future. She'd known he had issues. Carrie had warned her that he couldn't commit to a real relationship. Had losing his girlfriend in the accident really crushed him that badly, that he couldn't risk loving again?

Oh, God. He wanted to buy a lover because it put him in the position of control, and that way he wouldn't be hurt again. Was that why he was so adamant about staying in his Master persona?

Gradually, she became aware that the room was silent, and Rikard was watching her intently.

"You're crying. Why are you crying?"

"It's just so sad."

"But sad in a good way?"

Gayle gave a strangled laugh as she wiped her cheeks. "I see what you mean about not being a good traveling companion. It's a powerful song. Who's it for?"

He hesitated, then turned away to shut down his equipment. Talking to the bank of dials and switches, he mumbled, "Amanda Tiegg."

"The pop princess?" Gayle squeaked.

"Yeah. She wanted something darker, to try and change her image."

"Well, that's darker, all right. But still perky, if you know what I mean."

"That's what I was going for. So her fans who want mindless dance music will still be happy. But the music critics will have lyrics they can take seriously."

"So how does that work? Did she give you the subject for the song?"

"Well, we talked about some general ideas. It had to be something believable. She mentioned how annoying it was for people who had treated her like dirt in high school to now be treating her like they'd been best friends."

Then maybe it didn't reflect his attitude. After all, mystery writers wrote believable murderers without ever killing anyone.

Gayle smiled. "I'm sure she'll love it. You can tell me all about it Saturday night."

"So I'll see you Saturday night, then? Instead of Friday?"

"You'll need a full night's sleep before your drive. And if I spend the night, you're not going to be doing a lot of sleeping. I'll see you Saturday. But speaking of drives, I need to start mine. Or I'll really be late for work."

"Go. I'll see you Saturday."

She moved forward, kissing him goodbye despite the foam covering most of his face. Laughing, she wiped her nose and cheek with her sleeve. "Finish shaving. I'll let myself out."

As she drove away, she caught herself humming "Gonna Buy Me a Lover". Great. Another earworm.

* * * * *

The good news was, pop princess Amanda Tiegg loved "Gonna Buy Me a Lover", and planned to use it on her next album. And in honor of the sale, Rikard and Gayle played a game where she was, as he put it, "a woman with love for hire". He ordered her to do a wide variety of sexually explicit tasks, including pleasuring herself to orgasm while he watched and offered direction, which she found unexpectedly liberating. But the bad news was that he stayed in his role of Master the entire time, even the next morning as he fed her the promised blueberry pancakes. The sex was incredible, but it did nothing to reassure her that he was interested in having a relationship.

She continued seeing him on Wednesday and Saturday nights, sometimes spending all day Sunday with him as well. They often played pirate-and-lady again, each time with her getting a thorough flogging that sent her sailing among the stars. They played Batman and Catwoman, and she finally understood why Rikard felt so powerful behind his mask. Knowing that your face was hidden allowed your true self to surface in a way she'd never expected. They played Spanish Inquisition, where Rikard tortured her with fiendishly erotic torments, making her come again and again until she finally passed out in exhausted delight—although she successfully refrained from admitting she was a witch.

The sex was phenomenal. All she had to do was hear his voice saying, "I have a special treat planned for you", or see his blue eyes sparkling with that telltale glint in the depths of his mask, and her heart pounded, her breath turned quick and shallow, her nipples tightened into hard nubs, and her pussy throbbed with wet heat. Pavlov's dogs had nothing on her for salivating on a signal. And every time, after the sex, it seemed as though he wanted more, holding her with fierce desperation, and starting half a dozen times to say something, only to fall silent, and, when she asked, insist it was nothing.

But Rikard dodged her every attempt to establish a relationship based on anything other than sex. He cooked for her, elaborate gourmet meals that were feasts for the senses of sight, smell and touch as well as taste. He helped her with her music for *Into the Woods*. Sometimes he sang for her, baring his soul until she bled for his pain and ached with his desire. But he wouldn't come to any of her rehearsals, like other cast members' significant others did, insisting he preferred to get the full effect on opening night. He wasn't interested in going out to the movies, or even renting a DVD and watching it companionably in his home theater, saying he'd spent too many months watching films to find them entertaining any longer. He saw no reason to eat out when he could cook a better meal at home.

Whatever they did, he did it as Master Rikard. Aside from that one morning she'd surprised him while he was shaving, he was never just Rikard. She liked Master Rikard. She needed Master Rikard. But she suspected she could love plain old Rikard, if he ever gave her the chance.

She woke up one Sunday morning, alone as usual. He'd admitted that he didn't sleep much since his accident, and what sleep he did get was restless. She'd peeked into his room once while he was still in the shower, and seen the shambles he'd made of his bed before he had a chance to tidy it. Restless was an understatement. The covers were on the floor, the bottom sheet torn off the mattress, and the pillows flung into the far corners of the room. She didn't mind not sharing a bed after sex, since unlike him, she actually needed something approaching eight hours of uninterrupted sleep.

Shrugging into her robe, she belted it loosely, so that he could reach inside it to fondle her during breakfast. She visited her bathroom, to brush her teeth and use the toilet, and finished the roll of toilet paper. Since the guest bathroom was a peculiar oversight of Rikard's—he entered the guest bedroom and studio through the hall doors, never through the connecting bath—she knew he'd never notice the roll was gone. She had to change it.

A brief inspection of the cabinets revealed towels, drain clearer, and more piano knickknacks, but no toilet paper. He must keep the spares in his bathroom.

She padded across to his room, ignoring the enticing aromas of breakfast drifting up the stairs. Something with bacon or sausage this morning. Mouth watering, she entered the master bathroom. This wouldn't take long.

Rikard's bathroom was divided into two sections by the marble basin and counter top, which was directly opposite the door. To the right was the toilet and a combination sit-in shower/steam bath unit. On the left was a lower counter and padded stool, originally designed to serve as a vanity, but which now held his whimsical collection of rubber ducks. There were two sets of cabinets, one below the basin and one on the wall facing the vanity. She guessed he'd keep toilet tissue in the cabinet near the vanity, since that was likely to be drier.

She opened the cabinet on the wall and looked inside. Rikard's face looked back at her.

Gayle screamed. Backing away, she bumped into the vanity, and sat on a duck. It quacked an insulting raspberry at her.

Footsteps pounded up the stairs.

"Gayle? What is it? What's…" Rikard's question faded into silence, as he saw the open cabinet. "Oh."

"Oh? That's all you have to say? Oh?"

She forced herself to look inside the vanity cabinet again. It wasn't his head on the shelf. It was an incredibly realistic mask, complete with hair, on a foam head. In fact, except for the fact that it had no eyes, and ended at the upper lip, it looked exactly like Rikard.

There was another mask beside it, but this one rested on a plaster head that bore Rikard's features. The second mask was made of clear plastic, with eye and nose holes and a tiny opening around the mouth, although half of it had been painted white in the style of the Phantom of the Opera's mask. Heavy straps secured it to the plaster head.

She shook her head. No. Impossible. And yet…

"Take off your Master's mask, Rikard."

His hesitation was all the confirmation she needed.

"I've never seen your face, have I?"

"Not all of it, no."

"You lied to me."

"No!"

"What do you call that?" She stabbed an accusing finger at the face in the cabinet.

He sighed, and pulled off the leather mask she'd grown so accustomed to seeing. She didn't know what to expect, but the features he revealed looked almost exactly like the ones she was familiar with. The only difference was on the left side of his face. Dark purple-red scar tissue covered from the corner of his eye to just below his cheekbone, shining dully in the florescent light.

"I call that a memory," he answered softly.

She hadn't asked, but he removed his gloves as well. His right hand, which she'd seen holding his razor, was as beautiful and graceful as she recalled. His left hand, though, was covered with a mix of thin white scars and shiny patches of scar tissue, especially across the palm.

"When the truck exploded, I instinctively threw my arm up across my eyes. It probably would have killed me if I hadn't. But that limited the third-degree burns to my cheek, instead of my entire face. And my arm. I also got shards of glass in my arm. They were so busy making sure I didn't bleed to death, lose my hand, or lose my eye, they didn't have time to worry about cosmetics."

He spoke in a toneless, matter-of-fact voice. Yet she could feel his pain and terror, the agony of being engulfed in a fireball, followed by the pain of recovery. Absently, she massaged her aching left hand.

His gaze tracked her motion, and a wry smile twisted his lips. "Sorry."

Abruptly, the sensations stopped.

She fumbled behind herself, searching for the edge of the counter to grip, scattering obscenely cheerful ducks in her blind quest for something stable and real to hold onto. "You did that. You made me feel…what you felt?"

He shrugged. "I didn't mean to. It's this thing I've been able to do since the accident. I picture something in my mind, and when I speak, people see it in their minds, too. For some reason, you seem to pick up on things even when I'm not trying to send them."

As he calmed down, the scar on his cheek faded to a dull pink, barely darker than his natural skin tone.

She frowned. Was it fading because he was growing calmer, or had it faded because he was no longer transmitting a mental image of what he believed his scar looked like?

This was insane. She couldn't believe she was actually considering his explanation. And yet, it explained so many things she hadn't even thought to question. If the accident had happened the way she'd felt it…

She shook her head, and stared at him. If she believed him, that she'd experienced what he'd experienced, then he'd been driving alone in that car.

"Who was with you when the accident happened?"

"No one."

"But when we were rehearsing 'Not a Day Goes By', you said you'd lost your girlfriend in the accident."

"Actually, I think I said I lost my love." He closed his eyes and drew in a deep breath. Gayle instinctively braced herself for whatever further revelation he was about to toss her way.

"I was a jazz pianist. An interpretive singer and songwriter. That's all I ever wanted to be, since I started taking piano lessons when I was three years old. I performed at music festivals around the world, and was just starting to build a real name for myself. My first CD had been released, to critical acclaim and decent sales, and I'd started working on a second one. I was sure I was one step away from success beyond my wildest dreams."

He swallowed audibly, and lifted his left hand, closing and opening it.

"I can't play anymore."

Gayle shook her head. "I heard your recording for Amanda Tiegg."

"Track after track of one note at a time, layered on top of each other. It takes forever, but when it's done, you can't tell they weren't played together. I build the bass that way, then play the treble against it, and record the words last. You must have noticed I only play the right hand line when we rehearsed your songs."

"Well, your left is usually occupied." She blushed. "I Googled you, and nothing came up about a CD."

"It was under Richard, not Rikard. The marketing gurus thought that would sell better. If I'd known it was going to be my only CD, I'd have insisted on my own name."

"Oh." Quickly, she changed the topic. "What's the other mask for?"

"I had to wear it for two years after the accident, pressing against the skin of my face so that it wouldn't grow back all knobby and gross."

"Didn't that hurt?"

"Compared to burning the skin off in the first place? No. Eventually, I found it comforting. The same with the gloves. It started as a pressure glove. When I no longer had to wear it, I found I wanted to wear a glove."

He didn't say it, but she could hear the unspoken end to that thought. He wanted to hide his scars, from the world, but more importantly, from himself.

She took a deep breath. "So that's why you didn't want to go out?"

He nodded. "I knew wearing that mask would be lying to you. And that's the real reason I didn't want you to go with me on my trip. I knew you'd notice it, confined to a car for eight hours. You almost spotted it on our first date, when the latex adhesive started to come loose."

"Your lip wasn't peeling."

"No. The mask was separating. The hot coffee, the steam, or both loosened the adhesive on the lip."

"Swear to me that that's the only thing you've lied about."

Rikard blinked. "What?"

"You lied about not being scarred. Did you lie about anything else?"

He frowned, thinking hard. "No. Just about that, or anything that touched on that, like not being able to play the piano anymore."

"And since the secret came out, everything you've told me is one hundred percent true?"

"To the best of my knowledge, yes."

Was this the secret he'd tried so many times to tell her after they made love? Or had it been this lie that kept him silent?

"Do you love me?"

He blinked again. "What?"

"It's a simple question. Do you love me?"

"Yes." He shrugged his shoulders and stared at his feet. "But I understand—"

"No, you don't."

"What?"

She smiled, and captured his hands in hers. Both hands, the one clutching the safety and security of his black leather mask, and the one revealed in all the scars of reality.

"If you don't stop saying 'What?' I'm going to think that accident affected your hearing."

His mouth moved, but he stopped the word before he actually spoke it.

"As I was saying, you don't understand. I love you, too. Or I'm pretty sure I could, if you let me close enough to find out. Will you do that?"

His eyes widened. Without his mask in the way, she could see that the scar pulled down the corner of his eye, which was why his left eye wouldn't open as wide as the right one. "But I lied to you."

"Yes. You did. Are you going to do it again?"

"No."

"It's okay, then."

He blinked rapidly. "You're not leaving?"

"I'm not leaving."

She released his hands, stepped forward, and cradled his face in her palms. He stiffened, eyes wide in panicked alarm that slowly changed to wonder as he realized she was not reacting with horror to the touch of his scarred flesh.

Leaning in, she brushed his lips lightly with her own, sealing her pledge.

"Now, can I finally get to spend time with just Rikard, instead of Master Rikard?"

"Whatever you want." He held out the mask to her. "I don't have to wear this if you'd prefer."

"Keep it. I think it's kind of sexy. Just don't wear it when we're not actually playing."

"You really don't mind...?" He gestured weakly toward his cheek.

"Honestly, it's not as bad as you think it is. When you're not upset, it's hardly even noticeable. And even when it is, it's no worse than a birthmark would be."

"You're amazing. You have no idea. What can I do for you to show you how much this means to me?"

"Well, I am kind of hungry. And breakfast smelled delicious."

"Shit!"

That wasn't the reaction she'd expected. Before he could elaborate, the strident bleep of the smoke alarm made his explanation for him.

"Go!" She shoved him toward the door.

He raced for the kitchen, and whatever disaster had occurred there. Idly, she wondered if his racing to clean up kitchen disasters caused by her distracting him was going to be a pattern of their lives together. Considering how much she usually enjoyed his distractions, she kind of hoped so.

Bending down, she picked up the mask he'd dropped in his flight. She cleared a space among the fallen ducks, and set the mask on the vanity counter. They weren't going to need that. Not today. But tonight...she was in the mood for a pirate captain and a very saucy lady.

The End

About the Author

෯

Email: yeep@aol.com

Website: www.jenniferdunne.com

Jennifer welcomes mail from readers. You can write to her c/o Ellora's Cave Publishing at 1056 Home Avenue, Akron, OH 44310-3502.

Also by Jennifer Dunne

෯

Hearts of Steel *(anthology)*

Hot Spell *(anthology)*

Luck of the Irish *(anthology)*

Party Favors *(anthology)*

R.S.V.P. *(anthology)*

Santa's Helper

Sex Magic

Tied With a Bow *(anthology)*

From Cerridwen Press

Fugitive Lovers

World Gates 1: Not Quite Camelot

World Gates 2: Shadow Prince

Gia in Wonderland

Dominique Adair

‽

For Zach ~ *if there was ever someone who could use a good spanking…*

ა

Trademarks Acknowledgement

~

The author acknowledges the trademarked status and trademark owners of the following wordmarks mentioned in this work of fiction:

Lexus: Toyota Jidosha Kabushiki Kaisha Corporation
Pellegrino: San Pellegrino S.p.A

Chapter One

ஐ

"This one is *so* you."

Gia forced open one heavy eyelid, mentally cursing the decision to ask her friend Constance to join her for the afternoon. So much for having a relaxing spa day as the other woman never stopped talking long enough to draw breath, let alone unwind. She stifled a yawn. No wonder Connie's own brother, Rick, affectionately called his sister "Constance Chatterley".

"What are you going on about, *cara*?" Gia's voice was slurred and her faint Italian accent thicker than normal—a side effect of the heavenly sea salt and lavender massage Connie had just interrupted.

"An ad in the personals section. It's as if this man wrote it with you in mind." Clad in a fluffy terrycloth robe, the other woman walked toward her with a newspaper in one hand.

"Since when do you read the personals?"

"I always have." Connie waved the paper at Gia. "There are some really twisted people out there and it makes me feel better about my sexual perversions."

Gia rolled her eye. "Uh-huh. And you think one of those twisted people wrote a personal with me in mind? Thanks but no thanks, *cara*." She allowed her eye to slide shut. "Only you would be reading the personals when you should be enjoying the mud room," she muttered.

"Yeah, well, one of us has to make an effort to get you laid," Connie drawled. "It's been so long since you've had anything other than battery-operated sex that your cherry has probably grown back."

Gia's masseur and close friend, Tyler, laughed then quickly tried to disguise it as a cough when she raised her head to glare at Connie.

"It isn't the getting laid part that I have a problem with," Gia said. "If I wanted straight vanilla, missionary sex, hell, that's available any time. All I need is ten minutes in a club and I can find some stud to prove his manhood."

"And if you're really lucky you might find someone who is proficient in up against the wall monkey sex," Tyler murmured. "My personal favorite."

Connie laughed. "Naughty boy. You get more sex than the both of us and I'm married."

"Well, I don't like to brag..."

Gia shook her head. "Let's face it, *cara*, finding a good, reliable bondage partner is hard to come by." She resumed her former position and settled her cheek against her crossed arms. "There has to be a certain level of trust in a relationship before it can progress into the bedroom. It just isn't that easy to find a good Dom." Tyler applied more lotion then began massaging her shoulders to work the oils deep into her skin. She groaned when he hit a sore muscle. Damn, she loved this man.

"Which is why I grabbed this to read." Connie held up the front page of the newspaper so Gia could see the title. It was a copy of The *Rose and the Thorn*, a local bondage paper.

"And what does your husband think about you still reading that, *cara*?" Gia's brow rose. "Now that you're off the market you need to give up your twisted pastimes."

"As if." Connie shook her blonde head. "He doesn't care since The *Rose* contains informational articles about the latest bondage toys. You know Len, he's always up for in-depth research."

Gia snorted.

"Hush now." The other woman straightened the paper. "Listen to this one, I swear it was written just for you. Artistic, Single, White, Dom looking for a Submissive Alice for some adventures in Wonderland. Dark-haired, non-smoker—"

"Maybe I should dye my hair blonde," Gia mused.

"—who is into Brazilian bikini waxes, spanking, bondage, fantasy games and multiple orgasms."

"That last part sounds pretty good," Tyler rumbled.

"And you already have the waxing part covered thanks to Madame Ruska," Connie said. "You're all set."

Gia shook her head. "I'm hardly an Alice in Wonderland type."

"Oh, I don't know." Tyler dug his fingers into her upper arms eliciting another groan from her. "I can see you tumbling down the rabbit hole in your best bondage wear."

"There's a number at the bottom of the ad." Connie held out the paper in Gia's direction. "I think you should call it when you get home."

"And I think you should head for the mud room, *cara*," Gia shot back. "Your pores are clogged and it's affecting your brain function."

"That might be, but at least I don't sleep alone at night." She waggled her finger in the air.

"Well, I should hope not as you're married—"

"My Dom is waiting for me at home—" Connie continued.

"Pffft!" Gia closed her eyes, determined to ignore her friend. "Go away."

"I'm lucky enough to be married to the most amazing man in the world. But how do you think I got that way, my darling? By dating men, doing the scene and actually going out in public once in a while."

Gia barely resisted the urge to grind her teeth. "Easy for you to say. You didn't have some crazed fool chasing you around trying to kill you. You'll have to excuse me if that makes me just a little hesitant to go out in public."

"True but that no-neck geek is somewhere back in California and you're here in New York. No one is ever going to find you among millions of people."

"Tell that to John Lennon," her tone was dry.

"Smartass." Connie dropped into a chair, a look of annoyance on her lovely face.

"You really don't get it, *cara*. You don't know what it's like to be a public figure and to be stared at and harassed, it can become tedious."

"I would imagine."

"You also have no concept of what it means to have your life threatened by someone you've never met. For the rest of my days I'll have to look over my shoulder until I know for sure he's dead and buried."

"But that doesn't mean your life is over." Connie leaned forward and braced her elbows on her knees. "If you're careful there's no reason you can't go out for some fun and games."

"*Merda!*" Gia shook off Tyler's hands then sat up, any hope for relaxation was long gone. "You still aren't hearing me, Connie. Every time I go outside my front door I have to watch anyone and everyone who gets near me. The Los Angeles police were never able to catch *le bastardo* and he's still wandering around somewhere possibly still looking for me. I will never, ever feel safe until he's caught."

"And pays for ending your career." Connie's voice was soft.

"That too. He destroyed everything I was when he forced my car into that telephone pole."

"That's not true, Gia—"

"It is true." Gia could feel the tension welling up in her chest and her hands began to shake. "Before the accident I was *somebody*, Connie. I was Gia Conti, prima ballerina with the largest dance troupe in Europe. I danced for kings, queens and the heads of state for almost every country in the world and *le bastardo* took everything away from me…"

"But you still are someone, Gia. Can't you see that?" Connie's expression softened. "What you lost was secondary to who you are on the inside. Yes, you were a ballet dancer but the sum of who you are as a person was not your job no matter how much you loved it."

"You still don't understand, *cara*." Gia rubbed her forehead as she struggled to regain her composure. "You didn't spend your entire life fighting to be the best ballet dancer and earn the most coveted position in a troupe, only to lose it less than a year later. Everything I ever wanted was on that stage and now it's gone thanks to my shattered ankle."

"At least you can walk again—"

"After many, many months of physical therapy. Trust me, I'm grateful every day that I can walk to the bathroom as I couldn't do that on my own for almost six months." Gia dropped her hand, her gaze meeting her friend's. "In that accident I lost every dream I ever had for myself just because someone decided I was the woman for them. When he failed to get close to me he made the decision that if he couldn't have me, no one would."

Connie rose and took her hand. "I admit I don't know what it is to suffer that kind of a loss. What I do know is now that your body is on the mend, it's time to work on putting your soul back together. You need to pick up the pieces of your life and a good place to start is to get out and back into circulation."

"Leave me alone, Constance." A slow ache sprang to life behind her left eye causing Gia to grind her teeth. "You let me worry about my love life while you go relax in the mud room. I'll join you as soon as I'm done here."

With a reproachful look, the other woman released Gia's hand then turned away. "Stubborn as a mule," she muttered as she left the room, the door slamming behind her.

"*Merda!*"

Behind her, Tyler cleared his throat and the noise startled her. She'd forgotten he was still there.

"She's right about that," Tyler said. "You're a stubborn one. Lie down and let me finish your massage. You'll feel better when I get done."

"I think you need to start from scratch." Weary, Gia stretched out on the table then laid her chin on her crossed arms. "Do you think I'm stubborn, Tyler?"

"Stubborn, irritating, fascinating, playful, irresistible, intelligent, funny and beautiful."

Gia stifled a laugh. "Being beautiful can be a curse my friend, never doubt that."

"We should all be so cursed." He gave her gentle swat on the buttocks. "Now, roll over on your back, Goldilocks, and let me soothe your cares away."

"That's Alice to you."

He chuckled.

Fully nude, she rolled onto her back, unconcerned about exposing herself to her masseur. She'd been coming to Tyler ever since she'd moved to New York two years ago, and in that time they'd developed a very special relationship. At this point he'd seen her in the buff more than any other person in her life, ex-boyfriends included.

"If only you could soothe my cares away," she said.

"Poor, poor, Gia." His blue eyes twinkled. "Just lay back and enjoy my handiwork. In minutes you'll feel like a new woman."

"Promise?"

"Yes, now quiet down."

She was smiling when she closed her eyes. Tyler picked up her foot and began massaging it. His strong fingers were gentle as they moved over the scars that marked the end of her dancing career.

As much as she didn't want to admit it even to herself, Connie was right by saying it was time for her to get back into circulation. While her accident had been front-page news for several weeks, very few people in America recognized her anymore. Most of the time she received those puzzled "Don't I know you?" looks. It had been weeks since she'd been approached by a stranger and since moving to New York, she'd worked hard to maintain a low profile just in case *le bastardo* was still looking for her.

She sighed and Tyler made a shushing sound.

Gia didn't remember much about the accident. Most of her knowledge had been gleaned from the newspapers and the accident report filed by the police. Both she and Ricardo, her now ex-boyfriend, had been out to dinner earlier that evening before stopping at a friend's house for a drink. He'd been driving them back to their home in Hollywood Hills and according to the police, he'd been speeding on wet roads. The slick streets had caused him to lose control on a curve they'd crashed into a telephone pole at more than fifty miles an hour.

Both she and Ricardo and had told the police about a black Lexus that had come at them at a high rate of speed from a side street. Both of them maintained that it was the other car which had caused Ricardo to swerve and lose control. The police had discounted their report, as both of them had hit their heads and were considered unreliable. Seeing that there'd been neither witnesses nor evidence of a second car, it went into the papers as an accident caused by alcohol consumption and slick streets.

In her heart she knew it wasn't the whole story. Several times a month in the dark of night she'd dream of the crash. In her dreams she was looking through the shattered windshield at a tall, dark-haired man staring down at her. A baseball cap had obscured his eyes and when she began to scream he'd give her an icy smile. Without a word he'd lay a pink rose on the windshield before walking back to his car and leaving the scene.

But was that what had really happened? Both of them had suffered concussions and she knew Ricardo had been unconscious from the moment they hit the pole. Both had survived though her ankle had been shattered badly enough to require four surgeries to repair it.

Humpty Dumpty had nothing on her.

Ricardo had gotten off lightly with a drunken driving conviction and, seeing that he wasn't an American resident, it had had no effect upon his life whatsoever. He'd stuck around long enough to learn from the doctors that her career was over then he'd jumped a plane to Europe as fast as his Italian leather shoes could carry him.

Arrivederci.

Devastated by the loss of her career, though not quite as traumatized by the loss of her boyfriend, Gia had come to New York to lose herself in the crowded urban environment while she learned to walk again and contemplate her future without ballet.

Somehow, while she'd been contemplating her future, two years had managed to pass without her noticing.

Ty's strong, oiled hands worked their way up to her thighs, kneading and massaging until she felt as limp as overcooked spaghetti.

Maybe Connie was right and it was time to venture back out into the dating scene. It had been a long time since Ricardo hit the door and while she didn't miss him, she did miss the sex, the closeness that came from being in a physical relationship. Since the accident the only men to touch her were Tyler and her doctors. A faint grin crossed her face as her thigh muscles loosened under his skillful hands. While an afternoon with Tyler could be very satisfying, it just wasn't enough for her.

She forced open one eye to focus on her handsome blond masseur. "Tyler, do you think it's time for me to take a lover?"

His expression turned mock mournful. "You're thinking of leaving me, aren't you, Gia?"

"I'm just thinking about it."

He shook his shaggy head. "Actually I think it's well past time." His hands worked their way across her belly, warming her skin. "If you remember, I've brought up your dating several times over the past year and you shut me down every time."

"I just—"

His big fingers tweaked her pierced nipples. "It's time, beautiful Gia. You are a loving, warm, delightful woman and you need a man to worship you." He began stroking her nipples until a soft ache blossomed between her thighs. "Though I shall miss this."

She gave him a lazy smile, surprised when tears prickled her eyes. "So shall I," she whispered.

"But you need more than what we have together." He released her and walked to the door to lock it. "I'm not ready to be faithful to only one woman and," he gave a self-effacing grin, "not to mention the fact that I've never wanted to spank a woman in my life." His lips brushed hers in a familiar, almost brotherly touch. "And if ever there is a woman in need of being spanked, it's you, my Gia."

He took one nipple into his mouth and her fingers tangled in his hair, digging the pads of her fingers into his scalp. Tyler was a virtuoso when it came a woman's body — then again he'd seduced half the female population of Manhattan. He knew exactly where and how to touch her to bring her the release she so desperately needed.

Working his way down her body, he paused for a nibble here, a suck there, until he parted her thighs. Sliding his fingers into her damp pussy, he lowered his head and she closed her eyes when he touched her with a slow stroke of his tongue. He entered her with his fingers, stroking, stretching, teasing, and filling her until she writhed on the table. Arching her back, she pressed her hand over her mouth to stifle her cries of release.

After a few moments, Gia sat up and swung her legs off the table. Taking Tyler's dear, handsome face into her hands, she kissed him gently on the lips. He was right, she was more than ready to move out into the dating world.

"I will miss you, Gia." His voice was husky.

"And I, you." She slid off the table and reached for her robe.

Watch out, New York, Gia Conti was coming out to play.

Chapter Two

ഔ

"I think I need a few more reassurances."

Drake jerked when the female voice shattered his concentration. Before his eyes the fragile clay vase he was molding collapsed beneath his fingertips. With a sigh he reached down and switched off the pottery wheel and the misshapen mass slowly came to a halt. The last hour of his life now resembled a second grader's school art project.

Damn, Constance.

He reached for a cloth to wipe his hands clean. Why had Jim let her into his studio again? Maybe he'd send his worthless assistant to the hardware store and buy the biggest deadbolt they carried.

"Again?" He rose from his stool and stretched. His back ached from sitting hunched over the wheel for so long. "I thought we hashed this out last week."

"Tell me again that you won't let Gia get hurt." Connie stalked toward him, a troubled look in her green eyes. "I want your word, Drake."

"Con, I don't know how much more I can reassure you other than what I've already said." He dropped the cloth onto a bench then held out his hands toward her.

"Don't even think about touching me with those dirty mitts." She glanced at his clay-streaked hands and he enjoyed her grimace. She'd never been the type who'd liked to get dirty.

"I told you last week that my intentions toward Gia are honorable." He turned away to wash his hands in the sink. "I want to tie her up and spank her until she comes over and over again."

"Drake—"

"Con."

She scowled and he couldn't help but shake his head.

"You don't have to worry, Con. Gia has nothing to fear from me either emotionally or physically." He picked up a nailbrush to scrub the residue from his hands.

"Probably, but she's just so vulnerable right now—"

"And you know I would no more intentionally hurt her than I would any other woman. I would've thought that you, as my best friend's sister, would know this as you've known me since you were in diapers. If I haven't proved myself to be trustworthy by now then I guess I never will."

She bit her lip, indecision written on her face.

"Have you ever known me to lie to you?" He reached for a clean towel.

Her eyes narrowed. "There was that time in high school when you swore to me the wasabi paste was mint."

He laughed. "And you still haven't forgiven me for that prank."

"Well, if my tongue hadn't taken three days to quit burning then maybe I would have. My first French kiss was the next night and I couldn't even enjoy the event because my tongue was on still on fire." Her lips quirked. "I don't think Fred Marchand has ever forgiven me for kissing him then immediately reaching for a glass of water."

"I'd reach for water too if I had to kiss Freaky Fred." He crossed his arms over his chest. "Do you feel better now?"

She sighed. "I'm sorry, Drake. You know Gia is very special to me and she's not like my other friends. Her life has been so sheltered, what with her constant practice and traveling—"

He held up his hand to stem the flow of words. "I'm well aware of her unorthodox background, Con. Trust me when I say, nothing bad will come of her answering my ad. She'll be as safe as a babe in its mother's arms."

She pursed her lips and exhaled loudly, fluffing the soft curls on her forehead.

He shrugged. "Besides, it remains to be seen if she will even pick up the phone. Let's face it, she might not be ready to start dating again."

A mischievous grin appeared. "That is a possibility but I slid the ad into the pocket of her jeans just in case."

"Then she'll wash the ad with her laundry and there'll be no need for you to worry anymore."

"Oh, please. As *if* Gia would do her own laundry. She has a housekeeper who takes care of it."

"Well, there you go, mission accomplished." He took her arm and steered her toward the door. "Now go home, relax and let Gia decide what is best for her."

"And you'll tell me if she calls?"

"Yes, but that's all you'll get from me."

She grinned. "Spoilsport."

"A gentleman never tells."

"As if." She hurried toward the door, her high heels clicking on the utilitarian cement floor of his studio. "I'll be waiting for your call." The door slid shut behind her.

"And I'll be waiting for Gia's," he murmured to an empty room.

With his concentration broken, Drake knew he'd get no more important work done this evening. Outside the windows of his studio, the sun had faded leaving only a narrow stripe of dark purple on the horizon. Maybe he'd call it an early night and close up.

Turning away from the impressive view of Manhattan, he headed for one of the doors in the far corner of his studio. Opening it, he flicked on the overhead light. The hum of a glass-fronted refrigerator sounded loud in the stillness of the room. The walls were stark white with the exception of one corner where he'd placed sheets of corkboard and covered them with dozens of photographs.

Every one was of Gia.

Most were professional photographs taken when she was the lead ballerina for a European touring group. His gaze moved over an eight by ten of Gia Conti's unforgettable heart-shaped face.

Taken approximately six months before her accident, the photo had captured her classic Italian beauty. Her dark hair, scraped back from her face into a complicated twist, accented her creamy pale skin and the soft blush that graced her high cheekbones. Her brown, catlike eyes were downcast, shadowed by thick, smoky lashes. Her nose was petite and her lips full. She had a mouth that proclaimed her sensuality accented by the tiny mole, which flirted with her upper lip. Her chin rested against her delicate wrist, her slim fingers with their pale pink polish were limp against the sharp line of her jaw. She was, in one word, exquisite.

His gaze moved over the other photos, most of which were of her dancing. Gia as Cinderella in a delicate white tutu and diamond tiara, and as Giselle, her long, supple limbs in perfect form. He smiled when he saw the photograph taken when she was only seven and she'd danced in the *Nutcracker*. By the time she was nineteen she'd captured the lead role in *Swan Lake* along with thousands of hearts all across Europe. At her peak, she'd been the most sought-after ballerina of the past fifty years.

Near the wall of photos was a small, round worktable upon which sat a tall cloth-wrapped object. He began removing the cloth, his movements slow and methodical.

Many years ago he'd briefly met Gia Conti. She'd been a fragile-looking thirteen-year-old who'd barely spoken a word of English though she'd possessed a grace and maturity level far beyond her tender years. She was already a fast friend of Con's and they'd all been invited to attend a birthday party for one of the Whitney heirs in Martha's Vineyard. Even then he'd been fascinated by the slim girl who'd watched everyone around her with massive brown eyes and a painfully shy smile. While all of the other kids had frolicked in the pool, she'd hung back almost as if she wasn't sure how to have fun with kids her own age.

When the boisterous Whitney heir decided to pick on Gia, Drake had seen the look of stark terror on her face when the boy had picked her up and threatened to toss her into the water with her clothes on.

Drake had stepped in and rescued her, shoving the Whitney heir into the pool instead. With one glance from those dark eyes coupled with her shy smile of thanks, he'd fallen head over heels into infatuation. For the duration of the party he'd watched her from afar, unable to think of anything to say to her as the language barrier had been insurmountable.

When the party ended, a stretch limousine had pulled up in front of the house and a uniformed driver had bundled Gia into the back. He'd never seen her again, face to face at least, though over the following fifteen years Drake had kept up with her, peripherally at least, and watched her grow from a shy, awkward teenager into a beautiful, elegant woman.

A wry smile crossed his mouth.

To think, he'd watched her for so many years yet they'd never said a single word to one another.

He shook his head. Late last year when the city of Brussels had commissioned him for a statuette of a ballet dancer for a new theatre, it was inevitable that he'd use Gia as his model.

The final piece of damp cloth fell away to reveal the three-foot tall, clay ballet dancer. With her head tilted, her back arched and her arms pointing toward the heavens, the figurine was possibly the best human sculpture of his career. One only had to look at the dreamy expression and her catlike eyes to notice the resemblance to the famous ballerina.

It was undeniably Gia.

Drake couldn't say he was in love with her. How could a man love someone he'd never spoken to? Even now, years later since he'd seen her in the flesh, he remembered how it had felt when he'd seen that look on her face when Whitney had snatched her off her feet. The look of pure fear on her lovely face as she'd clutched at his hair had ignited a protective streak in Drake that he hadn't been aware he'd even possessed. He'd only wanted to save her, shield her from ever experiencing that level of terror again.

But he'd never had the opportunity. She'd been whisked off to Europe and he'd been sent off to boarding school in Switzerland and slowly the memory of that magical afternoon faded.

He'd kept up with Gia's exploits through Con though it had become more of a habit than anything else. It wasn't until after the accident and Con's announcement that Gia was moving to New York that he'd even thought he might have a chance to meet her again.

He slid his fingers along the delicate clay curve of the dancer's arm.

Drake knew it was now or never. Con had mentioned she was pushing Gia about getting back into circulation and the thought of her with another man was one he didn't want to face. He had to know if there was anything, any spark of attraction between them. If there was, fine and if there wasn't, he'd move on with his life and forget about her.

After much thought he'd come up with the idea of the fake personal ad. This way it would give her a sense of security by letting her make the first move and create the illusion that she was the one in charge. Creating a custom version of The *Rose and the Thorn* personals had been a snap on his computer, convincing his best friend's sister had been a different story.

He stroked one slender foot.

When he'd approached Con about arranging an introduction with Gia, she'd baldly stated he wasn't her type. It had taken quite a bit of fast-talking to get her to admit that Gia was heavily into bondage games.

A slow heat ignited in his gut.

Little did Con know about his sexual proclivities…

He'd been celibate for the better part of the last six months and he was itching to get back into the game. Just the thought of Gia, nude, tied to his bed, her buttocks pink from his hand or a soft leather paddle, and his cock hardened. If she was as submissive as Con had hinted, Gia was definitely the woman for him.

He dropped his hand.

And who knew? Maybe Gia would decide he was just the man for her, permanently.

Chapter Three

ဆာ

Loaded down with shopping bags, Gia breathed a sigh of relief when her apartment door shut behind her. The cool, silence of her sanctuary soothed her weary soul and the mixed scents of lemon oil and lavender caused her to smile. How she was looking forward to taking a hot bath, donning her pajamas and curling up in bed with a good book.

"Manuela?" She dropped her packages on a chair near the library door. "Are you still here?"

"Sí. In the living room, Señorita Gia." Her housekeeper's familiar accent broke the stillness.

The scent of roses struck her hard and she recoiled, her stomach churning. *Le bastardo* had sent roses with every message he'd left and now, even after more than two years of peace, she still associated the scent with fear. Her gaze sought the source of the odor and she spied a clutch of pink roses in a vase near the stairs. Her mouth went dry.

There's no reason to believe he sent them…you're safe here in New York.

Her gaze danced around the familiar confines of the foyer. She lived in a secured building with twenty-four-hour security guards and cameras in the hallways and lobby. No one could gain access to her apartment unless she left their name with the guard and he'd ring her before granting them entrance. A small keypad near the front door was her direct link to the guard station and all she had to do was push three buttons and armed help would arrive in less than two minutes.

Pushing aside her fears, she rubbed a shaky hand over her stomach. Her housekeeper must've picked up the flowers, forgetting that she hated roses. It wasn't unusual for Manuela to stop and buy a bouquet on her way into work in the morning.

Walking into the living room she found her housekeeper loading her cleaning supplies into a small carrying caddy. The round, friendly-faced woman was dressed in her usual black polyester dress and comfortable shoes and her dark hair was arranged in its familiar braid.

"How was your day, Manuela?" Gia perched on the arm of the couch. Her ankle was aching from all the walking she'd done when she and Connie had hit the shops after the spa.

"Fine, fine, Señorita. I picked up your dry cleaning and put them away for you." She gave the coffee table one last swipe with her dust cloth before tucking it into the caddy. "I also took some phone messages and they're on your desk along with the mail."

"Excellent. Did a package arrive from my mother? She mentioned she was sending some old photographs and I can't wait to see them." Gia stretched her ankle and tried to ignore the ache that had set in. She'd have to take a pain pill or she'd never get any sleep tonight.

"Sí, there are several packages for you." Manuela picked up the caddy. "You did not leave instructions for dinner so I made a grilled chicken salad for you, okay?"

"Fine, Manuela, thank you."

Both women walked into the hall and the housekeeper turned toward the kitchen. "If you don't need me, I'll put away my supplies and head home, Señorita Gia."

Gia headed for the library. "Thank you for everything, Manuela. I hope you have a good evening."

"Thank you, Señorita."

The scent of leather and lavender engulfed her when she walked into the library. Her desk was situated before a wide window and her mail and phone messages were arranged in two neat piles. Ignoring the phone messages and the envelopes, she picked up two slim packages from the bottom of the stack. Glancing at the return addresses, she noted that one was indeed from her mother while the other was blank. She frowned. The post office stamp indicated it had been mailed only a day ago from a Manhattan zip code.

She sighed and tore the tab on the back. No doubt it was from her agent pushing her to sign the endorsement deal with a leading leotard manufacturer. He just couldn't understand that she didn't think it was necessary to put her face on a hangtag just to sell clothing. It wasn't as if she needed the money. She'd banked much of her dance earnings and had received a substantial inheritance from her maternal grandfather when she'd turned twenty-five. No, selling clothing was not her style but teaching was. For the past few months in the back of her mind, the idea of opening her own dance studio was slowly taking shape.

She reached inside the envelope and withdrew a folded piece of paper. Her breath caught when she saw the familiar handwriting.

Miss me?

With shaky hands, she dumped the remaining contents of the envelope onto the desk. Several photographs fell out and her blood ran cold when she saw they were all of her. She picked them up and flipped through them, her heart beating faster with each one. All of them had been taken within the past week or so. One was of her walking into her doctor's office on Fifth Avenue and another was of her and Connie at a bistro in the Village.

Stunned, Gia dropped the envelope. He was back. The man who'd caused her accident had tracked her to New York.

* * * * *

Sitting on her couch wrapped in an afghan, Gia was numb. Several police detectives were speaking in hushed tones as they gathered evidence in her library. Manuela hovered over her, wringing her hands and muttering colorful Spanish curses.

A rookie police officer was stationed in the entry near the front door, though why she wasn't sure. Did the detectives think *le bastardo* would try and break in? Or better yet, maybe that she'd try to make a fast getaway? It wouldn't surprise her if they believed she was a liar as their skepticism was evident as she'd made her report.

Weary, she rubbed her forehead trying to will away a burgeoning headache.

"Miss Conti?"

Gia dropped her hand into her lap as the taller detective, Gannon maybe, walked toward her with a black notebook in his hands.

"Yes?"

He stopped a few feet away, his pen poised to make notes. "What makes you think this is the same man who'd threatened your life in California?"

It didn't take a rocket scientist to see from the bland look on his face that he still didn't believe her.

"I recognized his handwriting." Her voice was faint.

"And you believe he's coming after you again?"

She fought the urge to roll her eyes. When she'd moved here her agent had urged her to notify the police of her background and the ongoing investigation in Los Angeles. Up until now her life had been quiet and there'd never been any need to call them to her home. No doubt he thought she was just some nervous Nelly or a fading celebrity in search of some tabloid coverage.

"Isn't that what it looks like to you? I receive an envelope of photographs of myself with a note asking if I'd missed him. This is not a common occurrence in my life."

"It would appear to me that you have an admirer who is handy with a camera or a practical joker trying to scare you." He shrugged. "While it is a little creepy, you are a celebrity and there's no law against taking photos of someone on a public street."

"You need to contact Sergeant Diaz at the Hollywood Hills police department. This man stalked me in Los Angeles and is a possible suspect in my accident several years ago." She spoke through gritted teeth. "I left LA because of this creep and I've gone to extremes to keep my new home private."

"Yeah, well." He flipped his notebook closed. "If this is the same man then I would say someone sold you out or you didn't do a good enough job in covering your tracks."

"Great," she muttered. "So now what do I do?"

"Well, you've done a good job of keeping your home safe. This building is secure, the guards are top-notch and I'd recommend that you don't go out alone at night. If this guy is for real, who knows what he might do."

Agitated, Gia rose from the couch, still clutching the afghan. "I know exactly what he'll do, he'll try to kill me."

"Miss Conti, let's not be hasty." He held up his hands as if that would calm her down. "We don't know for sure that this is the same man. What I would do if I were you is go away for a few days, relax, have some fun. My partner and I will work on this, dust the evidence for prints and see what we come up with."

"Nothing, probably." She sighed. She'd heard that refrain many times in Los Angeles. "I don't mean to sound ungrateful but I was just beginning to feel safe here and now," she waved her hand toward the library. "This is pretty disturbing."

He gave her an even smile. "No problem, Miss Conti. We'll get this back to the lab and I'll call you when we find something." He headed for the door, leaving her to follow. "In the meantime, if anything else does happen call the number on the card I gave you."

Yeah, and by the time you get the message I could be dead.

She forced a cool smile. "Thank you, Detective, gentleman. Have a good evening."

She locked the door behind them taking care to arm the security system. Manuela stood in the living room doorway with a worried expression as she continued to wring her hands.

"*Madre de Dios,*" she muttered. "What will you do? Will you go away this weekend?"

Gia shrugged. "I don't know where I would go."

"*Madre de Dios!*"

"It will be okay, Manuela." Sticking her hand in her pocket, she frowned when she felt something unfamiliar. Pulling it out, she saw it was the personal ad Connie had read to her at the spa.

That brat...

* * * * *

A tense twenty-four hours later, Gia spread out the ad on the coffee table and read it for the hundredth time. No doubt Connie had secreted the personals page in her pocket while she'd been showering at the spa. Her gaze moved over the text and the most titillating phrases caught her eye.

Spanking.

Bondage.

Fantasy Games.

Multiple Orgasms.

She groaned and fell back on the couch. For her it wasn't about orgasms as much as it was about simple human contact. She could masturbate herself to release in minutes — that had never been a challenge. What she longed for was the sensation of hot, male skin against hers, the feel of sweat and arousal as his cock plunged into her hungry body.

But this man would be a complete stranger…

It wasn't as if she'd never had a one-night stand before. She was twenty-nine years old and had spent over twenty years of her life on the road. Other than two steady boyfriends, all of her sexual encounters had been of the casual variety. What choice did a woman have when she moved between towns every week? It was hard to strike up a relationship when she knew she'd leave in a few days.

Exhausted, Gia rose and headed into her bedroom. Besides, she was tired of feeling trapped in her apartment waiting for *le bastardo* to make another move. Maybe calling this man who'd placed the ad would divert her from her current predicament and give her a much-needed mental and physical break.

The bedroom was filled with a golden glow from the burning candles. The scent of melted wax and vanilla beans teased her senses. Her bed was made up with cream sheets and the dark wine comforter pulled back, ready for her to climb in.

It wasn't that she desired a one-night stand, that wasn't the case at all. It was simply that most men wanted their women at home, not dancing for hours and hours on different stages every night. Gia made a face and reached for her toy drawer. Of course her circumstances had changed and now she could stay home if she chose to do so.

She withdrew her favorite toy, a purple dildo, and couldn't help but grin. After picking up a bottle of lube, she shed her silk dressing gown and climbed into bed. Pulling the ribbon from her hair, she shook the long locks free until they tumbled over her shoulders. Settling back against a mountain of pillows, she placed her toy on the bed. Situated near the footboard was a large dressing mirror, which afforded her an excellent view of the bed.

Spreading her legs, she stroked her fingers though the narrow stripe of dark hair that covered her mound. She loved waxing her pussy. The silky soft flesh covered only by that small patch of hair made her feel beautiful, sensual. Parting her pussy, she gave herself over to the sensations her fingers aroused. Her flesh grew puffy and wet as she stroked her clit then toyed with the lips of her vagina.

She loved this, the slow ascent, the erotic burn that came from careful arousal. Slowing only long enough to oil her hands and her soon-to-be latex lover, she continued stroking her clit with slippery fingers. Cupping one breast, she toyed with the nipples. They were pierced with tiny gold rings, one in each nipple. Giving one of the rings a tug, a sigh hissed through her clenched teeth. It was that mix of pleasure and pain that drove her.

Becoming a sub had never been a conscious decision on her part. Her first serious boyfriend, Eric, had taught her the line between pleasure and pain was very thin in the human psyche. He'd been the first to tie her up, the first to spank her and the first to show her the immense physical and psychological pleasure she was capable of experiencing. Gia had embraced the life of a submissive and from that moment on, she'd never looked back.

Picking up her dildo, she moved it against her vagina, flirting with the sensitive lips. Bracing her feet, she pushed it forward. Her breath came in a slow gasp as the purple latex stretched her delicate muscles and gave her that delicious full feeling. Leaning back, she withdrew only to push inside again. Settling into an even rhythm, she gradually increased the pace as her arousal grew.

Her back arched and she hammered away with the dildo, her body taking and yet wanting more. With a flick of a finger she turned on a vibrator inside the dildo and the sensations only increased her arousal. The pace was brutal as she fucked herself toward the edge of release. Sweat broke out on her skin as soft cries escaped her mouth. With her free hand she pulled hard at her nipple rings, the sensation just enough to toss her over the edge.

With a low moan she drove the dildo in deep. Her head snapped back and her cries echoed off the walls of her bedroom yet still it wasn't enough. Even though she'd reached her release, she couldn't bring herself to stop. Releasing her nipple ring, she began masturbating her clit as she worked the dildo in and out of her still-needy flesh. Swiftly she ascended the peak to a second orgasm and she howled as she came.

Panting, Gia went limp against the pillows, her dildo clutched in her hands. Flicking the off switch, her lover went silent and she rolled onto her side and curled up in a ball.

Why did she feel so empty?

Tucking her hand against her cheek, she inhaled the scent of her own release. Maybe, just maybe she'd call the number in the personal ad in the morning. Gia yawned. Who knew? At the other end just might be the Dom of her dreams.

* * * * *

Drake's attention was focused on his potter's wheel when the intercom buzzed. He cursed under his breath when the vase, for the second time, collapsed beneath his hands. Several times he'd thought about killing his assistant but the problem was he worked cheap and he was a cousin. His Aunt Clare would not be happy if he strung Jim up by the balls.

He rose and stalked toward to the intercom. Mindless of the wet clay on his hands, he hit the TALK button.

"What now?" he barked.

"Someone named Gia Conti called on that special phone line you installed," Jim's nasally voice sounded over the speaker.

His pulse quickened. "Yes, and?"

"I did as you asked and got her pertinent information and set up a telephone interview with her this evening at 8:00 p.m."

He held his breath as a rush of pleasure spread through his body to center in his groin. He glanced at the clock. In only nine hours he'd be speaking to Gia Conti, the object of his most erotic fantasies for the past few months.

"Excellent," he could hardly keep from shouting.

"I have her information out here on my desk."

"Great."

"She was very…perky."

"Perky?"

"Mouthy, quick on the uptake. She talked rings around me."

Drake grinned. In reality it wasn't hard to do where Jim was concerned. He wasn't exactly the brightest bulb in Aunt Clare's family but he usually meant well.

"Okay, thanks for the information."

"Is there anything else you want? I have an appointment with my allergist and after that I have to see my psychologist—"

"No, Jim. You can leave. Just make sure you lock the door behind you. I don't want any more unexpected visitors."

"Oh, okay. Bye."

The intercom clicked again when his assistant disconnected. For a moment Drake stood there with his hands covered in clay as he savored his small victory. While he was a long way from getting Gia into his bed, he was finally on his way. He looked down at his dirty hands. First he had to get cleaned up as he had a great deal to do before calling her this evening.

Chapter Four

🔊

Gia stared hard at her cell phone, torn between wanting it to ring or throwing it against the wall. Her grip tightened on her wineglass.

Waiting sucked.

Her gaze darted to the clock on the fireplace mantel.

7:58 p.m.

Damn Connie for slipping the personal ad into her pocket.

She didn't force you to pick up the phone and make that call this morning…

Concerned that the delicate stem of her glass would break, Gia relaxed her death grip. She'd never been much of a drinker before her accident as she'd always been in training. It was amazing how much life could change in the blink of an eye. Rubbing her thumb against the rim of the glass, she contemplated just what might happen in the next few minutes. Her stomach clenched.

When she'd called this morning a man who'd claimed to be an assistant answered the phone and after answering a few rudimentary questions, they'd set an appointment for a phone call from the gentleman who'd placed the ad.

Her gaze returned to the clock.

7:59 p.m.

Was it too late to turn off her phone?

Setting the glass on the coffee table, she leapt to her feet and began to pace. What in the devil did she think she was doing? Calling strange men to arrange for a sexual encounter...

Her toe caught on the leg of the coffee table and she yipped when pain shot up her leg. "*Merda!*"

Scowling, she dropped onto the couch to clutch her toe. For crying out loud, it was only sex. Sex was easy. He was a man, she was a woman and they were both looking for the same thing. She massaged her toe and the pain slowly ebbed away. They were about to have a phone conversation and if they connected then maybe they would meet in person.

She released her foot.

If they didn't then she simply hung up the phone and broke out her vibrator.

"It wouldn't be the first time—"

Her phone gave a low, tolling ring and she almost jumped out of her skin. As she stared at it as if it were a snake readying to strike, it rang again. With each sound a Monty Python line ran through her head.

Bring out your dead...

She gave a nervous twitter and reached for the phone.

"*Ciao?*"

"May I speak to Gia Conti?" The voice was definitely masculine, low and rumbling just the way she liked it.

"Speaking." Her voice came out squeaky, at least an octave higher than normal.

"Gia, my name is Drake and I believe I'm your eight o'clock appointment." His tone was smooth, assured. "Is this a good time for you?"

"Yes, of course." Her grip tightened on the phone.

"First, I want to thank you for answering my advertisement, it shows you are a woman of adventure." Approval laced his tone.

"Well, your ad was intriguing."

"Good. That was my intention." He chuckled, and the deep sound sent sensations of awareness down her spine. "And thank you for speaking with my assistant and agreeing to a meeting on the phone. I figured this would be less pressure and one cannot be too careful these days."

"You're right about that," she murmured. "Have you had many responses?"

"A few though yours is the only one I will be pursuing."

"And why is that?" Gia reached for the bottle of wine and refilled her glass. "I would think that you'd speak to several ladies before making a decision. What if I'm a dud?"

He chuckled. "Somehow I doubt that very much. There's no way a woman with a voice as lovely as yours could be a dud. Can you tell me what made you decide to respond to my advertisement?"

Well, a friend harassed me into it and then there's this madman I call le bastardo…

Gia took a deep drink of her wine before she answered though she hardly needed any more false courage. One more glass and she'd be passed out on the coffee table and Drake would only hear her snoring in his ear.

"Currently, I'm between serious relationships and I find I have an itch that needs to be scratched." Shocked that she could say such a thing to a complete stranger, she set the glass down on the table. No more wine for her.

"Mmm." His voice grew deeper. "Is that so? But why did you choose to answer a personal ad?"

"Actually a friend saw your advertisement then persuaded me to call you. I admit I haven't read the personals very much."

"Neither have I."

"And seeing as it isn't all that easy to find someone to perform as a Dom, and I'm not looking for a long-term commitment, *voila*, here we are."

"Sounds straightforward."

"Very much so." Gia stretched out her legs, bracing her heels on the low-slung coffee table. "So what made you choose me over the other respondents?"

"You're very beautiful, Gia."

Stunned, she sat upright. "How would you know what I look like?"

"I recognized your name. My mother is very fond of the ballet."

Damn! She'd never considered that he might recognize her name. Flustered, she cleared her throat and her voice came out husky.

"You have me at a disadvantage then. I don't even know what you look like."

"You will soon enough." He chuckled. "I have to admit that I did not choose you based solely upon your lovely face. My assistant said you were spunky and full of fun. After speaking with him I couldn't help but think that you'd be a pleasure to train."

Gia's brow arched. Slow down now, stud...

"And you think you're Dom enough for me?"

"Most definitely."

Heat curled along her spine at his confident tone. She enjoyed powerful, self-assured men.

"So, if I agree to become your sub, what will you do for me?" She reached for her glass.

"I will show you pleasures like none you've ever imagined..."

"Such as?" Gia took a drink, enjoying this conversation more and more. "You should know that I have a very vivid imagination." He chuckled and sparks burst forth in her lower belly. She loved a man with a sexy laugh.

"Are you trying to lead me into having phone sex with you?"

"Mmm, now that you mention it." Gia leaned her head against the back of the couch.

"If you need something, you only have to ask, Gia."

"Okay."

"I will make the decision as to whether your request is in our best interests, sexually speaking, of course."

"Fine with me."

"And you will call me Sire Drake or just Sire, whichever you prefer." His tone brooked no argument.

Her throat went dry and she gulped down more of her wine. "Sire Drake."

"Very good. What are you wearing this evening, Gia?"

She looked down at her rumpled robe. "Just a red robe, silk."

"Sire Drake," he prompted.

"Sire Drake." She leaned forward and put down her glass. Her stomach was tense while the rest of her body was liquid, waiting to see what would come next.

"And nothing else?" he purred.

"No, Sire."

"Excellent. You will open your robe for me."

Gia's gaze darted around the living room even though she was alone in her apartment. The blinds were drawn and there was no way anyone could see her during their private fantasy. She licked her lips and her palms were damp by the time she reached for the tie around her waist. The silk slid apart with no urging on her part, baring her body to the cool, air-conditioned air.

"It's open, Sire Drake." Her voice was faint.

"Now close your eyes, Gia, and listen to my voice."

She swallowed hard and allowed her eyes to slip shut.

"If I were with you now, I'd take your hand and bring you to your feet. I'd remove your robe from your body leaving you naked to my eyes, my touch. I'd adorn your beautiful throat with a narrow leather collar and I'd decorate your beautiful breasts with a matching pair of gold rings."

"They're pierced," her tone was breathy. "My nipples are pierced, Sire."

The sound of his indrawn breath was loud. Was he displeased?

"Sire?"

"Really? Pierced? Very nice." His voice was husky with approval. "I will enjoy that very much. Just thinking about your pierced nipples is making me hard, Gia."

She couldn't help but smile. Good, because just talking to him was making her hornier than hell.

"I would take your hand and lead you into the bedroom. Using black silk scarves, I'd tie you down, not so tightly that it would hurt but just enough to restrict your movement. I'd like to see you like that, your body open and waiting for my touch. At my discretion of course."

Gia bit her lower lip as a wave of heat ran down her spine.

"I'd touch you all over, stroking every inch of your skin until you quiver with anticipation. Then, only then, would I touch your pussy, parting your lips I'd lower my head between your thighs and taste your sex. I'd stroke your beautiful cunt with my tongue, sucking your clitoris until you're begging me to fuck you. But I'm not going to, not yet."

Her breathing grew deeper. She could well imagine the scene and her sex grew moist at the images her mind created. She spread her legs and began toying with the narrow strip of hair on her mound.

"First, I would fuck you with my fingers while my mouth suckled on your nipples. I will enjoy the taste of your flesh, your arousal. When you're ready to come, I'd stop and spread your thighs as far as your bonds permit. I'd kiss my way up your thighs until you quiver with your need for release but still I won't allow you to come yet. I want you to beg, beg me to touch your pussy, Gia."

"Please..." Without realizing it, she spoke aloud.

"Touch yourself, Gia. You may stroke your clitoris but don't come until I tell you it's time."

A soft whimper escaped her when she pressed her fingers over her mound before dipping inside.

"Then I'll lick you, tasting your arousal against my tongue. You'll be sweet and warm and I'll enjoy it very much. My cock is rock-hard just thinking of eating your pussy. I won't be able to get enough of you and I'll want to lick you for hours."

Her fingertip grazed her clit sending a trill of arousal up her spine.

"But still, I won't let you come, not quite yet. I'll remove my clothes and my cock will be so hard, so hot just for you. I'll slide it into your pussy, parting your sweet, slick flesh and filling you to the root. I'll begin to move, pushing deep inside you, fucking you into mindless arousal. Then I'll kiss you, allowing you to taste your arousal on my tongue, all the while my cock will be pounding into you. Then, only after you beg me, will I allow you to come."

A small moan of pleasure broke from her mouth, her thighs tight as she dangled on the edge of release.

"Please, Sire Drake," she whispered. "I need to come."

"This time you may, Gia," he purred.

With a solid stroke against her clit her body arched and a powerful orgasm washed over her. She sobbed out her release, her body spasming against her fingers as liquid release rained hot against her fingers. Her breathing was harsh and she was strangely lightheaded when she finally forced her eyes open.

"That's my girl. I can't wait to see you come." He gave a soft chuckle. "How do you feel, Gia?"

Her tongue felt thick and uncoordinated while her body was spent. "Hot," she whispered.

"Would you like to continue this conversation tomorrow? I would very much like to hear what you'd like to do with my cock in your mouth."

"Yes," she whispered.

"Excellent. I will call you tomorrow at 8:00 p.m." There was a pause. "Until then, dream of me."

She murmured her goodbye, torn between complete terror and total arousal. Just what was she about to get herself into?

* * * * *

Drake could barely contain his shout of excitement when he hung up the phone. Gia was more willing, so much more than he'd ever dared to dream. Her voice was husky, sensual and her responsiveness was explosive. His hands itched to get a hold of her and touch her in person.

But right now he had a more urgent problem.

His erection was pressed against the zipper of his jeans and it was becoming quite painful. He exhaled slowly as he released the closure and allowed his cock to escape.

Wrapping his hand around his thick member, he gave it a slow squeeze and felt his balls tighten. Automatically his hand began a slow, familiar stroke that caused his toes to curl.

No, not yet.

Exhaling, he forced himself to release his cock. A drop of precome glistened on the head. He'd allowed Gia to take her release, but he'd wait for his satisfaction until tomorrow night. His blood heated. He could hardly wait to hear what she'd say to him, what images her words would evoke in his mind as he imagined her taking his cock into her mouth, sucking, licking—

He groaned as his cock jerked, just barely on the edge of release.

Pushing to his feet, he stalked toward the bathroom and the cold shower that awaited him.

Chapter Five

ᡐᠥ

Just what had she gotten herself into?

By the next evening, Gia had lost count of the number of times she'd asked herself that question. Over and over again as she went through her daily routine, it plagued her.

Now, standing in the window of her penthouse apartment, she watched the sun sink in the western sky. She couldn't deny how much she'd enjoyed herself last night. Having phone sex with a stranger had been arousing, exciting and something she'd never tried before. The best part was for the first time in weeks, she'd gone to bed without thinking twice about *le bastardo*. Talking with Drake had been fun, easy, and it reinforced the beauty of this potential relationship, the effortlessness. No stress, no emotions to get in the way, just natural sensuality.

It's empty…

She winced at the voice in her head. Emotionally empty maybe, but she wasn't ready for an intense relationship. Right now she just wanted to have some fun. For the moment she was content to play Alice in Wonderland and Drake was just the man to be her Mad Hatter—

The phone rang and she darted a look at the clock. 8:00 p.m. on the nose. She snatched up her cell phone and tumbled onto the couch.

"*Ciao?*"

"Good evening, beautiful."

Gia's toes curled at the sound of his deep voice. "Good evening, Sire."

He chuckled. "I like how you say that."

"And I like that you like it." Her nipples ached.

"How was your day, Gia?"

"Quiet. I went shopping for some new lingerie."

"Hmm, for me?"

"Hardly, I don't know your size," she shot back.

He laughed again and the sound made her stomach flutter. "So what else did you do?"

"Ran some errands, had lunch with a friend." Gia didn't know why she was reluctant to tell him that she'd also endured two hours of grueling physical therapy on her ankle. It was a part of her life, which was intensely personal not to mention painful, and she tried to put it behind her the moment she left the clinic every Monday, Wednesday and Friday. "That's about it."

"Sounds stimulating." She heard the amusement in his voice.

"Oh it was. So what did you do all day?"

"Thought about you."

Her breath caught and a silken ache ignited between her thighs. "Is that so?"

"It is. I didn't get much work done otherwise. I spent most of my day wondering how you would taste. What you would feel like as you came apart beneath me."

Her mouth went dry.

"Luckily for me I'm caught up on my work." He chuckled.

She cleared her throat, her mind still transfixed by the powerful images his words had evoked. "Just what do you do for a living, Sire?" Her voice came out a little husky.

"I'm an artist."

"A painter?"

"Among other mediums, yes, I do paint."

"Really? Somehow that surprises me."

"How is that?"

She squirmed. "Well, I guess I don't envision the artsy type as a take-charge kind of man."

He chuckled again. "Don't be fooled by my soulful exterior, Gia. I am very much in charge. Now tell me, will you allow me to paint your portrait?"

She blinked. "You want to paint me?"

"I would love to paint you, to capture your beautiful face on canvas would be an honor."

Her teeth caught her lower lip. It wasn't the first time someone had asked her to model. When she'd danced the lead in *Swan Lake* her mother had commissioned a portrait that now hung in her parents' sitting room in Rome. For the most part it had been completed with photographs but she well remembered the painful hours she'd had to endure while the artist put the finishing touches on the portrait and had needed her to pose for him.

"Mmm, I don't know about that. Let me think on it."

"Fair enough." He didn't sound disappointed with her decision. "Now, tell me, Gia. Have you thought about our conversation this evening?"

"Yes."

"So tell me," his voice dropped. "What would you do to please your Sire?"

"First, I'd make you dinner."

"You cook?" Somehow he couldn't see it. According to Con, Gia was a pampered flower and consequently she was unschooled in the domestic arts.

"Yes, I cook. Not a lot but I can find my way around a kitchen." He heard the indignation in her tone.

"Will you be naked?"

She laughed and he enjoyed the silky notes of joy. "If you wish."

"I do indeed."

"Fine, I'm dressed only in our collar and my frilly white apron."

He grinned at the evocative image. "Lovely," he murmured, his cock already hardening. "Go on."

"I'll make you roasted lamb with Greek lemon potatoes and fresh asparagus. Sitting in your lap, I'd serve you with my hands, feeding you morsels of your meal and plying you with your favorite wine." Her throaty voice was warm, her tone intimate. "And just before you're full I'd present you with dessert."

He cleared his throat. "Just what would that be?"

"You'll have to wait and see…" Her singsong voice was driving him crazy.

He burst out laughing. "Go on."

"Afterwards I'd invite you to join me in the bedroom where I'd strip you naked and ask you to get into bed. I'd remove my apron and join you wearing only my collar and nipple rings. I'd slide between your thighs and ready myself to feast on your cock."

He wrapped his hand around his stiff member.

"I'd hold you in my hands and stroke until you were fully hard. Then I'd take you into my mouth. I'd run my tongue up and down your cock and before long I'd take you deep into my throat. Suckling you like hard candy, my tongue will move over you, savoring every inch, every flavor, every texture."

He began a slow stroke and his breathing deepened.

"Then I'd cup your balls, lightly dragging my nails against your skin. Moving my head over your cock, I'd free my long hair so that it would tickle the inside of your thighs. I'd slowly begin working the head of your big cock, my tongue pressing hard against the sensitive underside. You'd try and guide me but I wouldn't let you. I'm your slave and as such I have learned what my Master enjoys in bed. I know what really turns you on." Her voice grew huskier, her accent more pronounced.

"Yeah, you do," he whispered, his stroke increasing.

"Your hips arch toward me as I suck you. My hand encircles your shaft and you're only moments away from release. But it's too soon. I let you slide from my mouth as I switch positions. I straddle your chest, my naked, wet pussy mere inches from your mouth."

He groaned.

"I'd take you into my mouth once more, and I'd take you deep. With every stroke my wet pussy is pushed into your face. As you snake your tongue out to touch me, I slide my pinky into your anus and stroke from the inside out until you come deep in my mouth."

Thoroughly aroused and unable to help himself, his balls tightened and Drake came with a roar. His come jetted over his hand and he continued stroking, drawing out his climax until he could wrench no more feeling from his body. Slowly reality reasserted itself and the ability to speak and think coherently returned.

"Did you enjoy yourself, Sire?" Her coy little question elicited a bark of laughter from him.

"Yes, in case you didn't notice." His tone was wry. "Very good, Gia. You are a very obedient sub and I think you and I will enjoy each other's company quite well."

"I have to agree."

"Well then, are you ready to meet me for dinner tomorrow evening?"

There was a slight hesitation and he held his breath as he waited for her answer.

"Yes."

"Very well. Meet me at 7:30 p.m." He mentioned the name of a discreet Italian restaurant.

"I'll be there."

"I'll see you tomorrow night, Gia."

"Yes, and Sire," he caught a hint of teasing in her tone, "in the meantime, dream of me."

His grin nearly split his face when the line went dead. He'd already spent many hours dreaming of her and now, in less than twenty-four hours, his dreams would become a reality.

Chapter Six

🔊

Her photos didn't begin do her justice.

Drake took a sip of his merlot, enjoying both the flavor of the liquid and the sway of Gia Conti's hips as she walked toward him. Dwarfed by the tall hostess, Gia was perfection in motion. With her black hair in a sophisticated twist and her creamy, pale skin, she was the poster child for feminine beauty. Her dark catlike eyes were shadowed by lush lashes and accented with heavy liner. Her features were fragile, fey-like with winged brows, a petite nose and lush, red lips. Just looking at her made him think of raw, raunchy, sweaty sex.

Dressed in a simple black sheath that skimmed her slim curves, she walked with an easy grace. She wore no stockings and a pair of flat strappy sandals. In her hand she carried a slim ebony walking stick though he noticed she didn't seem to lean her weight upon it. She had a very slight limp, one that most people wouldn't notice unless they knew to look, a possible byproduct of her accident.

He set down the glass and was preparing to stand when a young girl intercepted Gia. The girl looked up at her with such a look of complete adoration as she held out a sheet of paper and an ink pen.

Gia gave her a slow smile and his gut clenched. That smile was lethal. She bent and spoke to the child for a few moments before signing the paper and giving her a hug. The girl clutched the paper to her chest as if it were more precious than gold then ran back toward her table.

It would appear he could add gracious to Gia's list of attributes.

He rose to greet his dinner guest.

"Mr. Whelan, your dinner guest has arrived." The hostess stepped to the side allowing Gia to precede her.

"Gia, you look lovely." He took her slim hand in his.

"Drake." Her perfume was subtle, sexy and she leaned in and gave him a quick kiss on the cheek.

"Please sit."

He took her hand and guided her to the padded leather seat of the booth. She slipped into the seat then leaned her cane against the end.

"I'll send your waiter right over," the hostess said.

"Thank you, Rachel."

One slim, dark brow rose. "You come here often?" Her voice carried the faintest of accents from Northern Italy, one of his favorite places in the world.

"Usually for lunch, my studio is right around the corner." Drake resumed his seat. "Can I offer you some wine?"

"Please."

He poured her a glass of wine then reached for a chilled bottle of Pellegrino.

"You never told me your last name." Her tone carried a hint of reproach.

"At the time I didn't think it was important." He filled her water glass then refilled his own.

"Oh really? The fact that you are and I quote, 'One of the most innovative artists of modern time'—I believe that is what the *New York Times* said about you—wasn't important?"

"It's my job, but it doesn't define who I am." He shrugged. "I wanted us to get to know one another on a more basic level, one without all the tags society forces upon us."

One perfect brow arched. "This is a bit awkward."

"Think so? We know the rudimentary details of each other's lives. Part of the thrill of meeting someone new is taking the time to get to know them and to ferret out the interesting details of their lives. If we know everything up front, where is the mystery in that?"

Her gaze danced away.

"Just for the record, I'm divorced, no children, no pets. I have a sizeable income, impeccable credit record and I play football, racquetball or Frisbee golf on the weekends with college friends. I don't smoke, drink only socially and—"

She held up her hand, a wide smile curving her luscious mouth. "I believe I've heard enough."

He smiled. "Good, I was running out of statistics and was about to start making some up."

She tipped her head back and gave an unrestrained laugh. In that moment Drake knew he was about to be charmed by her.

* * * * *

Gia was surprised at how quickly they settled into comfortable conversation. Any sign of awkwardness melted away when he began telling her humorous stories about his time abroad. One of the most amusing of which was when, as a struggling artist, he'd been commissioned to paint a fresco and found himself the object of lust by the middle-aged wife of the homeowner. Upon completion of the project he'd received his first big check and a kiss that had left him reeling for days.

Charmed, Gia shared a few harried tales of her own, including the time a prominent head of state equated ballerina with prostitute and she'd clouted him over the head with a priceless Ming vase. She'd often wondered how he'd explained a broken family heirloom to his wife.

The waiter arrived and distracted Drake long enough to give Gia the opportunity to study him. He certainly was handsome which made her ask the question, why would he have to use the personals as a way of finding a lover?

He was quite tall, well over six feet and he wasn't built as she'd envisioned a painter would be. This man was powerful with his broad shoulders and thick chest. His arms were heavily muscled and his hands calloused. His dark brown hair was long enough to brush his shoulders and a diamond stud twinkled in one ear. His features were even, and his eyes were the most beguiling shade of blue.

She took a sip of her wine. There was something dangerous yet reassuring about him at the same time. He exuded strength and confidence and she'd hazard a guess that he was as at home in a suit or jeans. With the dark stubble on his chin, all he needed was a leather jacket and he'd look like the ultimate bad boy.

Heat pooled between her thighs.

There was something familiar, almost comforting about him. She stared hard at him and racked her brain to think if they'd met before but she came up with nothing. Surely if they'd met previously, Drake would've mentioned it.

Picking up a cracker, she smoothed a healthy dollop of pâté over it. When she bit into the savory treat she felt a warm hand touch her knee. Startled, her gaze darted toward Drake and the waiter. Both were still talking as if nothing were amiss even as the hem of her dress was lifted and his calloused hand touched her thigh.

Their table was private enough with the high back of the booth and an arrangement of palms obscuring the view of the rest of the room. The long white tablecloth would also serve to hide anything going on beneath their table. A slow ache built between her legs.

The waiter finally walked away before Drake spoke.

"How is the pâté this evening?" he asked.

"Hmm, very good." She fixed another cracker and handed it to him. Their fingers brushed and it sent a shiver of awareness up her arm.

"Excellent."

The pressure against her thigh increased as he silently urged her to part her legs. A rush of liquid heat invaded her pussy when she relaxed her thighs.

Part of her was shocked. Secluded booth or not, it was still a restaurant and anyone could walk past and see what they were up to, not to mention the fact the waiter could return at any moment. Another part of her, the part longing to break free and be wild again, didn't care what anyone might think as she was enjoying his touch too much to back down now.

She parted her legs to allow him better access and she sucked in a noisy breath when his hand covered the strip of silk that comprised her panties. Pushing aside the narrow band of elastic, one thick finger breached her damp flesh to zero in on her clit. Her back arched ever so slightly and she leaned into his touch. With his right hand he continued eating, his gaze focused on the plate of pâté and crackers. His talented fingers began stroking her hardened clit in a slow stroke that aroused her even more.

The waiter arrived with his soup and her salad before vanishing again.

Gia reached for her water and took a hasty gulp. It would be so easy to just lean back and give herself over to the mastery of his fingers, not caring that anyone else might hear her come. Wouldn't that shock the dinner-eating public? Probably not, it was New York after all. But, something still held her back and she pressed her lips together. Even though she wanted to break free, too many years of strict training and lessons on deportment were too intrinsic to her personality to just cast them aside now.

She glanced at Drake's handsome face. He offered her a warm smile, his eyes dark with sensual promise. Dipping his spoon into the soup, he offered her a bite.

"Try this, it's delicious. The texture is creamy, and the flavor is complex."

Gia leaned forward and took the offering, barely tasting the soup as his fingers continued their slow strokes. She could so easily imagine him kissing her with that wicked mouth and stroking her flesh with his tongue. She stifled a moan when he caught her clit with two fingers.

"Gia." His warm breath caressed her cheek and sent tendrils of sensation across her body. "What I'd like to do is pick you up and fuck you on this table."

Her thighs tightened, trapping his hand.

"I'd strip you naked so that everyone could admire your beauty. I'd suckle those nipples of yours and tease your piercings with my teeth. I'd work my way down your body, licking and kissing you all over. You'd spread your thighs for me because you're a well-trained sub and you know that your pleasure is linked with mine."

He entered her vagina with one thick finger. Gia gasped and leaned forward, her hands landing on his arm and her nails sunk into his suit jacket.

"I'd have the waiter bring me a bowl of chocolate mousse with which I'd paint your pussy. When I was done I'd lap at you like a dog until you were clean."

Gia swallowed hard. The need to come was strong now and she could feel the tension creeping up the back of her legs, a delicious heady sensation that grew more insistent as it reached her thighs.

"When I was done, I'd unleash my cock. Pressing it against your delicious cunt, I'd revel in the feeling of your hot, wet flesh giving way before me. You'd wrap your legs around my waist and I'd thrust into you hard, fucking you until you were coming again and again, screaming out my name."

Gia bit her lip and a whimper escaped.

"Other people would be watching us." His lips brushed the sensitive skin near her ear and she shuddered, her orgasm bearing down hard on her. "The men would be jealous of your tight pussy around my cock while the women would be masturbating against their panties. It wouldn't matter that they were watching us as the only thing that would concern us is reaching release. With my cock filling you, stretching you, it would only be a matter of moments before you lost control—"

Stiffening, her nails dug into his arm as a powerful orgasm exploded over her. Biting her lip, she managed to stifle her screams but just barely. Snatching up her napkin, she buried her face in it as she struggled to catch her breath.

When the moment passed, she lowered the napkin, her cheeks as hot as fire. Drake's fingers were still buried in her flesh and when their eyes met, he gave her clit one final stroke then removed his hand. Raising it to his lips, his tongue snaked out to taste her arousal.

She was unable to speak because her mouth was dry, and she reached for a glass of water. She was both shocked and pleasantly surprised by the recent turn of events. In the past twenty-four hours she'd had two explosive orgasms with this man and it just wasn't enough. She wanted more, much more.

The waiter reappeared. "Your entrees will be out very shortly—"

"Thank you, Greg. Can you please box everything up and have the car brought around? Something very important has come up."

Gia darted a quick look at his lap then had to stifle her laughter with her napkin. Something very important, and very large indeed.

Chapter Seven

🔊

Like two horny teenagers, Gia and Drake tumbled into the back of the limousine. She landed in his lap and the moment the door was shut and locked, they were on each other. Their first kiss was more about raw need than finesse. Her fingers clawed at his jacket as if she wished to climb into his skin while their tongues tangled in a dance of sensual excess that stole her breath away.

His hands seemed to be everywhere at once, on her hips, touching her thighs before skimming up her sides. Tugging the pins from her hair, he tossed them on the floor. The silken mass tumbled about her shoulders and he stroked her throat and the line of her jaw. Their limbs tangled and he twisted until she found herself flat on her back on the seat with Drake leaning over her.

She moaned into his mouth when he stroked his thumb over one erect nipple. Through the silk of her dress he located the ring and gave it a tender tug. She responded by nipping at his lower lip. Her fingers threaded through his hair for a better grip when his knee pressed against the seam of her legs and she parted them without hesitation.

Her pussy heated with moisture when he moved his thigh against her. Her nails dug into his scalp, her body automatically moving against him, desperately needing the pressure and sensation he was arousing within her.

Gia laced her leg around his waist, bringing him closer and he made an appreciative sound deep in his throat. His erection pressed into her lower belly and she longed to feel it in her hands, her mouth, her—

"Mr. Whelan, you're home."

She froze when the driver's voice sounded over the intercom and Drake broke the kiss.

Oh my God, she'd almost had sex in the back of a moving limousine!

Drake reached over and hit the intercom button. "Thank you, Doug."

Her cheeks were blazing when their gazes met. His dark hair was tumbled over his forehead giving him a boyish look that she found both endearing and sexy at the same time. With her lipstick smeared over his mouth and that slow dark look in his eyes, anyone seeing them would know what they'd been up to in the back of the car.

"Look at us acting like two sex-starved high-school kids." His voice was deep with arousal.

"Yeah well, the difference being if you play your cards right, you will get lucky tonight." She shimmied out from beneath him, enjoying his bark of laughter at her impudent words.

"I have a feeling I hold the winning hand."

He reached around her and opened the door. Almost immediately the doorman appeared and offered Gia his assistance in exiting the car. She avoided meeting his gaze knowing she must look a wreck or, at the very least, like a woman who'd been thoroughly debauched in the back of the sleek black limo.

Drake followed and took her arm then led her to the entrance. His apartment building was like most in the upscale locale. Gleaming marble floors, polished glass and a towering floral arrangement in the center of the lobby. Near the elevator stood a man in a dark suit with gold lapels. He nodded at them as they stepped into the elevator then followed. Her brow rose when she saw the brocade couch in the elevator.

How…handy.

"Good evening, Rand," Drake spoke.

"Evening, sir, and it is mighty fine one tonight," the older man spoke as the doors slid shut. He removed a small gold key from his pocket, slid it into the console then pressed the one button that was unmarked.

"That it is." Drake slid his arm around her waist and pulled her closer. "And how is your granddaughter doing? Last you mentioned she was in a tizzy over starting second grade in the fall."

The other man chuckled and Gia allowed their easy conversation to fade to a soft buzz. Her body was almost unbearably aroused and the elevator ride seemed to be taking forever. If they didn't get to his floor soon she was seriously thinking about tossing Drake on the couch and fucking him, audience or not.

He must have sensed her lascivious thoughts as his hand slid from her hip to cup one buttock. Giving her a gentle squeeze then a soft pat, his hand returned to its former position.

She shifted, pressing her thighs together as hard as she could without the movement being noticeable. The two men were still talking when the elevator slowed and the doors opened.

"Have a good evening, Mr. Whelan." He gave her a nod, his eyes friendly. "And young lady."

"Thank you, you do the same." Gia gave him a wide smile.

Drake flicked on the lights as they exited the elevator and stepped directly into his living room. "Welcome to my home, Gia."

"Thank you," she murmured.

The room was spacious and the wooden floor was polished to a high gleam. Two brown couches facing each other in the center of the room with a smoked glass coffee table in between. The outside walls were entirely made of glass and they offered a breathtaking view of Central Park and the glittering skyline of New York. The interior walls were a pale cream with paintings and wall hangings every several feet. Her eyes widened when she saw a Monet only a few feet from a Picasso.

"Can I get you a drink?" he asked.

"No thanks." Gia tossed her purse onto the couch and leaned her walking stick against the arm. "Is there anything I can do for you?" Kicking off her shoes, she walked toward him.

"Well…" His gaze skimmed her curves and the air fairly sizzled with tension as he ran his tongue over his lower lip.

Gia stopped barely a foot away from him. Her gaze dipped and she presented him with her back.

"Can you…unzip me?"

"With pleasure." His voice was deeper than normal.

He took her thick hair and gently moved it over her shoulder out of the way. With tantalizing slowness he lowered the zipper until it reached the bottom. Gia allowed the bodice to sag before letting it fall to pool around her feet.

"Thanks," she spoke in an airy tone over her shoulder.

She turned and didn't miss the fact this his eyes moved over her as if he were a starving man. She'd dressed deliberately in a red lace demi bra and matching thong. The bra was fitted so that a glimpse of her matching gold rings could be seen through the lace.

"You're welcome," he rasped.

She started to walk away when he grabbed her arm and pulled her against his hard body. Her breath caught when his arms tightened around her and he brought his mouth down in a kiss that rocked her world. With each torrid suck of her tongue, her arousal spiraled higher until she was just short of swooning and she was forced to cling to him. When her knees buckled, he lifted her and she twined her legs around his waist. The harsh ridge of his arousal jutted into her belly and she thought she just might faint with delight.

He began walking and she clutched at his shoulders, enjoying the sensation of his erection rubbing against her. They continued to kiss, slow drugging kisses that made her head swirl and her body ache.

She whimpered when he broke the kiss and slid his hands along her legs indicating he wished her to stand.

"I want you in my bed," he whispered, his breath warm against her temple. "Remove your lingerie and climb in."

Not even thinking of refusing, Gia released her grip on his waist then walked toward the oversized king bed. The covers were pulled back to expose snow-white sheets of pure silk. She removed her clothing then climbed onto the bed to settle down against a pile of pillows.

"I have a gift for you." He moved to a chest of drawers and picked up a slim black velvet jeweler's box. "This gift is to symbolize our new relationship and your willingness to please me as your Dom." He sat on the edge of the bed before opening the box.

Gia leaned forward to peer into the box. On a bed of blue velvet was a gold chain with a large loop at one end and a ruby heart with a key at the other. He removed it from the box then placed it around her neck, before sliding the heart through the loop to secure it. The chain was snug to her throat and the heart and key dangled between her breasts.

"Beautiful." He ran his finger along her jaw and his expression was tender. "Of course, when you disobey me you must be willing to pay the price—either option will be pleasurable to me."

The liquid heat in his voice caused a rush of arousal to streak through her body.

"Yes, Sire."

He reached for the bedside stand then opened a drawer to remove a red silk scarf. He threaded the silk through his fingers before pulling it free. "Lie down, Gia, and raise your arms over your head."

Her throat tightened with excitement and she slid down the pillows until she was on her back. Crossing her wrists she raised them over her head.

"Very nice." He wrapped the silk around her arms. Her breasts began to ache and she pressed her thighs together at the feel of the cool cloth against her skin. He tied the scarf to the headboard before giving the silk a tug to ensure it was secure. "Comfortable?"

She gave them an experimental tug as well. "Yes, Sire."

"Good." From the open drawer he removed a leather strap with wide loops at each end. Sliding one loop around her leg, he slid it up to her knee then tightened the padded loop. "Lift your hips just a bit." When she did so, he slid the strap behind her back to secure her other knee in the opposite loop.

Lying down again, she was surprised to realize her new position was comfortable. The strap held her knees up toward her shoulders leaving her thighs spread and her sex open. She wiggled, unused to such a provocative bound position. Never had any of her previous lovers been quite this inventive. It was both erotic and empowering yet it left her feeling vulnerable and painfully aroused all at the same time.

His eyes were dark with desire when he reached for her. His big hand covered her pussy and he gave her a gentle pat before cupping her. He licked his lips then slid a finger inside. She moaned when he gave her a gentle stroke. Her hips arched toward him as much as she could manage. He withdrew his hand and raised it to his lips to inhale her essence.

"Nectar."

Heat raced through her when he licked his finger clean.

"I think you enjoy being bound. This is very good. A good sub knows how to remain still, respectful while she awaits her Dom's pleasure." He ran his hand over her thigh, the curve of her buttocks. "Are you ready to serve your Dom, Gia?"

Wordless, she nodded.

"Answer me, Gia."

"Yes, Sire." Her voice was little more than a whisper.

"Much better." He rose to remove his jacket. "Tonight I'm going to show you what it means to be my woman." He began unbuttoning his shirt. "I'm very pleased that you enjoy being bound, Gia."

He removed his shirt to reveal a muscular chest lightly covered with dark hair. A tattoo of a Celtic cross marked his left arm. She licked her lips when he reached for his pants. Opening his trousers, he pushed his pants and boxers down then kicked them off. Her eyes widened when she took in his lean, wiry build. His legs were deeply muscled with round buttocks she longed to sink her teeth into.

Her gaze went to his groin and her breath caught. In one word, he was enormous. His cock was big, a thick delicious toy arching up from a thatch of dark hair and the color was a deep rose. A drop of liquid smeared the head, a sign of his obvious arousal. The head was broad and the stem was thick and for a moment she felt panic. How could she take all of him into her mouth, her body?

"Bondage is about anticipation." He reached for a small bottle on the bedside stand. "It is about learning and understanding the capacities of your body and your mind. Teasing yourself into such a state of arousal that it becomes almost an out-of-body experience."

Gia bit back a whimper.

"That is what you will experience this evening." He opened the bottle and took a small drink, holding it up so she could see. "Brandy. One of the most perfect sexual aids ever invented."

Her brow rose.

"I am going to show you exactly what your body is capable of."

He took another drink but this time he did not swallow. Instead he set down the bottle before he climbed onto the bed between her thighs. Lowering his mouth to her pussy he opened his mouth and the soft trickle of brandy dripped over her aroused flesh.

"This will burn, sting and bring your arousal to a new level." He soothed the liquid over her flesh with his fingers. Once he removed them the burn began immediately.

She squirmed as heat raced upward. It caused an itch, a heat that was distracting, arousing and she was unable to do anything to assuage it.

"Remain still, Gia. I'll take care of you in due time."

He repeated the process, taking more brandy into his mouth then dribbling it over her nipples before rubbing it in with his fingers. She was shivering with need when he was done.

In her position with her arms over her head and her thighs splayed wide and unable to close, she was totally vulnerable to him. She couldn't touch herself to relieve the burn he'd awoken in her—she needed him to do the job.

"Please," she hissed.

His brow arched and he replaced the bottle on the table. "It burns, doesn't it? But it feels so exquisite at the same time." He bent and licked at one nipple, catching the ring between his teeth and giving it a gentle tug before releasing her.

"Please..." she whimpered.

"I want to fuck you, Gia," he whispered. "I like you like this—bound, helpless in the face of my need."

His mouth was hot on hers and their tongues fought for supremacy. He settled his hips between her thighs, his cock coming to rest against her burning orifice. He pressed the broad head against her, moving his hips ever so slightly to delve inside a few centimeters. She whimpered.

"Is this what you want, my pet?" His breath was hot against her throat. "My cock inside you?"

"Yes," she moaned, needing him to enter her more than she needed her next breath.

He pressed forward, the width of his head stretching her aroused flesh. "Sire," he hissed.

"Sire," she sobbed.

"You're very tight, I don't want to hurt you."

'I don't care—"

He pushed forward, his cock stretched her pussy and she moaned. Throwing her head back, the only part of her body she could really move, she strained to arch her hips and take him deeper, faster. He ignored her movements and continued his slow, torturous entry until he was fully inside her.

He moved his arms beneath her shoulders to brace his upper body. She wanted to savor the feeling of him covering her, but her need was too great. She whimpered in the back of her throat and he seemed to understand what she needed. He shushed her with a quick, hard kiss then lowered his forehead to hers. Their gazes meshed and he began to thrust.

Within seconds she came, a deep hard release that threatened to tear her apart. She strained beneath him as he picked up the pace. His lips drew back from his teeth and his hips hammered at hers. Freeing one hand, he tweaked a nipple before giving the ring a tug, sending a powerful jolt of sensation directly to her clit. She came again with a scream, her body straining against the restraints.

He dropped his head, taking one nipple into his mouth as the final shudders of her release faded. He stiffened, a low groan that seemed to start from his knees rolled out of his throat and she felt his release fill her.

Struggling to catch her breath, she was replete yet still hungry. She clenched her pussy around him, surprised to find him still hard inside her.

"We're not done yet," he whispered. "I am a man of very healthy appetites."

She moaned when he began to stroke again, a lazy, sleepy stroke of burgeoning arousal. His skin was flushed and his hair clung to his sweat-dampened face. He had a dazed, dreamy expression and his eyes were closed as he moved inside her.

"Come for me again, Gia," he whispered.

The stroking continued and her arousal increased in a slow, inexorable tide. With each movement, each touch, her release beckoned. Taking her nipple between his teeth he worried the nub sending a rain of fire straight to her clit. He moaned against her breast and the animal sound was all she needed to tumble over the edge.

Sensation crashed through her body and his pace increased, his hips slammed into her bringing her yet another release. She felt him stiffen, his cock moving as if it had a mind of its own when he shot into her with a muffled cry.

When the storm settled, Gia felt him release her from her bonds. He rubbed her wrists and massaged her legs until she felt boneless. She rolled to her side, too tired to even open her eyes.

He lay beside her, spoon fashion. His cock was still semi-hard against her buttocks and his arm was heavy against her waist.

"Beautiful, Gia," he whispered. "Thank you."

She couldn't help but smile. "It is I who should be thanking you." Her words were slurred.

He chuckled. "Sleep now and we'll see about your thanking me when we wake up."

Chapter Eight

∾

Drake lay on his side watching Gia sleep. Her dark hair was a tumbled cloud about her slim shoulders and her lips were slightly parted. She was exquisite, even more so than he'd ever dreamed. He drew the back of his index finger over the tender curve of her belly. Gia's breathing hitched then smoothed.

The reality of being with her was more than he'd ever imagined. She was funny, intelligent, warm and sexy and he wanted to know everything about her. What her favorite color was, if she liked pineapple on her pizza and if she enjoyed film noir. Did she enjoy making love on a stormy afternoon or eating ice cream in bed?

She stirred, her lips pursed and she made a soft noise deep in her throat.

When he'd concocted this plan he'd hoped that they'd create at least a spark of attraction. He touched the tender skin of her inner elbow. This was much more than just a spark, it was an explosion of attraction that took his breath away. He twined a silky curl around his finger. He could only hope she felt the same way about him when this weekend was over.

She stirred again, a frown wrinkling her brow. Her head moved against the pillow and she whimpered as if something were bothering her in her sleep. Her hands fisted and her body tensed.

Concerned, he began stroking her arm. "Gia, wake up. You're having a bad dream."

Another whimper escaped her then her dark eyes flew open. They were muddled with sleep and the remnants of her dreams. She blinked several times before focusing upon him.

"Drake?" Her voice was rusty.

"It's me."

She sat up and looked around, her hair a silky halo about her head. "What time is it?"

"Around two maybe." He sat up and shoved his pillows against the headboard. Settling back, he roped an arm around her shoulders. At first she resisted him then she settled against his side, her head coming to rest on his shoulder. "What was your dream about?"

She hesitated and he felt the tension in her body. What had her so hesitant to speak to him?

"Gia?"

"It was my accident."

"Ah, I see." He stroked her hair, enjoying the silken texture. "Do you want to talk about it?"

She shrugged.

"I read bits and pieces in the paper." He tangled his fingers in the long tresses. "It was in California, wasn't it?"

"Hollywood Hills. I really don't remember much about that night."

"Mmm. What do you remember?"

She sighed. "Well, we'd gone out to dinner then stopped at a friend's house for a drink. We left and the accident happened only several miles from my house. I hit my head on the windshield and I don't remember much after that." She began rubbing her forehead as if it were giving her pain.

"And your dream is about the accident?"

"Sort of. I keep having this vision over and over, but it gets jumbled in my mind. I don't even know if it's real or not."

"Why don't you tell me about it."

She burrowed a little closer as if the memories made her uncomfortable. "I'm trapped in the car, my ankle was crushed, you see. I couldn't get out because my side took the brunt of the damage."

He continued stroking her hair. Contrary to what he'd told her, he'd read every newspaper account he could find and watched dozens of television reports on her accident. Seeing that she'd received a concussion, he probably knew more about the details than she did.

"I'm in the car and I look up through the shattered windshield. There's this man looking down at me. He smiles and it's the coldest smile I've ever seen." A soft shudder ran through her body and he hugged her closer. "Then he lays a pink rose on the windshield and then walks away."

He kissed her on the forehead. "Do you think it was real?"

"It sure feels real to me."

"Well, if it feels real then maybe it was." He leaned his head against the headboard. "Who do you think this man was?"

She hesitated again, her body tense against his side. He continued stroking her hair, patiently waiting for her to break the silence.

"A man has been stalking me."

He stopped, stunned. She had a stalker? Who? Where? A million questions raced into his mind and he had to force them to the side for the moment. Right now he wanted to let her get this out before he'd start asking questions.

"And you think this person in your dream was him?" He began stroking her hair again.

"Yes, I think so. I just can't explain it." He heard the frustration in her voice. "Don't ask me how I know, I just know."

"When did it begin, this stalking?"

"About three years ago. I'd taken a few months off to heal from a hamstring injury and I'd just bought a house in California. Flowers began arriving from a man who called himself an 'ardent admirer'. At the time I didn't think much of it. Let's face it, it's easy to find out where the stars live in Los Angeles as you can buy a star map every ten feet." She shook her head. "After a few months he started sending me dinner invitations and I refused them. That's when it began to escalate and soon he started threatening me. It got really bad when I started dating Ricardo and that's when he started making serious threats."

Rage simmered just below his skin and Drake had to struggle to keep his tone even. "And the police never found this bastard?"

She shook her head. "They knew he existed because of the letters, flowers and such. By the time of the accident I'd already made several police reports but they had so little to go on. Because I'd had a head injury from the accident and there were no other witnesses, they didn't believe my story. They chalked it up to my hitting my head, and that's where it stands now."

He cupped the back of her head. "And what a beautiful head it is." He dropped another kiss onto her hair.

She sighed and snuggled closer, her slim arms snaked around his waist. "I'm so tired."

"Sleep now. You're safe here and that's what matters."

"Thank you," her voice was silky soft.

She fell silent and he held her until she fell asleep, his mind working like a dervish. In the morning he'd call his cousin who was a private detective and have him look into this stalker business. If there was some crackpot out there trying to harm his woman, Ryder would be able to track him down. Drake's grip tightened on Gia's slim shoulders. He'd spare no expense to keep her safe.

He looked down into her sleeping face. It was also time to confess what he'd done to lure her into his bed. He needed to come clean about the fake personal ad and the one time they had met so many years ago.

Tomorrow, he'd talk to her tomorrow.

* * * * *

Gia fingered the heart necklace, her mind in turmoil. She wasn't sure what had made her tell Drake about her stalker. After the LA police had discounted her story the night of the accident, she rarely ever spoke of *le bastardo*. Seeing that her memories of that night were sketchy at best, there were many times that she doubted herself.

She looked across the room where her lover was sleeping. His dark hair obscured his rugged features and his tanned skin looked erotic against the crisp white sheets. A frown tugged at her lips. There was something so familiar about him, something she couldn't quite put her finger on.

She looked out the window again, the lights of New York gleaming against the dark velvet sky. What she felt for him was more than just sex. While she couldn't quite define it, she did know that she felt secure with him. It was in the way he carried himself, his sense of humor and his attention to her pleasure as well as his.

In short, Drake was a man she could trust.

Her gaze drifted back to the bed. In her experience, a man who could be trusted was a rare commodity. She knew she could trust him with her body, but could he be trusted with her heart as well?

She dropped the heart pendant and it landed between her breasts. She'd learned that when dancing with a new partner, there was only one way to find out if they were trustworthy — she'd have to take the leap and see if he would be there to catch her.

Chapter Nine

ରୁ

"Are you sure you want to do this?"

Gia's husky voice slid over his skin like oiled silk. Drake looked up from the canvas, a palate in one hand and a brush in the other. He was sitting on a platform roughly eight feet in the air, which enabled him to have an aerial view of his subject. She lay on her back, her dusky limbs tangled with creamy silk sheets in the middle of the bed. Sunlight poured in through the studio skylights illuminating her flawless skin. Her dark hair was tumbled across the pillows, and with a naughty expression she was sex incarnate.

"Are you kidding?" He dabbed his brush against the palate. "I'm enjoying every minute of this."

She sighed and tossed her head. "I'm getting tired of just lying here…"

"A few minutes more and you can get up for a while. Let me capture the curve of your arm then we can order up some lunch from a Chinese place around the corner."

Gia made a soft humming sound that made him smile. He couldn't blame her for being restless, they'd been at it for over three hours, and anyone would be tired.

"Amuse me while I finish up. Why don't you tell me about your last boyfriend," he said.

She wrinkled her nose. "Why would you want to hear about him?"

"He left you after the accident."

"No real loss there. He knew the money train was coming to a halt. My ankle was shattered and the doctor had just told me I would never dance again." Drake didn't miss the shadow of sadness that dimmed her lovely features. "So the next day Ricardo showed up at the hospital and announced it just wasn't working out between us. He kissed me on the cheek and headed straight for the door. I promptly called my friend Constance and made arrangements to come to New York." Her dark gaze met his. "So there you have it."

"No broken hearts?"

She laughed, a silky sound of amusement. "No, no broken hearts. Ricardo was good-looking, energetic in bed and he adored me as long as the money ran his way."

"He was a wuss," Drake said. "No real man would have done that to a woman."

She gave a startled laugh. "Well, he was that." She shifted her legs and the sound of silk against her flesh set every hair on his body to alert.

"So tell me, what does the future hold for Gia Conti?"

"Mmm, I don't know for sure. I have some options." She bit her lower lip and a rush of heat raced toward his groin. He loved her mouth.

"Such as?" He dabbled his brush in the scarlet paint.

She squirmed. "I've been toying with the idea of opening a studio to teach children ballet."

"Really?" She'd surprised him again. Con had always claimed that Gia was a little bit of a prima donna and he'd yet to see any signs of it. "I think that's a great idea, Gia."

A slow smile moved across her face. "Yeah, it is, isn't it?"

"The second floor of this building is empty. It would make a great space for a dance studio."

She blinked. "Do you think so?"

"Yes, I do." Drake set the palate and brush on a small table near his elbow. "I also think it is my duty to do everything I can to erase that fool, Ricardo, from your memory." He climbed down the ladder then walked toward the bed he'd set up in the middle of his studio. "Starting with, kissing you from head to toe."

She squealed when he grabbed the sheet and pulled, baring her body to the brilliant sunlight. "Stop!"

"Mmm, lunchtime." He dove onto the bed and gathered an armful of warm, fragrant female. "This nipple will hit the spot."

Her fingers tangled in his hair when he suckled her nipple, teasing the gold ring with his tongue. He released her and she grabbed onto the front of his shirt, pulling him close for a kiss that threatened to rock his world. Nibbling on her lips, he wanted inside her mouth. His tongue snaked out and just as it touched her lips, she twined her legs around him and rolled to the side. Taken by surprise, he allowed her the movement and she ended up sprawled on top of him.

Drake grasped her by the waist while her busy hands tore at his shirt. Her hair hung long and tangled and he couldn't resist twining the locks around his fingers. He pulled her toward him, their lips meeting in a greedy kiss of need. A soft moan sounded from her throat and she sucked his tongue, driving sensation directly to his throbbing groin.

"Let me," she hissed, her fingers tearing at his pants.

He lay back and propped his head on his hands, willing to let her take the lead for once. "Do you have any idea of how beautiful you are?"

To his surprise, she rolled her eyes. "Beauty is highly overrated. I can't take credit for genetics." She leaned forward and teethed his nipple, eliciting a hiss from him.

He grabbed her head and forced her mouth back to his. Every time they were together it was like this, as if it were the first time. Drake felt as if he couldn't get enough of her. Like a starving man he wanted to spread her across the bed and feast on her. Her nipples would —

All thoughts of tasting her flew from his mind as her hand plunged into the front of his pants and her fingers encircled his cock. She squeezed gently, causing licks of fire to race over his body.

"I think I like you like this," she purred. "At my mercy."

He spanked her on the ass and chuckled. "Don't get too used to it."

She sat up, her thighs parting to bracket his hips. Her breasts shimmied as she moved onto her knees over him. Wrapping her hand around the base of his cock, she positioned him at the entrance of her pussy and, with a heady sigh, sank him deep.

He grabbed her by the hips, glorying in the raw beauty that was Gia. She began to move over him, her body angling to capture her clit. With her head tipped back, she lifted her body from his only to return, barely giving him time to draw breath. A dreamy smile curved her mouth and she moved easily, her pace slowly increasing.

Her release came hard and fast, her tight muscles caressing him with mind-numbing accuracy. His teeth gritted, as her silky cries threatened to send him over the edge.

No, it was too fast.

He grasped her waist and rolled, catching her by surprise, and she ended up beneath him. Tangling his fingers in her hair, his hips began to hammer into hers. Heat raced through his body when she wrapped her legs around his waist urging him deeper.

Together they scaled the peak, heat rode low and hard in his body and when he felt her come apart, he lost another piece of his soul as he came inside her.

* * * * *

The dream came as it always did, sneaking up on her while she slept.

Once again she was trapped in her shattered car, paralyzed by pain from her broken angle and the metal wrapped around her lower body. Through the windshield she saw the shadow over her and even though she didn't want to look up she knew it was inevitable.

The figure was in shadow and the rain fell from the sky. The ball cap was pulled low and he moved toward her. A bolt of lightning streaked across the sky illuminating him and a scream lodged in her throat when, for the first time, she saw his face.

It was Drake.

Gia came awake with a start, her breathing harsh. Sweat bathed her limbs and she was shaking from head to toe. Tilting her head back, the night sky shone through the skylights and reality slowly gained a foothold in her consciousness.

She was safe.

She was in Drake's studio.

All was well.

Forcing herself to relax, she concentrated on slowing her breathing. Beside her Drake was still sound asleep with his arm tossed over her waist. She looked down at him and her stomach twisted.

Now why had her subconscious fabricated Drake as her stalker?

She smiled and reached out to touch one of his tumbled locks. Talk about running scared, she'd probably conjured him up because falling in love with him was the last thing she'd expected. Then again, wasn't that what usually happened? When you least expected to find love, that's when it appeared. Soft, contented warmth stole through her body.

Imagine that, Gia Conti was on the verge of falling in love.

Taking his hand, she gently removed his arm from her waist then slipped from the bed. He made a sound as if he objected to her leaving. On the floor near the foot of the bed she found his shirt. Smelling of turpentine and man, she pulled it on to cover her naked body. Her heart lifted and the remaining darkness brought on by her dream vanished.

Yeah, she was in trouble all right.

With a silly smile on her face, she turned away. Right now she had more pressing matters to attend to, like finding a bathroom. The room was full of shadows and she walked carefully across the dim expanse. In the corner were two doors. Now which one was the bathroom again? Grasping the handle of the closest one, she opened the door then flicked on the light. She winced when the fluorescent lights came on and threatened to blind her.

"Wrong room," she muttered when she saw the nearly empty space. She reached for the light switch when a corkboard of photographs caught her eye, an eight by ten in particular.

She tilted her head, confused. Now why would Drake have a photograph of her? Her gaze moved to the others on the board and her heart dropped when she realized they were all of her.

What was going on here?

As if in a daze, she entered the room, allowing the door to slide shut behind her. With her heart pounding in her throat, on leaden feet she walked across the room, her gaze glued to the corkboard.

There were at least two dozen photographs and every single one of them was of her. With a shaky hand she reached for one of the publicity photos. Tearing it from the board, she stared down into her own glossy face. This one was taken while she'd danced as Juliet on her last tour. As far as she knew, this photograph had never been released to the press.

Just where had he gotten these?

Her arm dropped and she allowed the photograph to fall to the floor. A feeling of unreality slipped over her as images from her dream flashed before her eyes.

Trapped in the car.

The rose.

Drake smiling down at her from beneath a ball cap.

No, it couldn't be…

Heart pounding, she turned and stumbled against a small worktable. The tall, towel-draped object rocked on its turntable and part of the wrapping fell away revealing one slim clay hand. A feeling of dread came over her and she stared at it with her heart in her throat. Even though she didn't want to, she knew she had to look. Her arm felt alien when she reached for the wrappings. Pulling them free, she saw a clay statue of a ballet dancer.

She didn't have to look at the face to know that it was she. The tutu was similar to the one she wore as Giselle. Her fingertip brushed over the delicate curve of one leg. Drake was sculpting her likeness in clay.

Why? Why would he do this to her?

Miss me?

The words from the packet of photographs drifted through her mind. Was it true? Could it be that Drake was her stalker?

Her gaze wavered as her heart began to pound. Her own face mocked her from the glossy photos on the corkboards.

Everything in this room pointed to that being the case. Why else would he have all of these photos of her on the wall? What other reason would he have for creating this statue of her if he wasn't obsessed with her?

Turning away, she saw the glass-fronted refrigerator and her eyes widened at the sight of a dozen pale pink roses in a vase. Her heart almost stopped as images of the night of her accident sliced through her mind. She hadn't seen him very clearly. She'd been left with just the vaguest memory of dark hair and piercing eyes. It had been dark and she'd never been able to shake the feeling that she'd seen Drake somewhere before.

Had it been on a dark, rainy road in Hollywood Hills?

Her hands began to shake and her breathing grew harsh.

Damn him…

Stalking over to the refrigerator, she wrenched open the door and cool, rose-scented air blew out. She snatched the roses from the vase and tossed them onto the floor, barely feeling the prick of thorns against her palm. Shaking from head to toe, she grabbed an Exacto knife from a worktable and walked toward the ballet dancer. Raising her arm over her head, she drove the knife straight into the heart of the statue. Damn him for being the man who'd destroyed her life. Damn him for lying to her.

And damn him for making her love him.

A sob caught in her throat and Gia had to fight for calm. On the verge of screaming, she knew she had to make her escape or she wouldn't be accountable for her actions. Slipping back into the studio, she saw Drake was where she'd left him. Suddenly he didn't look quite so innocent, quite so loving anymore.

You don't know for sure that he's guilty…

Sure, everyone keeps photos of her on the wall. She pushed that thought away and began gathering her strewn clothing. She had to get out of there. She had to think and she couldn't do that when she was with Drake. She stripped out of his shirt and hurriedly pulled her clothing on. Carrying her shoes and her cane, she slipped out the studio door without a backward glance.

As luck would have it, a man was getting out of a cab just half a block away from the front door of the building. He held it for her and she flashed him an absent smile before climbing in the back. After giving her address to the driver, she was shaking by the time the cab pulled away from the curb.

Don't think…don't think…

The drive to her building was a blur and by the time she reached her destination she was freezing cold. Even though it was still in the eighties outside, her teeth were chattering. After giving some bills to the driver, she stumbled into her apartment building. The guard desk was empty but this wasn't an unusual occurrence. Sometimes security stepped out to assist a resident or to visit the bathroom.

At the elevators, she pushed in her code and the doors slid open. Stepping in, she pushed the button to her floor and the doors closed. Looking up at the glowing lights over the door, the elevator seemed to be moving slower than usual. A whimper caught in her throat as tears scalded her eyes.

Just a few more minutes and then you can fall apart…

The doors slid open and Gia stumbled out into the hallway. Her hands were shaking so hard that she could barely handle the keys. Finally she slid her key into the lock and opened the door to her apartment. Stumbling inside, she slammed the door, desperate to lock herself away from the world before the damn broke on her emotions.

Flicking on the light, reaching for the keypad, stopping when she saw the blinking green light. She frowned. Had she forgotten to set her alarm?

The scent of roses reached her nose and her stomach churned. A feeling of dread washed over her body.

"Good evening, Gia."

As if in slow motion she turned. A stranger stood in the living room doorway. In one hand he held a dozen pink roses and in the other was a gun pointed directly at her chest.

* * * * *

Drake was disappointed to wake up alone. Overhead, moonlight streamed in through the skylights and the sheets next to him were cool. He rolled over and buried his face in her pillow, inhaling the intoxicating fragrance of her hair. His cock stirred. He hadn't meant to fall asleep but with all the nocturnal activities of the past two days, there hadn't had much time to sleep.

A slow grin spread across his face. Gia was intelligent, funny, sweet and beautiful. In short she was everything he'd ever imagined and more. Just thinking about her made him want her beside him. He raised his head.

Now, the question was, where was she?

He rolled over and sat up on the edge of the bed. The studio was dark with the exception of the light spilling from an open doorway. It was the room where Gia's sculpture resided.

Damn.

He rose and walked toward the smaller room, mindless of his naked state. He knew he should've told her about the project. She was probably in shock and thought he was some freak like the one who'd been tormenting her. How he'd like to get his hands on that one. He'd gladly tear the bastard limb from limb for even thinking of hurting or scaring his woman. He still needed to call his cousin in the morning and put him on the case.

Drake pushed open the door and blinked against the glare of the fluorescent lights. A quick glance told him the room was empty. He frowned. Where was she?

Roses were scattered across the floor and he walked toward them. What was going on? A few feet away was a photograph of Gia that had been torn from the board. A feeling of foreboding spawned in his stomach. She wouldn't even begin to understand—

He turned away when he saw the knife sticking out of the sculpture's chest. A chill crept across his skin.

She had misinterpreted what he was doing. No doubt she'd decided in the face of this damning evidence that he was just another person who'd wanted to steal a piece of her soul. He reached for the knife. All of this because he'd fallen asleep and failed to have the conversation he knew they'd needed to have. Gently dislodging the knife, he allowed it to fall to the table. He'd have to go after her, to explain what was really going on with the statue.

He could only hope it wasn't too late to salvage their relationship.

Chapter Ten

ఴ

How could she have been so wrong?

Numb, Gia sat on her couch, her nails dug into a pillow on her lap. Across from her sat the man who'd tried to kill her once before and was now back to finish the job. In that moment, she knew that thirty years on this earth wasn't enough. There was so much she wanted to do, to see, to accomplish.

And just when she'd met Drake.

Her heart constricted. How in the world she could've mistaken Drake for this man, she'd never know. He was at least four inches shorter than her lover and at least fifty pounds heavier. His dark hair was overgrown and thick stubble marred his chin. He wore blue jeans and a white button-down shirt that was stained with something on the front that looked suspiciously like blood.

"I'll bet you never thought this day would come, did you, Gia?" His voice was low and it sent chills over her skin.

Mute, she shook her head.

"I have dreamed of this moment." His smile was slow, unpleasant. "At night when I lay in my bed and I think of you, I fantasize about what it would be like to sit with you, to touch you."

He rubbed the side of his gun against his thigh and her knotted stomach tightened even further. The roses lay on the coffee table between them, the scent from the half-opened buds making her nauseous.

"H-h-have we met before?" Her nails dug deeper into the pillow.

"Not really, not like this at least." His smile remained in place. "I've been in the same room with you on many occasions but a dancer of your caliber would never have paid attention to a prop man such as myself."

"P-p-prop man?"

He nodded, still stroking the gun against his thigh. "I worked with you on *Romeo and Juliet* as well as several others." His smile faded. "At least until I was fired. It almost killed me knowing I wouldn't see you anymore, be able to hear your voice…"

Gia swallowed hard. Madness glimmered in his eyes and her muscles tensed. As he spoke, his expression turned distant. Her gaze darted around the room looking for anything to aid her escape. The security keypad with its green light mocked her from across the room. It was too far away and she'd never make it before he'd shoot her in the back.

Her gaze darted toward the fireplace. Another possibility was the poker, which was certainly much closer. Her cane was also beside her but would the slim ebony stick be capable of inflicting enough damage to enable her to get away?

"Gia, are you listening to me?" His voice was soft, crooning.

She forced a pleasant smile. "Sorry, I was thinking about having to go to the bathroom." She pushed the pillow onto the couch and got to her feet. "If you will excuse me — "

"I think I will accompany you, if you don't mind." He rose.

"I really don't think that is necessary — "

His smile was cold. "I insist."

With shaky knees, she began walking toward the front hall. With her cane clutched in her hand, she leaned hard upon it as if she were more dependant upon it than she really was. With every step the front door grew closer and she knew if there was ever a time to try and make her escape, she had to seize it now. All she needed to do was get him behind her then strike from the left which meant he would fall to the right and it would buy her a few more seconds to get away.

Would it hurt to get shot?

He fell into step behind her and together they walked into the entry. Her grip tightened on the cane, and just as she was about to make her move, a loud knock sounded on the door.

* * * * *

Gia's scream sent Drake headlong through the door. His boots skidded on the polished tile and his heart almost stopped when he saw his woman fighting with a strange man who was at least double her weight. The other man hit her hard on the jaw and she fell back with the man on top of her.

Drake lunged as she went down and slammed into the stranger, to send him flying off her with two hundred pounds of enraged, territorial male on his back. Drake heard Gia scream something but the only word that registered was "gun". Beneath him the man twisted and fought like a tiger. His arm came up and Drake snagged his wrist.

"You bastard," the other man screamed. "You can't have her, she's mine."

"Over my dead body," Drake snarled.

"That can be arranged."

Leaning his considerable weight onto the man's upper body, Drake slammed the other man's hand against the marble floor in an attempt to break his grip. The man roared and Drake repeated the movement, slamming his hand harder. He felt the other man's grip tighten just seconds before the sound of the semiautomatic report rang out.

Stunned, Drake felt something wet hit him in the face and the man went limp.

Slowly Drake rose, taking the gun from the stranger's hand. The man lay still on the marble floor, a slowly spreading pool of blood around his head in a macabre halo. Moving forward, Drake leaned down and checked for a pulse.

There was none.

Straightening, he saw Gia standing near the door, a look of horror on her beautiful face. To his relief, she appeared to be unharmed.

"Gia, are you okay?" he asked.

Slowly, as if in a dream she looked over at him. Blinking several times, she finally nodded. "*Sí.*"

Not wanting to think about how close he'd come to losing her permanently, he wrapped his arms around her, grateful to hold her once more.

* * * * *

The sun was high overhead and Gia tipped her head back to enjoy the warm rays on her face. She was weary to the bone and while she longed to sleep, every time she lay down and closed her eyes, she saw *his* face.

A shiver ran down her spine.

In the meadow, children were playing a lively game of Frisbee. With their brightly colored clothing and infectious laughter, her gaze was drawn to them over and over. A fuzzy dog resembling a pile of dirty cotton balls ran from child to child barking and leaping like mad. Gia couldn't help but smile at the animal's antics.

On the bench next to hers was an older woman feeding the birds and chipmunks while a homeless man lay asleep on the grass under a tree just a few yards away. Only in Central Park could one see both ends of the human spectrum within a few hundred yards of each other.

Even in the bright light of day, Gia still couldn't wrap her mind around what had happened last night. Her jaw ached from *le bastardo* hitting her with a right hook, and her shoulder throbbed from landing on it when he'd tackled her. If it weren't for Drake's timely arrival, the outcome would have been so much worse.

She tilted her head and rotated it, trying to relieve the tension in her neck and shoulders. Her nightmare was over and her tormentor had bled to death in her foyer. Her stomach churned. She'd never be able to sleep there again. Movement to her right caught her attention and she saw a man walking toward her. Black boots, worn jeans and a plain white T-shirt accented his broad shoulders. His dark, wind-ruffled hair was loose and he walked with a swagger that Gia recognized well.

Drake.

Dark sunglasses shielded his eyes and his jaw was set. Her heart sank. She'd let him down. She wouldn't blame him if he'd followed her to the park to dump her for acting like a ninny. He'd been nothing but upfront with her and she'd run away at the first misunderstanding. Her head dropped and she focused her gaze on her shoes.

At the sound of footsteps, every hair on her body leapt to attention. Dark boots stepped into her line of vision and stopped directly in front of her.

"I let you down." Her voice was soft.

"You think?"

She looked up at him, squinting against the sun. "You don't?"

"I don't." He dropped onto the bench beside her. "Regardless of what happened, the reality is that we barely know one another." He shoved his sunglasses up onto his head. "With everything that has happened to you where that freak is concerned, I don't blame you for running away from me. In your shoes I might have done the same thing."

"Really?"

"Really."

Gia exhaled loudly. "Thank you."

"You're welcome."

"Even though I left, you were there for me when I really needed you." Her voice trembled.

"And I will be in the future if you'll let me." He reached over and brushed her tangled hair away from her face. His fingertips gently touched her forehead. "Are you okay?"

"When I couldn't dance anymore, I thought I'd lost everything I'd ever wanted in life." Her lips trembled and she gave a jerky nod. "I defined myself by my ability to get up on the stage and command an audience." She shook her head. "I sat there on that couch across from *le bastardo* and all I could think was that I wasn't ready to die yet. That there were so many more things I wanted to accomplish with my life, and in that moment I wanted to live so badly, more than I'd ever thought possible."

He smiled and the corners of his eyes crinkled with laugh lines. "I'm glad."

"Yeah." She smiled. "Me too."

"Since we're having confession time, I feel the need to confess something to you while we're at it."

She gave a startled laugh. "What on earth would you have to confess to me, Drake?"

"A lot actually." A soft flush moved over his cheekbones.

Wow, this must be good.

"I haven't been straight with you from the beginning. You and I have met before, when we were children."

She frowned. "When was this?"

"It was the first summer you spent in the States and you and Con were already bosom buddies."

"You know Constance?"

"Very well, since she was a toddler."

Her eyes narrowed. "Go on."

"You were thirteen and you attended a party on Martha's Vineyard for the Whitney birthday party. I also attended the party with Con's brother, Rick. Everyone was playing in the pool and you were standing on the side—"

"Oh no..." Images flashed through her mind of that day. The sickening smell of birthday cake icing melting in the sun, feeling alien because she didn't speak the language and she'd clung to Connie like a lifeline, and the one boy who had saved her from being tossed in the pool while still clothed in her new party dress. A feeling of unreality crept over her. From the moment she'd met him she knew there was something familiar about it yet she'd never been able to put her finger on it.

Drake had been the young man who'd rescued her.

"*Merda!*" She slugged him in the shoulder, wincing when the pain shot up her arm and to her sore shoulder.

He leaned away. "Easy now, I'm wounded."

"Yeah, right." She rolled her eyes. "If you had been straight with me from the beginning none of this would have happened." Crossing her arms over her chest, she scowled at him. "You were the boy who rescued me from Whitney."

"Yes, that was me."

Her gaze narrowed and his blush rose. "Go on."

"Well…" He looked away. "I wanted to talk to you so badly that day but I didn't speak Italian and you didn't speak English." He chuckled. "I sure as hell didn't want to use Con as an interpreter, and I let you get away. Over the years I've kept tabs on you through Con and the newspapers. When she said that you were moving to New York, I'd hoped she would reintroduce us but it never happened.

"A few weeks ago she announced you were thinking of getting back out into the dating scene and I knew it was now or never. I created that personal ad on my computer and I convinced Con to read it to you—"

"Connie was in on this too?" Stung, Gia sat up, her back ramrod straight.

"Hey, it wasn't easy to sway her. It took well over a week to convince her that I wasn't going to hurt you—"

"You're hurting me now. It's so nice to know who my friends *aren't*."

"I'm sorry, Gia. Truly I am. I never should have lied to you."

She didn't have to look into his eyes to know that he was telling the truth as sincerity rang in every word. She shook her head. "I don't understand why you would do all of this."

He reached over and cupped her cheek, his calloused hand warm and reassuring against her skin. "I knew there was something special about you the moment I rescued you from Whitney. I let you get away that day and I was determined to not make the same mistake again. All these years I'd kept an eye on you from afar and I wanted to know once and for all if there was any spark of attraction, any common ground between us."

She blinked and in that moment her heart melted. "Really?" she whispered.

"Really."

A goofy grin split her face. "What do you think now?"

An answering grin curved his mouth. "I think I was incredibly smart even at fifteen."

"Oh yeah?" She took his hand and pressed a kiss against his palm. "How smart were you?"

"Well." He looped an arm around her shoulder and she leaned into him, her head coming to rest over his heart. "I was smart enough to have picked out the prettiest girl at the party—"

"And not talk to her." She giggled and slid her arms around his waist, content to sit close to him. "So where do we go from here?"

"I'm thinking we'll head back to my apartment and sleep for many, many hours."

"Mmm, sounds like a plan to me." She closed her eyes, comforted by the rumbling of his voice and the steady beat of his heart.

"After that we can have dinner, get to know each other a little better."

"Fabulous."

"Then, I will tie you up and paint your body with chocolate mousse—"

She started laughing and raised her head. "How did you find out what Gia Pie was?"

His brow rose.

"Of course, when I make dessert," she pulled away from Drake and rose, "it wouldn't be me that was covered in mousse." Her gaze dropped to his lap before meeting his once more. "If you know what I mean."

"I think I do..."

About the Author

જી

Dominique Adair is the pen name of award-winning novelist J.C. Wilder. Adair/Wilder (she chooses her name according to her mood — if she's feeling sassy and brazen, it's Adair; if she's feeling dark and dangerous, it's Wilder) lives just outside of Columbus, Ohio, where she skulks around town plotting her next book and contemplating where to hide the bodies (from her books, of course — everyone knows that you can't really hide a body as they always pop up at the worst times).

Dominique welcomes mail from readers. You can write to her c/o Ellora's Cave Publishing at 1056 Home Avenue, Akron, OH 44310-3502.

Also by Dominique Adair

✂

Holly

Last Kiss

Party Favors *(anthology)*

R.S.V.P. *(anthology)*

Tied With a Bow *(anthology)*

Xanthra Chronicles: Blood Law

Writing as J.C. Wilder

✂

Ellora's Cavemen: Tales From the Temple II *(anthology)*

In Moonlight *(anthology)*

Men of SWAT: Tactical Maneuver

Men of SWAT: Tactical Pleasure

Things That Go Bump in the Night 2004 *(anthology)*

Why an electronic book?

We live in the Information Age — an exciting time in the history of human civilization, in which technology rules supreme and continues to progress in leaps and bounds every minute of every day. For a multitude of reasons, more and more avid literary fans are opting to purchase e-books instead of paper books. The question from those not yet initiated into the world of electronic reading is simply: *Why?*

1. ***Price.*** An electronic title at Ellora's Cave Publishing and Cerridwen Press runs anywhere from 40% to 75% less than the cover price of the exact same title in paperback format. Why? Basic mathematics and cost. It is less expensive to publish an e-book (no paper and printing, no warehousing and shipping) than it is to publish a paperback, so the savings are passed along to the consumer.

2. ***Space.*** Running out of room in your house for your books? That is one worry you will never have with electronic books. For a low one-time c ost, you can purchase a handheld device specifically designed for e-reading. Many e-readers have large, convenient screens for viewing. Better yet, hundreds of titles can be stored within your new library — on a single microchip. There are a variety of e-readers from different manufacturers. You can also read e-books on your PC or laptop computer. (Please note that Ellora's

Cave does not endorse any specific brands. You can check our websites at www.ellorascave.com or www.cerridwenpress.com for information we make available to new consumers.)

3. *Mobility.* Because your new e-library consists of only a microchip within a small, easily transportable e-reader, your entire cache of books can be taken with you wherever you go.

4. *Personal Viewing Preferences.* Are the words you are currently reading too small? Too large? Too... ANNOYING? Paperback books cannot be modified according to personal preferences, but e-books can.

5. *Instant Gratification.* Is it the middle of the night and all the bookstores near you are closed? Are you tired of waiting days, sometimes weeks, for bookstores to ship the novels you bought? Ellora's Cave Publishing sells instantaneous downloads twenty-four hours a day, seven days a week, every day of the year. Our webstore is never closed. Our e-book delivery system is 100% automated, meaning your order is filled as soon as you pay for it.

Those are a few of the top reasons why electronic books are replacing paperbacks for many avid readers.

As always, Ellora's Cave and Cerridwen Press welcome your questions and comments. We invite you to email us at Comments@ellorascave.com or write to us directly at Ellora's Cave Publishing Inc., 1056 Home Avenue, Akron, OH 44310-3502.

THE
☥ ELLORA'S CAVE ☥
LIBRARY

Stay up to date with Ellora's Cave Titles in
Print with our Quarterly Catalog.

TO RECIEVE A CATALOG,
SEND AN EMAIL WITH YOUR NAME
AND MAILING ADDRESS TO:

CATALOG@ELLORASCAVE.COM
OR SEND A LETTER OR POSTCARD
WITH YOUR MAILING ADDRESS TO:

CATALOG REQUEST
c/o ELLORA'S CAVE PUBLISHING, INC.
1056 HOME AVENUE
AKRON, OHIO 44310-3502

ELLORA'S
CAVEMEN
LEGENDARY TAILS

Try an e-book for your immediate
reading pleasure or order these titles in print from

WWW.ELLORASCAVE.COM

ELLORA'S CAVE
THE BEST IN TODAY'S ROMANTICA™

Make each day more *EXCITING* With our

ELLORA'S
CAVEMEN
CALENDAR

www.EllorasCave.com

COMING TO A BOOKSTORE NEAR YOU!

ELLORA'S CAVE

Bestselling Authors Tour

UPDATES AVAILABLE AT

WWW.ELLORASCAVE.COM

Cerridwen, the Celtic Goddess of wisdom, was the muse who brought inspiration to storytellers and those in the creative arts. Cerridwen Press encompasses the best and most innovative stories in all genres of today's fiction. Visit our site and discover the newest titles by talented authors who still get inspired - much like the ancient storytellers did, once upon a time.

Cerridwen Press

www.cerridwenpress.com

Discover for yourself why readers can't get enough of the multiple award-winning publisher Ellora's Cave.

Whether you prefer e-books or paperbacks,

be sure to visit EC on the web at www.ellorascave.com

for an erotic reading experience that will leave you breathless.